S0-BAK-969

"Matt, we need to talk."

"What good will talking do? Will it change the past?"

"No. We can't change the past. But it could help you build a future."

"Leave it alone, Honey." He turned to leave.

Suddenly afraid that if she let him go, she'd never see him again, Honey dashed across the room and grabbed his arm. If she couldn't make him understand with words that love didn't have to hurt, maybe she could show him.

Pressing her lips against his, she said a silent prayer that she still had enough power to prove that he was wrong, that love only hurt when it wasn't returned.

Dear Reader,

March roars in like a lion this month with Harlequin American Romance's four guaranteed-to-please reads.

We start with a bang by introducing you to a new in-line continuity series, THE CARRADIGNES: AMERICAN ROYALTY. The search for a royal heir leads to some scandalous surprises for three princesses, beginning with *The Improperly Pregnant Princess* by Jacqueline Diamond. CeCe Carradigne is set to become queen of a wealthy European country, until she winds up pregnant by her uncommonly handsome business rival. Talk about a shotgun wedding of royal proportions! Watch for more royals next month.

Karen Toller Whittenburgh's series, BILLION-DOLLAR BRADDOCKS, continues this month with *The Playboy's Office Romance* as middle brother Bryce Braddock meets his match in his feisty new employee. Also back this month is another installment of Charlotte Maclay's popular series, MEN OF STATION SIX. Things are heating up between a sexy firefighter and a very pregnant single lady from his past—don't miss the igniting passion in *With Courage and Commitment*. And rounding out the month is *A Question of Love* by Elizabeth Sinclair, a warm and wonderful reunion story.

Here's hoping you enjoy all that Harlequin American Romance has to offer you—this month, and all the months to come!

Best,

Melissa Jeglinski
Associate Senior Editor
Harlequin American Romance

A QUESTION
OF LOVE
Elizabeth Sinclair

HARLEQUIN®

TORONTO • NEW YORK • LONDON
AMSTERDAM • PARIS • SYDNEY • HAMBURG
STOCKHOLM • ATHENS • TOKYO • MILAN • MADRID
PRAGUE • WARSAW • BUDAPEST • AUCKLAND

If you purchased this book without a cover you should be aware that this book is stolen property. It was reported as "unsold and destroyed" to the publisher, and neither the author nor the publisher has received any payment for this "stripped book."

To Kim Kozlowski for the inspiration for this story and her enduring friendship. To Pattie Steele-Perkins for her faith, her hard work and her friendship. And, as always, to my personal hero and the love of my life, my husband, Bob.

ISBN 0-373-16916-7

A QUESTION OF LOVE

Copyright © 2002 by Marguerite Smith.

All rights reserved. Except for use in any review, the reproduction or utilization of this work in whole or in part in any form by any electronic, mechanical or other means, now known or hereafter invented, including xerography, photocopying and recording, or in any information storage or retrieval system, is forbidden without the written permission of the publisher, Harlequin Enterprises Limited, 225 Duncan Mill Road, Don Mills, Ontario, Canada M3B 3K9.

All characters in this book have no existence outside the imagination of the author and have no relation whatsoever to anyone bearing the same name or names. They are not even distantly inspired by any individual known or unknown to the author, and all incidents are pure invention.

This edition published by arrangement with Harlequin Books S.A.

® and TM are trademarks of the publisher. Trademarks indicated with ® are registered in the United States Patent and Trademark Office, the Canadian Trade Marks Office and in other countries.

Visit us at www.eHarlequin.com

Printed in U.S.A.

ABOUT THE AUTHOR

Elizabeth Sinclair was born and raised in the scenic Hudson Valley of New York State. In 1988 she and her husband moved to their present home in St. Augustine, Florida, where she began pursuing her writing career in earnest. Her first novel reached #2 on the Waldenbooks bestseller list and won a 1995 Georgia Romance Writers' Maggie Award for Excellence. As a proud member of five RWA affiliated chapters, Elizabeth has taught creative writing and given seminars and workshops at both local and national conferences on romance writing, how to get published, promotion and writing a love scene and the dreaded synopsis.

Books by Elizabeth Sinclair

HARLEQUIN AMERICAN ROMANCE
677—EIGHT MEN AND A LADY
787—THE OVERNIGHT GROOM
827—THE PREGNANCY CLAUSE
916—A QUESTION OF LOVE

Don't miss any of our special offers. Write to us at the following address for information on our newest releases.

Harlequin Reader Service
U.S.: 3010 Walden Ave., P.O. Box 1325, Buffalo, NY 14269
Canadian: P.O. Box 609, Fort Erie, Ont. L2A 5X3

Tess's Special Oatmeal Cookies

Set oven at 350°F.

Sift together:
1 1/2 cups flour
1/2 tsp baking soda
1 tsp cinnamon
1/2 tsp salt

Stir in:
1 egg, well beaten
1 cup sugar
1/2 cup melted butter
1/2 cup melted lard or other shortening
1 tbsp molasses
1/4 cup milk
1 3/4 cups oatmeal
1 cup seeded raisins and 1 cup of broken nut meats

Arrange by teaspoonfuls on buttered cookie sheet.
Bake until the edges are brown (about 12 minutes).
Makes about 75.

Chapter One

Honey Logan dropped like a rock onto the Victorian settee and stared in horror at her mother-in-law. From the placid expression on Amanda Logan's aged, but still lovely face, she seemed to have no idea that she'd just announced the impending end of Honey's world.

"Now, dear," Amanda said, tapping Honey's hand lightly with the tips of her well-manicured nails, "this shouldn't take too long. A few weeks at the very most."

"A few weeks?" Amanda might as well have been suggesting a few centuries. Honey tried, without too much success, to erase the desperation from her voice. "Isn't there anywhere else he can go?"

"I was so hoping that you would agree to this." Amanda leaned back in her wheelchair and sighed. "I'm afraid there is nowhere else. His house hasn't been lived in for over two years, and it needs cleaning and fixing." She smiled at Honey. "He *is* my nephew, dear. Family. I couldn't very well turn him away, now, could I?"

Yes, you could have, Honey wanted to yell. *You could have told him to get a motel room in the next town, the next state, another country, anywhere but here.*

Regretfully, she knew she couldn't make that kind of demand. No matter how much she loved Amanda and Amanda loved her, her mother-in-law owned the house. Honey resided there purely as a guest. Despite her efforts to make Honey think of it as her home, she lived here at her mother-in-law's pleasure, as her home-care nurse. As such, Honey felt she had no more say in what went on here than the gardener or the housekeeper. Her mother-in-law's innate consideration for everyone in the house was the only reason they were even having this conversation.

"Of course you couldn't," Honey finally managed to murmur.

"I knew you'd see the sense of this." Amanda squeezed Honey's hand reassuringly. "It'll work out for the best. You'll see." Heaving a tired sigh, she settled back in her wheelchair. The light from the Tiffany chandelier overhead played in the facets of the diamond rings adorning two of her fingers. "I'm exhausted. I think I'll go to bed early. I hate to bother her at this late hour, but would you mind finding Tess and asking her to get the spare room ready? I'm afraid Matt will be here first thing tomorrow morning."

Seeing that the conversation had overtaxed Amanda, Honey didn't try to prolong it. Besides, she couldn't come up with an argument that wouldn't sound frantic and interfering. "Would you like some help getting back to your room?"

The older woman shook her head, then raised her chin in a way Honey knew indicated pure stubbornness. "No. I'll manage on my own." The curve of her lips and the love in her eyes softened the crisp words.

Smiling inwardly at her mother-in-law's refusal to give in to the infirmities of old age, Honey nodded. She had a tendency to be overprotective of those she loved, but Amanda always found a way to gently remind Honey that she wasn't quite ready for a nursing home.

Honey followed the electric wheelchair into the hall. The soft hum of the motor grated on her frazzled nerves. She saw Amanda safely seated in the chairlift that would carry her to the second floor, then stowed the wheelchair in a nook beneath the stairs. After making sure Amanda reached the top safely, where her walker waited. Honey headed down the hall in search of Tess, Amanda's long-time friend and housekeeper, to tell her of the arrival of their visitor tomorrow morning.

Tomorrow morning.

A sense of doom washed over Honey. In a few hours the secure life she'd made for herself would crumble around her.

She'd spent years forgetting the touch of Matt Logan's lips, the caress of his hands, the way his smile warmed her soul, the afterglow of his tender lovemaking. But most of all, she'd fought hard to forget the pain she'd endured when he'd left town without a word to her.

Now, after seven years of silence, he planned to stroll back into her life as if he'd never left. To make matters worse, he'd be staying with them.

Matt under the same roof with her...and Danny. Oh, glory, she'd forgotten about her son. With concentrated effort, she tamped down the panic that followed on the heels of that thought, and fought for stability. She straightened her spine, forcing courage to the surface, courage she didn't really feel.

You'll deal with it, she told herself. *You'll deal with it just like you dealt with your father and your brother, Jesse.*

But Matt, for all his flaws, had in no way resembled either her domineering father or her silent, brooding brother. Matt had been warm and understanding, and though he hadn't known it, her emotional bulwark against her father. Matt had been…everything, or so she'd thought.

Suddenly, she felt like she had when her father had forced her to marry Stan Logan, Amanda's spoiled son—as if her world had spun out of control, leaving her helpless and vulnerable. And with that vulnerability came dread.

She stepped into Tess Martin's domain and found it deserted. Honey's gaze darted to the kitchen wall phone. *Emily.* She'd call her sister. After all, not long ago, Emily had had to contend with having a man she'd once cared about walk back into her life. Maybe she'd know what Honey could do. In any case, talking to someone might help her regain her focus, and right now, she desperately needed focus. Focus and a plan.

Picking up the receiver, she held it to her ear with shaking hands and dialed Emily's number. Emily's mother-in-law answered.

"Rose, I know Emily is probably busy putting the twins to bed, but can you ask her to come over as soon as she's finished? I need to talk to her. Danny's father is coming home."

Before Rose could answer, Tess came into the kitchen. As if she'd been doing something wrong,

Honey abruptly hung up. Bad enough that she felt like a complete fool for allowing the sudden reappearance of Matt Logan to throw her for a loop. She didn't have to broadcast it to one and all.

Tess grinned at her. The housekeeper's apple cheeks dented into deep-set dimples. Honey had always felt apple-cheeked women were a product of children's literature, until she met Tess. But then, a lot of kid resided in Amanda's Irish cook.

"Secret admirer?" Tess asked with the familiarity acquired over the twenty-plus years she'd been with Amanda. The housekeeper had long ago adopted the entire Logan clan as her own, and treated them accordingly, including Amanda. Going to the sink, she began rinsing the cups Honey and Amanda had used for tea earlier.

"No. Just talking to my sister. She's coming over." Honey suddenly had too many hands and nowhere to put any of them. "I'll make some coffee."

As she started the mindless task of assembling a pot of coffee, she could sense Tess watching her. Knowing how possessively Tess ruled her kitchen, when she finally spoke, it shocked Honey that her words held no reprimand. "Something wrong, dear?"

Honey jumped at the unexpected question. "Huh? Oh, no, what makes you ask?"

Gently, Tess removed the pot from the coffee-maker, then swung the basket open. "Even though she makes coffee strong enough for a mouse to trot across, Miss Emily prefers it on the weak side. But I'm thinkin' this might be just a wee bit too weak even for her." They both stared down at the empty filter. "You sure there's nothing wrong?"

Shaking her head, Honey stepped aside and allowed Tess to add coffee grounds to the basket. "I'm fine, just a little distracted."

That had to be the understatement of the century. Distracted didn't come close to describing her confused mind, her rolling stomach, her throbbing temples and the need to run anywhere as far and as fast as she could, as long as it was away from here, away from Matt.

"Miss Amanda wants you to freshen the spare room. Her nephew is coming to stay for a while. He'll be here tomorrow morning." Was that really her voice sounding so calm and in control?

"Matthew? Coming here?"

Honey nodded.

Tess huffed impatiently. "Why didn't she wait until morning to be tellin' me? Nothing like giving a body notice."

"We just found out a few hours ago."

"Oh, well." Tess's frown turned into a grin. When she spoke again, her lyrical Irish accent became even more pronounced. "I shouldn't be at all surprised. Never could figure out what that lad was up to. He hasn't changed a jot. Sure and it'll be lovely to have him home again."

Delving under the sink for the basket with all her cleaning aids in it, Tess extracted it, hooked it over her arm, then grabbed her broom and headed out the door. As she passed into the hall, she continued a discourse on Matt's virtues.

Honey didn't hear what she said, nor did she care that Amanda's housekeeper proclaimed Matt to be the greatest thing since bottled water, or that everyone else in the house took immense delight in his unexpected visit. Honey had her own opinion of Matthew

Logan, and it didn't come anywhere close to being charitable or delighted.

When she thought about the mess he'd left her to untangle, her anger began to rise to the top of her thoughts like cream in a milk bottle. The angrier she got, the less shaky she felt, so she gave her temper full rein, enjoying being back in control. By the time Emily walked through the door, Honey had summoned up a full head of steam. All of it aimed at Matt Logan.

MATT STEERED HIS BLACK pickup truck to the side of the road, right next to the sign that read Welcome to Bristol, New York, Population 3,000 & Growing. He grinned at the optimism of the town fathers. Unless things had changed drastically, Bristol had remained relatively the same size for over thirty years. With the exception of when the town fathers allocated funds for an occasional spring touch-up, the sign had also remained unchanged.

He took in the familiar mountain skyline, sighed contentedly, then did a quick check of the motorcycle tied down in the back of the truck. His hometown felt good, right, familiar. He planned on proving to all those naysayers that you could return to your roots, even if it meant doing battle with demons from the past. Maybe that bull had done him a favor when it gored his leg and forced him to take early retirement.

Memories crowded into the interior of the truck. For a long minute he just sat there, staring out the windshield at the town from which he'd fled. He hadn't come back, not once, not even for Stan's funeral a year ago or his father's funeral two years before that.

He sincerely regretted not being there for his aunt when Stan had died, but coming would have meant seeing Honey again, and he hoped to avoid that for as long as possible. Besides, he'd been in Australia with the rodeo, and by the time he got back, it would have been all over. When he'd spoken to Aunt Amanda a few days ago, he'd expressed his regret, and she'd assured him that under the circumstances, she'd understood his absence. But it didn't erase the guilt from his conscience. Stan had been his best friend, and despite what he'd done, and the fact that Matt hadn't forgiven him, Matt should have made the effort to attend for his aunt's sake.

His father's funeral was a different matter. He'd stayed away intentionally. What good would it have done to be there? The old man wouldn't have cared one way or the other. Matt's existence had never been of any great importance to Kevin Logan during his life. Why would it be any different at his death?

Matt stirred restlessly, then stretched his right leg over the seat. The long ride straight through from Texas had cramped the muscle in his injured limb. As he gingerly massaged the cramped calf muscle, he recalled the doctor warning him that this would happen for a while. The ache finally eased.

A full moon, hanging like a large ripe lemon in the sky, turned the treetops behind Osgood's Market to silver. Funny, but that moon never quite looked the same from anywhere else.

Suddenly anxious to once more become a part of the slow-paced, sleepy hamlet, Matt pulled back onto the road and steered his truck toward The Diner. He knew it would be the one place in town open at this hour, the one place that served the best cup of coffee and the biggest burgers in four counties. Once he'd filled his rumbling stomach, he'd head to Aunt Amanda's and then, in the morning, he'd go to the town hall and pay up the overdue taxes on his father's house.

No. Pushing the past out and moving in new memories, happy memories, meant starting to think of it as *his house.*

Jim, a fellow rodeo rider, had warned Matt that he would need to settle up with the past before he could start a future. Matt didn't believe that. If he just concentrated on redecorating and stopped thinking about the unhappiness he'd known in that house, the memories would soon fade away. Besides, how do you settle up with a man who's dead and buried?

"So, WHAT DO YOU PLAN on doing?"

Honey avoided Emily's gaze and her question. The silence in the kitchen grew louder. She occupied her hands by stirring her cold coffee. Her shield of anger had dissolved as quickly as it had materialized. Uncertainty had returned with a vengeance.

"Honey?"

She gave an abrupt shake of her head. "I don't know."

"Well, I hate to be the one to point this out, but you don't have a whole lot of time to decide." Emily stopped Honey's nervous movements by placing a hand on her arm. "He'll be here in the morning."

"I know that," Honey snapped. Immediately contrite about her sharp tone, she flashed a weak smile at her sister. "I know," she repeated more softly. The role of the one needing advice did not sit well with her.

She stood, walked to the sink, then poured out the cold coffee. Turning, she grabbed the coffeepot and refilled her cup. "What right does he have to come back here and intrude in my life?"

"The same right my husband had to come back. Like Kat, this was Matt's home, the town where he grew up."

Knowing her statement had been totally unreasonable, Honey refrained from replying. Slowly, she shifted her gaze from the dark liquid in her cup to her sister's worried face. "Do you think he'll notice— about Danny, I mean?"

"Unless he's gone blind in the last seven years, I'd say the odds are very good that he'll catch on. You better prepare for it."

Honey nodded, unable to speak past the knot that Emily's warning brought to her throat.

Emily glanced at Honey, then at her cup, then back to Honey. She played absently with the end of her long, brown braid. "There's something that always bothered me, but you never wanted to talk about Matt, so I never asked. Why didn't you tell him?"

Honey sighed, then took her seat across from Emily. She stole thinking time by carefully arranging the base of Danny's superhero mug to fit inside a group of green gingham squares on the place mat. She smiled sadly. Even Danny had heroes, but in all her life, she could not ever recall having one herself. Shaking away the unusual wave of self-pity, she directed her thoughts to Emily's question.

"Dad told me not to tell anyone. Said it would just make matters worse." She rolled her eyes. "Not that they could have gotten much worse. I tried to tell Matt, anyway." She plucked nervously at a loose thread in the place mat. "Problem was, no one in town knew where to find him. He'd just vanished." She held her palms up and hunched her shoulders. "After a few years went by, I just felt it would be better not to disrupt anyone's life. What was the sense?" She almost added, Would it have brought Matt home?, but thought better of it.

"What about Matt's dad? Did you tell him?"

She shook her head. "Mr. Logan never took much of an interest in Matt." She stared off into a mental world devoid of any memories of Matt and his dad interacting. "I never saw any sign of affection between them. Sometimes I got the feeling that Matt didn't exist for his father. After Matt left, Mr. Logan became more unapproachable than ever. I went there a couple of times, but he wouldn't answer the door, so I gave up. I sent him a letter, but since he never acknowledged it, I don't even know if he read it."

"What about Matt's mother?" Emily shifted to a more comfortable position in her chair, then crossed her denim clad legs. "I was too young to remember her. Did she leave them or what?"

"She died suddenly when Matt was ten." Honey sipped her coffee and made a face. Cold again. She set the cup down and pushed it away, then looked at her sister. "All this reminiscing is not solving my immediate problem, Em. How did you handle Kat showing up? I know you were so angry at him you wanted to beat him to within an inch of his life, then you ended up marrying him and having his twin daughters, but what did you—"

"Whoops. Wait a minute." Emily held up her hand. "The circumstances were a bit different."

"Sure, you wanted him to father your child so you

could fulfill the conditions of a crazy old man's will and keep your home.'' Honey smiled for the first time that evening, then shook her head. ''You never did anything simply. Leave it to you to go overboard and have twins. Dad would be very happy.''

At the mention of her twin daughters, a beautiful smile transformed Emily's face. ''Best bargain I ever made. I got a man I adore and two delightful children. And don't forget Rose. My best friend turned out to be my mother-in-law. Not bad for a girl who was ready to hit the panic button when she found out about the codicil to Dad's will.''

''Ready to hit it? To my recollection, you slammed your fist into it.''

Both women laughed. The laughter died slowly, but when it did, Honey still had not found a solution to her dilemma. How did she contend with Matt coming back into her life?

''So, what's my answer?'' she said, looking at Emily.

Emily checked her watch, then stood, slipped her purse strap over her shoulder and smiled weakly at Honey. ''I don't know that there is an answer, at least not one you can turn into a concrete plan. I'd say play it by ear. Go with your gut.'' She started to turn toward the door, then paused. ''Better yet, go with your heart.''

Honey frowned.

MATT STOOD ON THE FRONT porch of his aunt's house. He glanced at his watch: 1:00 a.m. He should have left The Diner sooner, but he'd enjoyed talking with friends he hadn't seen in years, remembering old times, rehashing the trouble he and his cousin Stan had gotten into as kids. He'd missed that while wandering from place to place. That friendliness, that familiarity was what he'd come home to recapture. Certainly that would chase the unhappy ghost from the corners of his house and his life.

He glanced at Amanda's front door and reached for the knocker, then hesitated. He knew a dynamite blast wouldn't wake Tess, but his aunt had always been a very light sleeper. He hated to wake her just to let him in. However, the one other place he could hope to find a soft bed for the night happened to be located in a motel thirty miles away. After driving for hours, he didn't want to even think of getting on the road again. They'd find him in the morning wrapped around a pole somewhere, his injured leg swollen to the size of a small tree trunk.

He continued to stare at the door, trying to work through his problem, then an idea came to him. He stepped back to inspect the rose trellis on the side of the house. It had frequently provided him and Stan with late night access to Stan's bedroom during their senior year in high school. Should he? He'd probably be arrested for breaking and entering and get thrown in the Bristol jail. Oh, hell, at least he'd have a warm bed to sleep in until he could make bail.

Quietly, he limped to the side of the house and grabbed the first set of slats on the trellis. Pulling himself up, he bounced experimentally, testing the strength of the makeshift ladder and his leg. He had gained a few pounds since his senior year and wasn't sure that time hadn't rotted out the trellis.

Though it creaked a bit and his leg throbbed slightly, he decided that both would support his weight for the short climb. Slowly, he inched his way up, cursing softly at the bite of an occasional thorn piercing his skin, then boosted himself over the balcony of Stan's old room. The French doors stood open. Tess had no doubt been airing the room for his arrival.

NEXT DOOR, Amanda Logan had heard the telltale creak of the rose trellis, a noise she'd grown familiar with when Stan and Matt had used it as an emergency entrance after their twelve o'clock curfew had come and gone. She'd recognized her nephew's voice cursing the rose thorns, just as he had years before. Just to make sure she wasn't wrong about the identity of their midnight visitor, she slipped from her bed and, with the aid of her walker, shuffled to the window.

Just as she pushed the curtain aside, Matt launched himself over the balcony rail. For a moment, she waited for Stan to follow on Matt's heels, as he would have years ago. Back then, she'd have stood here watching the two teenagers scale the balcony railing, all the while thinking they'd pulled the wool over her eyes.

But Stan didn't appear. Stan never would appear again.

Tears threatened. Though a year had passed since Stan had been killed in his race car, the pain sometimes felt very raw, the emptiness overwhelming.

She shook the tears and the poignant memories away, then maneuvered herself back to the bed. No time now for sorrow. Now was the time for new memories, new adventures, new loves.

She lay back against the pillows, quietly picturing the scene in the next room.

Tomorrow, thanks to fate and her slight intervention, this dreary old house would bear witness to an old wrong being set right, and perhaps, in the process, a new beginning.

MATT STEPPED OVER the threshold of his cousin's old room and stopped dead in his tracks.

There, spread out over the discarded bedcovers, lay a woman clad only in a T-shirt and bikini panties. One long, shapely leg stretched out across the white sheet. The other, bent at the knee, helped to expose a good portion of her naked bottom.

He crept closer, then moved to the side to allow the moonlight to bathe her supine body. He felt like a voyeur, but he couldn't help himself. Something about her called out to him, something familiar. When he stood at the foot of the bed, he knew why.

Honey Kingston lay deep in sleep, her hand cupping her cheek, her glorious honey-blond hair splayed over the pillow in loose tangles.

Despite the shock of seeing the one woman he'd hoped to avoid, he had to admit that she still had the power to take his breath away—and to provoke that churning fear that had sent him running from her years earlier.

He could not recall ever seeing a woman who equaled Honey's beauty, and he'd seen many on his travels. His stomach felt bottomless. His heart threatened to implode. Old emotions rushed forward. Emotions Matt had tried to kill in every way he could for over seven years. Emotions he'd been certain he *had* dealt with—until now.

As if it were yesterday, memories of her soft flesh sliding over his buffeted him. Almost unconsciously, he moved to the bedside. Something drove him, something he couldn't seem to control. He touched her cheek with the pad of his thumb and ran it slowly and gently over her creamy skin. She moaned and stirred in her sleep. He pulled back, half from fear of waking her, but more from that old sensual magnetism that spelled trouble and gave life to that gut-wrenching need stirring deep within him.

Despite his fear, emotions he'd thought never to experience again where Honey was concerned ran rampant through him. His groin tightened. He wanted to climb into bed with her and kiss her to wakefulness, hear the little noises she used to make when he made love to her, feel his heartbeat join hers.

He jumped back as if scalded. He had to stop this—now. *Damn her!* What was there about this woman that stole his common sense, his shield of protection, his pride? Even if he could get past his base inclinations, the fact remained that she'd married his cousin before Matt's trail dust had had time to settle. Pain sliced through him, as sharp and agonizing as it had when he'd first gotten word of her betrayal.

The clipping that announced the wedding had come in a plain white envelope with no return address. Only a postmark stamped Bristol, NY, and the date. He'd recognized the handwriting as his father's, the only one who knew where he was. Matt still didn't know why he'd contacted his father and sent him the post office box address. Maybe he'd hoped the old man would change. Maybe…

He whirled and headed for the door. He shouldn't have come here. Could those naysayers he'd scoffed at known what they were talking about, after all? Perhaps you couldn't come home again. Perhaps the ghosts of his childhood were much stronger than any human's resolve to banish them. Perhaps he hadn't gotten over Honey Kingston and, God help him, maybe he never would.

Chapter Two

Wide awake, Honey lay staring at the dark bedroom ceiling. Her heart beat a heavy rhythm in her chest. At first, when she'd heard the scuffle of footsteps on the balcony, she had feared an intruder had scaled the rose trellis. But when the shaft of moonlight illuminated Matt Logan's face, she knew a totally different kind of fear, the kind that made her heart ache with bitter loss, even when she'd declared her heart empty.

Recalling how, when Matt had stood over her a few minutes earlier, she'd managed to remain stone still, she congratulated herself. Then she remembered suppressing a groan of pure passion when he touched her, and the trembling inside returned. Aftershocks, she told herself.

With her skin still tingling where he'd smoothed her cheek, and her insides tangled into knots of dread, it surprised her that she could be flippant. But flippancy helped her contend with the concentrated effort she had to exert to keep from touching the spot his fingers had caressed. Somehow, she felt that if she gave in on this one small urge concerning Matt Logan, she would cave in on the important stuff, too, and she couldn't afford to.

She rolled to her side and stared into the darkness. Dear heavens, how would she get through the next few weeks and survive? How could she stand being in the same house with him, when she wanted to feed his carcass to the turkey buzzards that populated the woods behind Amanda's house?

Impelled by her lack of anger at the man, she bolted upright. Had she totally lost her mind? One touch and she'd been charmed again. Why had fate deemed that she should have men in her life that only knew how to hurt? Other women had heroes. So far, all Honey had were the throwaways. Well, she swore for the thousandth time, Danny would *not* turn out to be one of them.

To reinforce her anger, she rattled off a mental laundry list of all the reasons she had to detest Matt Logan. Because of Matt, she'd had to stand alone against her father's wrath. Because of Matt, she'd been too heartbroken to fight her father and had ended up enduring six years of hell as Stan Logan's wife, just so Frank Kingston could hold his head up in town. Because of Matt, Jesse's rage with their father had forced her half brother to storm from their house, and she'd lost another faux hero. Because of Matt, she'd had to struggle to raise her son as a decent human being, with values and a sense of responsibility. Because of Matt her heart lay dead in her chest.

And as if he hadn't done enough to make her life miserable, Matt's return to Bristol had aroused the memories of a self-centered, uncaring father who had run his family with a tyrannical hand.

She sniffed the air experimentally. At times like this, when the pain of what her father had done to her returned, raw and burning, she imagined she could smell cigarette smoke. Since no one in Amanda's house smoked, Honey knew it wasn't real, just her pain manifesting itself in her imagination. But even knowing it was not real, fear of opening her eyes and finding herself back in her father's house and under his rule, seeped through her.

The smell brought with it other things: memories of the night she'd found her father sitting alone in a dark room, smoking, while his wife—her and Emily's mother—lay in bed waiting. His silent presence had seemed to fill the big house. The red glow on the tip of his cigarette was the only visible sign that he was there in body, if not in mind.

For a long time Honey had stood there, just outside the door, wondering where his thoughts had taken him, willing him to allow her to reach beyond the icy barrier around his heart. When she couldn't, she'd credited her failure to being less than adequate in his eyes. She'd cried herself to sleep that night and innumerable nights after.

It took years for her to understand that her father's hell was of his own making. That neither she nor Emily nor their mother had caused it. But they'd all paid for it with his lack of understanding and his angry silences.

She recalled how alone she'd felt back then. When Jesse, her half brother, had come to live with them after his mother's death, they'd hit it off quite well. They hadn't been terribly close, just intuitive about each other's needs. Honey had thought she'd finally found a champion, but she'd soon realized that the sullen child felt about as much at home in the Kingston house as she did. Then Jesse walked out in a rage, and another of her heroes donned the tarnished armor of a fallen knight.

But despite the disappointments she'd suffered in those around her—her father's iron fist, Jesse's self-absorption, Matt's desertion, Stan's immaturity—Honey had emerged a stronger person. She came to realize that she and she alone controlled her happiness, and that heroes existed only in movies and novels.

She shook away the memories and lay back against the pillows. Being a pragmatic person, she couldn't go on fooling herself. She knew what had robbed her of a night's sleep, and it wasn't only the ghosts from her past. She'd learned to live with them long ago. Neither was it seeing Matt again. After years of practice, she'd become an expert at handling the residual feelings around Matt that surfaced from time to time.

Deep in her soul, she knew that her apprehension stemmed from more than the tiny spark of excitement that seemed to grow at the very idea of coming face-to-face with the man she'd once loved. The source of her growing fear generated far more serious consequences than merely meeting an old flame after seven years.

"MATT'S HERE, you know."

At Amanda's words Honey's hands stilled. Carefully, before she dropped it, she placed the glass of water Amanda had used to take her morning medication on the night table. Should she tell Amanda she knew? That he'd been in her bedroom last night?

Amanda chuckled from her bed and saved Honey the trouble of coming to a decision. "I heard him crawling up the rose trellis last night, just as if he were back in high school.'' She looked pointedly at Honey. ''He came right through your room. Didn't you hear him?''

As if she hadn't heard the question, Honey quickly carried the pill bottles into the bathroom before Amanda detected the truth in her expression. She placed the bottles in the medicine cabinet, then leaned on the sink for support.

Lifting her face, she stared at her white complexion in the mirror. She had to stop this right now. Matt was here. Matt would be here for an indeterminate length of time. She had to pull herself together before she went downstairs and came face-to-face with him. She turned on the faucet, scooped up a handful of cold water and splashed it on her face. She could do this.

Determination in place, spine ramrod straight, she patted the water from her skin with one of Amanda's fluffy towels, then returned to the bedroom. ''Are you ready to get dressed for breakfast?''

Pulling the lilac, quilted coverlet higher on her body, Amanda shook her head. ''I'm still a bit tired. I think I'll be decadent this morning and steal a few more hours sleep. Six-thirty is an obscenely indecent hour to ask anyone to get out of bed.''

''But what about Matt?''

''I'm sure you can entertain him for me, dear. Just make my apologies and tell him I'll see him at lunch.''

The idea of entertaining Matt in any way sent butterflies careening around Honey's stomach, but concern for her mother-in-law helped her ignore them. Amanda was traditionally an early riser. Honey had never heard her complain about the early hour before. "Are you sure you're all right?"

"Fine, just a bit tired." Amanda waved her hand at Honey, then snuggled down and closed her eyes. "You go ahead. Danny will be up soon and wanting you to have breakfast with him."

Danny!

Honey had totally forgotten that Danny would be going down for breakfast soon. She moved quickly to the doorway, turned off the light, then closed the door behind her. Hurrying down the hallway, she passed the spare room, noting the still-closed door. Thank goodness. Maybe Matt had decided to sleep in as well.

ENJOYING THE SILENCE of the early morning hours, Matt sipped his coffee and stared out the large dining room windows overlooking the vast expanse of lawn fronting his aunt's house. A mangy orange cat wandered aimlessly across the grass. Matt wondered if the animal had a home or, like him, just wandered from house to house looking for the next meal. But that had changed for Matt as soon as he'd arrived at Aunt Amanda's.

He had always felt at home here. When things had gotten beyond bearing at his house, Aunt Amanda had opened her arms to him and filled the void left by a mother who'd died when he was a small child and a father who found so much lacking in his small son. Matt had found love here with Amanda and Tess. Love and family and continuity. Things that had been painfully missing in his own home.

He smiled. Was it any wonder that when he decided to come home, he'd called Amanda? From all reports at The Diner last night, his father had done little to keep the place up after Matt left. It didn't surprise him. His father had mourned the loss of his wife and Matt's older brother deeply, and had waited many years for the release of death. For Kevin Logan, the house that should have been a home had become nothing more than a way station on that journey.

Matt shook off his dismal memories and instead turned his thoughts to the woman he'd found in bed last night, the woman who had married his cousin and best friend two weeks after Matt left town.

Like an old companion, he welcomed the familiar swell of anger inside him that inevitably came with the reminder of how quickly Honey had forgotten him. That alone confirmed that he'd done the right thing by leaving before she broke his heart. His anger cleansed him, burning away the ghosts of yesterday, making room for the promise of tomorrows that didn't include his father or Honey Logan.

A sound from behind him stopped his musings.

He lifted his gaze to the reflection in the window. Honey stood just inside the door, her glorious hair cascading over shoulders left bare by the spaghetti straps of a cornflower-blue sundress, her face devoid of makeup. Some women had to be groomed to the teeth to be classified as beautiful. Not Honey. She'd been blessed with natural beauty. In Matt's view, even though she had a heart as black as the night, no other woman could compare to her.

An image of her in bed last night flashed through his mind. His body stirred in response. To his utter annoyance, an overwhelming urge to touch her again, feel her silky flesh under his callused fingertips, burned through him.

"Hello, Matt." Her voice seemed to come from a distance, but the sound danced up his spine. She glanced quickly around the room. "You're alone?"

He took a fortifying sip of his coffee to wash down the knot that clogged his throat, while stalling for time to get his traitorous body back in line. Then he slowly turned to face her. "Honey, seems you and I are the only early risers around here. Oh, and of course, Tess. But then you always were up and out with the birds."

Honey felt the barb of his words bite deep. She knew he referred to the nights they'd spent making love and the mornings she'd dressed and dashed home before her father awoke.

Not ready to exchange unpleasantries with Matt, she went to the mahogany sideboard, poured herself a cup of strong, black coffee, then took a seat at the opposite end of the table, as far from him as she could get without moving into the kitchen.

"Amanda sends her apologies. She's feeling tired this morning and wanted to sleep a bit longer. Normally, she'd be down here before anyone."

He sat a bit straighter, his eyes showing his concern. "She's not sick or anything, is she?"

Honey shook her head, the sound of his voice doing strange things to her ability to speak. Beneath the table, she placed her palms firmly on her legs to stop them from shaking. Despite all her pep talks to prepare herself, the sight of Matt by daylight had a stronger effect on her than she'd anticipated. But that unguarded moment had passed, and now she had her control back...or so she thought until she looked at him again.

Basically, he looked the same, but his work-toughened, solid biceps straining at the short sleeves of his blue shirt were not those of the twenty-seven-year-old who had held her close. Nor had his skin been quite that shade of warm, golden brown back then. His eyes drew her attention. While still strikingly blue, they contained a sadness, an emptiness that she'd never seen in them before.

As if aware of her discovery, he blinked, then turned back to the window, effectively dismissing her presence and hiding his feelings behind a blank wall. Nothing new there. In all the time they'd been together, Honey knew surprisingly little of Matt. Obviously, he planned on keeping it that way. And that was fine by her.

She adroitly avoided thinking about the hours they'd spent making love and saying little.

A puddle of sunlight bathed him, glinting in blue-black flames off his ebony hair. She swallowed hard and clenched her fists to still the itch that had invaded her fingers. She'd once taken great pleasure in caressing the silky strands and teasing him about being blessed with such beautiful hair, when so many women would have killed for it.

The sound of pots clattering in the kitchen brought her out of her sensual haze. She straightened and picked up her coffee to give her something to do with her hands. "Amanda tells me you're going to be living in your father's place."

"*My* place," he corrected crisply. Without even glancing her way, he stood, walked to the sideboard and refilled his coffee cup from the silver pot.

As he headed back to his chair, the scent of his musky aftershave wafted to Honey. She held her breath until he was reseated. This simple act provided her with a distraction that kept her gaze from wandering to his tight posterior.

Finally, she could force words past her trembling lips. "Excuse me?"

"I said, it's *my* place."

"Oh? I wasn't aware of a distinction."

Ignoring her, he turned his attention beyond the windows again.

Honey glanced toward the stairs, then checked her watch. The tingle on the back of her neck told her exactly when his attention swung back to her.

"Am I keeping you from something important?"

She looked at him, but before she could answer, he turned away again, as if he couldn't stand the sight of her.

Miffed at being ignored, she met his sarcasm head-on. She glared at him, relieved at the appearance of an emotion she could count on, could control. "No. My son's bus will—"

His dark gaze snapped to her. "Son? You and Stan had a son?"

She frowned. "You didn't know?" She'd been so certain someone would have told him. Why hadn't Amanda mentioned her beloved grandson? She had never been reticent before about expounding on his virtues to anyone she could corner into listening. Why not Matt?

He turned toward her, his expression interested and definitely accusing. "No. Apparently no one thought it important enough to mention to me."

His words bit deep into her conscience, making her react defensively. "Maybe because no one knew where you were." She could have bitten off her tongue. "I'm sorry. I don't want to spar with you, Matt."

He set his coffee cup forcefully on the table, rose and strode to her side. She had barely enough time to notice his slight limp. Placing both palms on the mahogany tabletop, he leaned down till their eyes were level.

"Oh yes, you damned well do, lady. You want to demand answers and rip my head off. Well, I have my own list of questions, Honey. Like why did you marry Stan before I'd passed the town limits?"

She drew in a deep breath and stared into his cold, angry eyes. Why did he care? Determinedly, she vowed that nothing would make her fall apart now, not even his intimidating tactics. She stood, pushing her chair back so roughly that it nearly tumbled over. Her hand shot out to catch it. "That didn't concern you seven years ago, and it's none of your business now."

She started to walk away, but he grabbed her upper arms and swung her around to face him. "I think it *is* my business."

She struggled to free herself, not because he held her too tightly, but because his touch drained her energy to fight him. And she needed to fight him with all of the inner strength she had. That became more apparent with each passing moment. If she wanted to survive this, she had to fight. "Well, think again."

Then she made the mistake of making eye contact with him. The old magnetism that had drawn her to him to begin with reared its ugly head, holding her paralyzed in Matt's gaze. All rational thought vanished.

Matt could feel the heat of her skin burning into

his palms. Touching her had been a stupid move. But he couldn't let go. No matter how hard he willed himself to do it, he could not let Honey go. For what seemed like hours they just stood there, eyes burning, chests heaving. In anger or in renewal of an old passion? He didn't know. He didn't want to know.

What he did know was that if he didn't let her go in the next ten seconds, he'd press his lips against that sugar-sweet mouth of hers and kiss her to within an inch of her life.

That realization made him abruptly release her.

For a moment more she stood there staring at him, as if trying to find her center of balance. Then she took an unsteady step backward, one hand reaching blindly for her discarded chair, the other clutching her throat. Her chest rose and fell quickly, pressing her breasts against the thin fabric of her sundress.

"M-M-Mom?"

In unison they turned toward the doorway. Honey heard the catch in Matt's breath. She forced her lips to curve in a smile and made her feet move to stand beside her son. "Danny, this is your dad's cousin, your...Uncle Matt." The control in her voice astounded her.

She waited, her breath imprisoned in her burning lungs. She watched as Matt's gaze traveled slowly over features so like his own, and nothing like hers or Stan's blond hair and fair skin. Did he recognize his son? Except for a twitch on the right side of his lips, he kept his emotions hidden behind an enigmatic mask.

"Shake Uncle Matt's hand," she forced herself to say.

''How d-d-do you d-d-do?'' Danny extended his small hand.

Matt took it, his gaze never leaving the child's face. When Matt smiled, she finally exhaled the trapped air.

''How do you do? I'm so glad to meet you.''

''W-w-why?'' Danny let go of Matt's hand.

Matt's eyes widened, as if he was shocked by Danny's question. He squatted down to be on the boy's level. ''Well, because your...dad and I were great friends, and I hope we can be, too.'' His gaze shifted to Honey with a burning look so intense, she knew she'd counted herself safe too soon. He knew.

She looked away. ''Danny, you need to get your breakfast, sweetie. The school bus will be here in a few minutes. You don't want to be late for school on the first day of rehearsal.''

Matt stood. ''Rehearsal?''

''For my s-s-school play.'' Danny explained. ''M-M-Mom wants m-m-me to be in it, b-b-but I—''

''Don't tell me you don't want to.'' Matt raised his eyebrows, as if in surprise. Before Honey could do it, Matt poured milk on the bowl of oat cereal dotted with tiny technicolor marshmallow stars and moons, then carried it to Danny's place.

Danny lowered his gaze to the table. ''The k-k-kids will l-l-laugh at me.''

Matt took his seat and centered his full attention on Danny. ''Why would they do that?''

Honey couldn't believe he'd asked such a question. Wasn't it obvious Danny had a problem? Why underline it by making him explain? She stepped forward to intercede for her son.

''Because I t-t-talk funny.''

Frowning, Matt leaned back in his chair. ''Do you?

I hadn't noticed. What's funny about the way you talk?''

"That's enough, Matt!" Honey couldn't stand to see Danny put through this.

"It's okay, M-M-Mom. I can tell h-h-him."

For a moment, Honey hesitated. Then she saw Danny smile at Matt. He usually didn't talk to strangers. This was a first. "If it's okay with you. But you don't have to explain to anyone," she stated.

The boy glanced at her. "I kn-kn-know." The empty spot left by the tooth he'd lost last week winked up at her. Then he looked back to Matt. "I stutter."

Matt's brows dipped deeper. "Hmm. You didn't stutter just then. Are you sure you stutter?"

Danny laughed out loud. Honey hadn't realized how long it had been since she'd heard her son's unbridled laughter. He took a big spoonful of cereal and chewed. Milk dribbled out of the corner of his mouth. He caught it with his fist, then went back to eating his cereal.

"Use your napkin, Danny." She handed him the white linen square.

"So, tell me about this play. What's your part?"

Danny swallowed. "A t-t-tomato."

As Danny expanded on his debut into the world of "Farmer Jones's Vegetable Garden," Matt listened raptly to every word.

Honey suddenly felt invisible. And she wasn't at all sure she liked that feeling. In fact, she knew she didn't.

Danny had just finished relating the play's grand climax, describing how all the vegetables came on stage for their final bow, when a horn sounded out front.

"Danny, the bus is here. You can tell Uncle Matt more later."

Jumping up, Danny grabbed his knapsack and turned back to Matt. "You'll be h-h-here when I g-g-get home?"

"Right here," Matt assured him, then smiled a smile that Honey hadn't seen in over seven years.

Danny beamed from ear to ear, first at Matt, then at his mother. It was like looking at a smaller version of Matt. For the second time that morning, she needed the chair for stability.

Glad for an excuse to escape Matt and his smothering charm, she walked Danny to the door and down the front steps of the house. She leaned down and straightened his collar while offering her cheek for a goodbye kiss. With a sigh and rolling eyes, he obliged, leaving a milk smear on her skin. As she straightened and wiped it off, she noted Danny waving to the dining room windows. Turning, she found Matt, curtain pulled back, watching Danny climb aboard the yellow-and-black bus.

MATT NEVER TOOK HIS EYES off the bus as it moved down the driveway, the sound of exuberant children's voices spilling from the open windows.

"My son." The words slipped from his lips experimentally.

Suddenly, a gut-wrenching ache seized him. The pain nearly doubled him over. He'd missed six years of Danny's life. She'd stolen it from him, and he could never, ever get it back. He curled his hands into fists and drove one against the window frame to still the agony that sliced through his chest and ate deep into his heart.

He wanted to go after Honey and demand to know why she'd never told him, but he was afraid of what he'd do. Instead, he took deep breaths until the ache eased and he could stand upright again. Through the curtain, he could see Honey, her back to him, her gazed centered on the spot where the bus carrying their son had last been visible through the line of red oaks bordering the drive.

How could a woman he remembered as being sweet and sensitive have done something so cruel? Then he recalled how, seven years ago, she'd professed to love him, then barely waited for him to clear the town line before she'd married his best friend and cousin. Sweet and sensitive hardly fit Honey Kingston.

His mouth set in a grim line of determination, Matt strode from the room, determined to learn the truth. His angry steps ate up the distance between him and the woman who had betrayed him, not once, but twice, and in the cruelest way possible.

Careful not to alarm her of his approach, he walked up behind her, then laid his hand on her shoulder. When she seemed to ignore him, he spun her to face him.

''Come inside. We need to talk…about *our* son.''

Chapter Three

Honey looked around Amanda's large, Victorian living room. Almost two years ago, this room had held her sister, Emily, Honey's soon-to-be brother-in-law, Kat, and all their wedding guests. Now the same room suddenly seemed much too small to hold just Honey, an irate Matt and all the unanswered questions hanging in the air about the small boy who'd just climbed on the school bus.

Honey glanced cautiously at Matt. Though she'd known that she'd have to deal with this issue from the moment Amanda had announced that Matt would be coming to live with them, she'd fought against it. Now she couldn't sidestep it any longer. Oddly, the idea of finally letting go of her secrets almost came as a relief. She'd only held on to them to protect Danny and his grandmother from heartache.

Logically, despite the fact that Matt had walked out on her, he had not walked out on their son, since he had no knowledge of his existence. Although her personal opinion of Matt Logan wouldn't win him any awards, deep down, she knew he would not have deserted Danny had he been given the choice. And Danny should not be deprived of his father's love because she and Matt had their problems, problems that in no way involved Danny. However, even after she divulged all that Matt would demand he be told, there was one more stumbling block that she knew Matt wasn't going to be happy about.

Whether she liked it or not, the time had come to do what she'd tried to do seven years ago, and whether or not Matt would believe she'd made that attempt remained to be seen.

Squaring her shoulders, she faced him. "What do you want to know?" Her voice quivered. *Damn!* She hadn't wanted to let her apprehension show. She cleared her throat, hoping that he'd read the crack in her voice as physical, rather than emotional.

"Everything. Start at the beginning." Matt stood just inside the closed door, waiting, one hand on the door frame above his head, the other thrust deep into the pockets of his jeans, pulling the denim tight across the lower front of his body.

Tearing her gaze away from temptation, Honey took a deep breath and swallowed. The trembling in her legs made the need to sit apparent, but she stood, refusing to give him even that much of an edge. She cleared her throat. "You're right. Danny is yours, not Stan's."

Matt cursed softly and covered the space separating them in three long strides. "I hardly needed that confirmed. I have school pictures of me that could easily have been taken of Danny. The kid's a miniature of me. How long did you expect to keep me in the dark?"

"I didn't expect any such thing." She glared at him. This was hard enough without his sarcasm. "Do you want to hear this or not?"

Taking a seat on an overstuffed chair, Matt leaned forward, his elbows on his knees. He clasped his hands tightly in front of him, as if by immobilizing them he could harness the anger tightening his shoulder muscles and blazing from his eyes. "Go on. I'm anxious to hear your excuses for keeping my son's existence from me for almost seven years."

Grateful for the support of a sturdy piece of furniture, she dropped onto the sofa. "You have no right to judge me on this, Matt. You walked out, not me. I would have told you, if you'd been here."

Matt leaned back. He couldn't fight her on that score. Neither could he tell her why he'd walked out. How could he tell her that he'd run like a frightened rabbit because his father thought him a poor excuse for a son, and that loving her scared the hell out of him? Even if he told her, what would it change? She hadn't cared enough even to wait and see if he'd come back. She'd married Stan and cheated Matt out of his son.

The bottom line was that, unless he wanted to get into the whole thing about his father, something he'd never told anyone, he had no choice but to allow her to think what she would about him. But that didn't explain why she'd never told him about Danny.

"Did you even try to find me, or did you just figure that you'd trick the first guy with heavy pockets who came along into marrying you, and let him think the kid was his?" Even as the words left his mouth, Matt could have kicked himself for giving his frustration a voice. He knew Honey well enough to know that, if he pushed too hard, she'd close up tighter than a clam.

Bolting to her feet, Honey glared at him. Her hands twisted together, as if she was putting forth a superhuman effort not to slap him. Her furious words confirmed it. "How dare you imply that I tricked Stan or that I married him for money?"

To his utter annoyance, her marriage to Stan infuriated Matt. Dangerous territory, but he couldn't resist asking the question that had burned itself into his mind all those years ago. "So why did you marry him?"

Honey turned away. "That's none of your business. We're discussing Danny, not my reasons for marrying Stan."

Matt strongly disagreed with her reasoning. The two were so tightly entwined that he couldn't have pried them apart with a crowbar. But he let that go—for now. Insulting Honey wouldn't encourage her to tell him about his son and why Matt had been robbed of the first six years of the boy's life. As hard as it might be, he had to hold back his anger and let Honey talk.

Shaking his head, he stood. "Listen, we're not going to accomplish anything with a war of accusations about things that can't be changed." He motioned to the sofa. "Sit down and tell me what happened."

For a long moment, Honey glared mutinously at him. He didn't blame her for not wanting to continue. His remarks had been far from civil, and if he'd been in her shoes, he'd have walked out. To her credit, she hadn't, telling him without putting it into words that she wanted to get the air cleared as much as he did. "Please."

She backed away from him and sat, acutely aware that he hadn't apologized for his words. Let him believe what he would. Matt Logan's opinion of her didn't matter at all, she told herself, but her anger simmered beneath her surface calm.

Folding her hands in her lap, she looked at him. "I never tricked Stan into anything. He knew up front that Danny wasn't his, but it never made a difference to him. He loved him just as much as if he had fathered him naturally."

"That still doesn't answer my question. Why didn't you try to find me? I had a right to know I had a son."

The edge in his voice acted on her conscience like a finely honed rapier. Honey smoothed the material on the arm of the sofa, trying to find the words to tell him that she had tried, that she'd asked everyone in town if they knew where he'd gone. But just the thought brought memories pouring back—painful, agonizing memories of drowning in the desperation of being absolutely alone, of having no one to turn to, nowhere to go. Maybe that was why she'd welcomed Stan's friendship, and later, with her father goading her on, his proposal. Then again, maybe after Matt left, she just hadn't cared enough about anything to fight either of them.

In the end, she settled for the simplest explanation. "I did try. But no one knew where you'd gone."

He stood and loomed over her. "Not good enough. My father knew where to contact me, Honey. Why didn't you just ask him?"

She felt the tiny fissure in her heart—the last evidence of her long healing process—split wide-open. If only Mr. Logan had answered the door. If only…

How could she explain? How did she tell Matt that his father had become a sick, sullen old man, a virtual hermit who'd shut himself away from her and the rest of the world? "I tried to speak to your father, but I didn't think—"

"Didn't think? You didn't think what? That I'd want my own kid?" Matt strode across the room to the window and shoved back the lace curtain. His face in profile concealed the grim line of his mouth and the rage flashing in his eyes, but the stiffness in his broad shoulders broadcasted his feelings.

Matt saw nothing beyond the window. Instead his sight had turned inward, to the memory of a small boy standing outside the door waiting for his father's notice. He saw a teenager proudly presenting a handmade tie rack to his father, and the man simply glancing at it and nodding. He saw a young adult offering his love to a lonely old man, hoping to fill the void left by the loss of a young wife and a son, and having that love brushed aside. He heard the words *You'll never be what your brother was* echoing through his mind.

But Honey knew nothing of that, and Matt wasn't about to tell her, not even to prove he wouldn't have walked out on his son. He would have loved Danny with every fiber of his being—because he knew too well what it was like to be deprived of that love. Those very memories were the ghost he'd come home to exorcize, and talking about them would only grant them life. And granting them life would put him through the rigors of hell again, and he would never go back there, not even for Honey. Not even for Danny.

Slowly and methodically, as he'd trained himself to do for so long, he tucked the memories back into the far reaches of his mind, safely hidden from him and everyone else.

"So, where do we go from here? Do we tell Danny I'm his father?"

Honey sprang from the sofa. "No. No, we can't tell him, at least not yet. Danny's stutter is a manifestation of his grief over losing his…over losing Stan. Dr. Thomas says that any more emotional upheaval could make it a permanent condition. As long as we don't push, he can overcome this."

Although Matt understood what Danny was up against much better than she thought he did, he had hoped that he could claim his son. Considering Danny's problem, Matt had no choice but to wait until the boy could emotionally withstand the news that he was his father.

"Dr. Thomas? Isn't he the old GP who had an office on Main Street?"

She nodded.

"What does he know about this kind of problem?" Matt glanced at Honey.

"Enough that I have the utmost faith in his diagnosis."

Matt disagreed, but kept his opinions to himself. They had other fish to fry. "How long will this take?"

She shifted her gaze away from his and began fussing with some flowers in a vase on a nearby table. "We don't know. Maybe months, maybe years."

"And in the meantime?"

She turned fully toward him. "In the meantime, we wait and try to keep him on an emotionally even keel."

"Which means not telling him about me."

"I'm afraid so."

Matt stared at her for a long time. Something in

her eyes caught his attention, something like pity. No, not pity. Compassion.

"Matt, I know this isn't easy for you."

Before he could respond, she turned away and headed for the door. With her hand on the knob, she stopped. "I wish…"

He waited for her to finish, but she didn't. "What?"

She looked at him for another moment, shook her head, then left the room.

HONEY STOOD IN THE LARGE front hall, her back against the living room door. What had she wished? That those seven years had never happened, that she'd never met Matt Logan, that he could have been around for all those wonderful years of Danny growing up, that a bitter old man had reached out and opened the door for her? That Matt had loved her as much as she'd loved him?

She shook her thoughts away. She had no more power to alter the past than she'd had to make Matt stay all those years ago. The past had to remain as it was—unchanged. Right now, she had more important things to worry about. How would she tell Amanda that her beloved grandson was not really her grandson? Amanda had centered her world around Danny after Stan died. How would she take the news?

Honey had been right to dread Matt's homecoming. Life had been so simple before his reappearance. He'd been here for less than a day and nothing was the same anymore.

She sighed, pushed herself away from the door, then started for the kitchen. The soft whirr of Amanda's chair-lift stopped her. Waiting until the elderly woman reached the bottom of the stairs, Honey hurried to pull the wheelchair from its nook, then position it for her mother-in-law.

"Amanda, you should have called me to help you dress."

"Why? So you could avoid the unavoidable?" Amanda levered herself out of the chair-lift and into the wheelchair. As she adjusted the throw over her legs, she studied Honey with a knowing look. "Come into the dining room and have a cup of coffee while I eat breakfast."

Amanda's wheelchair moved smoothly over the polished, wide pine boards. With a skill born of spending the last five years in the chair, Amanda maneuvered it through the double dining room doors to the spot left vacant at the table. Silently, Honey went about filling a plate for her mother-in-law from the chafing dishes on the sideboard. When she returned to Amanda's side with her usual breakfast of fruit and toast, the older woman's fingers closed around Honey's free hand.

"Did you tell him?"

"Tell him what?"

"About Danny."

Honey sighed. "I told him Danny's stutter—"

"No, not that. Did you tell him Danny is his son?"

Only with concentrated effort did Honey manage to set the plate on the table and not drop it on the floor. Shock waves ebbed through her. She sat heavily in the chair that was, thank goodness, right behind her, and stared at Amanda. "How…"

Amanda chuckled, released Honey's hand, then spread a napkin over her lap. "My dear, I've suspected for some time. The older the child got, the more he looked like Matt as a boy. I knew you'd been seeing Matt before he left town, and the rest was just a simple matter of deduction as to why my son had gone from best friend to groom in a very short period of time.''

Honey couldn't believe her ears. She'd spent the last six years walking on eggs to make sure no one, especially Amanda, knew that Matt was Danny's father. She'd been holding on to a secret that hadn't been a secret at all.

''How many other people know?''

Amanda spread orange marmalade on her toast. ''I'm sure no one but me and maybe Tess, although she hasn't said anything one way or the other. As for anyone else, you can bet if they'd guessed, it would be all over town by now, and it isn't. So it's safe to say none of them picked up on the resemblance as being anything more than family genes. After all, I used to have black hair myself when I was younger.''

Honey was relieved that she hadn't become the talk of the town and that the likelihood of anyone pointing out Danny's heritage to him was slim. But it didn't assuage the guilt she harbored because she hadn't told Amanda. Not that she hadn't wanted to tell her from the start. Stan had insisted that they keep it a secret from his mother. It had taken a few years for Honey to realize that his request had little do with concern for his mother's feelings and a lot to do with his male ego.

''Why didn't you tell Matt?'' Honey asked.

Amanda sighed the sigh of a mother who had done everything she could to make her son happy, including turning a blind eye to a little boy's true father. ''Selfish reasons. Besides, it wasn't my place to tell him about something I only suspected was true, even if I had known where to contact him. Was it?''

"I guess not. I'm so sorry we didn't tell you, though. Stan never wanted you to know, and after he died, I didn't see the point in telling you. You'd already gone through enough pain, and I didn't want to have to tell you that you'd lost a grandson as well as a son.''

Laying her fork down, Amanda turned squarely to face Honey. "I will never lose my grandson. That child has his own special place in my heart. He's as close to me as if Stan had fathered him.'' Tears welled in her eyes.

Honey's heart swelled. "That's the one thing I can safely say that I think Matt and I would agree on. Danny will be your grandson as long as both of you want it that way.'' She kissed Amanda's cheek. "Thank you.''

"Posh!'' Amanda waved her off. "Go see if Tess has made fresh coffee.''

Knowing Amanda hated sappy scenes, Honey headed for the kitchen, but not without wondering what she'd done to deserve such a wonderful woman in her life.

MATT RAN THE CLOTH over the shiny black fender of his motorcycle. Other than a sizable bank account, a game leg and this bike, he had little to show for his years on the rodeo circuit. But then, that seemed to be the pattern of his life—he'd had nothing to show for anything until today. Now he had Danny.

He stopped rubbing the fender and allowed his fantasies to take over. He pictured himself patiently teaching Danny to ride a horse, to pitch a baseball, to handle this bike. All the things that every father had ever dreamed of teaching his son—except Kevin Logan. Matt's father had dreamed of nothing except the woman he'd lost to breast cancer, the son he'd lost in a plane crash, and how he could turn Matt into his brother, Jamie.

But Matt's perfect visions of life as Danny's dad contained a flaw he couldn't seem to erase. In the background of every fantasy, Honey appeared, smiling, laughing, her love for both of them shining in her eyes.

He shook away the disquieting family pictures. Neither Honey nor any other woman could ever be a part of his life. Hadn't he decided that when he left here? A woman in his life would mean he'd have to love her, and he would never surrender to that weakness again—for anyone. Never. Nor would he ever try to live up to someone else's expectations, or leave himself open to the disappointment that would inevitably come to both of them.

He just wished he didn't have to wait to hear Danny call him Dad. But he understood why Honey had asked him not to tell his son just yet. Matt knew all about stuttering. He'd stuttered himself after his mother died.

Thanks to a very special speech teacher, he'd managed to overcome it. Danny would, too. And Matt would help him all he could, whether Honey liked it or not.

FROM HER WHEELCHAIR, Amanda held Matt's big hands and smiled up into his face. "Lord, how I've missed you, Matthew."

He reminded her in many ways of Stan, with his

large, broad-shouldered frame, in his strong hands and gentle grip. But in many ways, he was Stan's opposite. She'd often thought of them as night and day. Stan's shock of blond hair and sparkling blue eyes reminded her of sunshine and bright blue skies, while Matt's dark good looks and brooding mouth had always brought to mind the night sky, where secrets could hide. Stan had always been quick to smile and tease, while Matt had been quiet and thoughtful.

Matt had grown into a fine young man. Stan had continued to be a boy, and his little-boy attitude had killed him…. At the thought, Amanda felt tears threaten. Shuffling the memories aside, she concentrated on the man who had been more to her than merely her brother-in-law's son.

Part of the reason she'd been able to accept Danny as her grandson, even though she'd suspected differently, was because she'd always regarded Matt as her second son, loved him and wanted his happiness as much as she did Stan's.

When Matt had left without a word, it had hurt her deeply, but she knew too well what he lived with in Kevin Logan's house. What did surprise her was that it had taken so long.

"Amanda, I'm so sorry I didn't—"

She placed her fingers over his lips. "I told you before, no regrets, Matt. I knew why you didn't come back for the funeral, and I don't blame you one bit."

He kissed her cheek, then backed away to sit across from her wheelchair. Where did he start, in telling her about the events of the morning? "I know about Danny."

She smiled. "Honey told me about your little chat this morning. I'm glad the air is cleared."

"Amanda…why did Honey marry Stan? Was it just because of Danny?"

Amanda straightened the throw over her legs, then centered all her attention on him. "No, but that's all I'll say on the subject. This is between you and Honey. I have no right telling her story."

Impatient, Matt frowned at her. "You had no problem inviting me to stay here when you knew I'd find out about my son."

She shook her head, her mane of perfectly coiffed, snowy hair turning golden in the afternoon sunlight coming through the sitting room windows. "Ah, but that was just some innocent maneuvering to get two stubborn people to face their problems. I'm an old woman who is not above a little meddling, Matthew Logan. However, I will not divulge confidences."

It irked him that Honey would trust Amanda enough to tell her why and not him. Honey didn't trust him. He should have guessed. Still, the realization brought with it an almost physical pain. "Then she told you?"

"Not everything."

"Then—"

"I'm old, not stupid. I did figure some of this tangle out for myself. Then Honey filled in the blanks this morning after she spoke with you." A serious expression transformed her face from the gentle woman who had held his hand, to the woman he had faced as a teenager after sneaking into the house after curfew. "Just remember, Matt, you're not the only person in this world with problems."

Now, what did that mean? Before he could ask, she went on. "So, what are you going to do about your son?"

Matt had spent the better part of the day thinking about Danny. He would not turn his back on his son. He wanted to be part of his child's life. "I'm not sure, but one thing I do know, I won't walk out of Danny's life, no matter what. Honey be damned." He sighed heavily and stood, then bent to kiss Amanda's cheek. "In the meantime, I guess I'd better check on the house and see what needs to be done. See you at dinner."

Amanda, noting the pain in his expression, watched Matt leave, then shook her head. She never doubted that Matt would want to be a part of his son's life. But did he realize that he'd have to learn to love himself before he could love the child—and quite possibly the child's mother?

Through the window, she watched as he shooed the stray orange cat off the hood of the truck, then climbed in and drove away. For the first time since she'd agreed to Matt's coming here, she wondered if she'd done the right thing. Had she given those she loved an opportunity to heal old wounds or had her interference paved the way for new ones?

Chapter Four

The rumble of his truck's motor filled Matt's ears, but the noise couldn't block out the childhood memories tripping through his mind. Memories that had begun buffeting him the minute he'd pulled into the driveway of his former home. Gripping the steering wheel with white-knuckled hands, he stared at the weathered building that had haunted him for seven years.

The ghosts had assembled like a ghoulish welcoming party. The dogwood tree he and his mother had planted on his fifth birthday. The porch swing where he'd presented that handmade tie rack to his father, who had merely grunted and set it aside, reaching for the Giants tickets Matt's older brother, Jamie, had given him.

Matt managed to combat most of them, but one persisted. Before him, as if projected on the landscape by an invisible camera, his father and he stood on the lawn. His father threw a baseball, and Matt strained to catch it in the oversize mitt. He missed.

"Put your glove in front of you. Remember the way Jamie taught you? You can do it," his father had instructed in a gruff and impatient voice.

"I'm trying," Matt had replied.

"You're not trying hard enough. Don't be afraid of the ball."

Holding the glove exactly as he remembered Jamie had instructed him, he waited for his father's pitch and put every ounce of effort he had into catching the ball. Again he missed. He could still hear his father's words as he'd thrown his mitt to the ground, glared at his young son and then stalked off in disgust. "You're not even trying. You're never going to be able to do it if you don't concentrate."

What Matt heard was *You'll never be your brother.*

No one had to tell him he'd never take the place of the older brother he'd loved and admired, sometimes hated and envied, and missed to this day. In an effort to fill the gaping, empty spot in Kevin Logan's heart, Matt had lived through a repetition of that day, trying against all odds to live up to his father's expectations. But Matt had been fighting a losing battle. No matter how much he wanted to please his father, he would never be his brother. Finally, he'd just stopped trying.

With a heavy sigh, Matt reminded himself of his vow not to let the past ruin his homecoming. He climbed down from the truck, then headed toward the one place that had brought him the small measure of true happiness he'd known as a kid—his mother's greenhouse. As he made his way toward the back of the house, tall weeds snagged at his jean legs, leaving dried burrs clinging to the material. A rabbit scurrying from the recesses of the vine-covered woodpile startled Matt, then hurried out of his way.

As he neared the rear of the house, the annoying racket of a machine coughing and sputtering to life shattered the silence. Curious, Matt slowed his pace and peeked around the corner. The back lawn spread out before him, mowed and neatly trimmed. A portly man in bib overalls guided a gas-powered weed-whacker around the foundation of the small green-house, its recently cleaned glass glittering in the morning sun.

Matt studied the man's stooped body. When he'd paid the back taxes, not an hour ago, the clerk had told him the house belonged to him. So who was this guy?

Just as Matt opened his mouth to call to the man, the weed-whacker went silent. The man turned. His ruddy face, half hidden beneath a Yankees baseball cap, broke into a broad grin. Matt immediately recognized Sam Thatcher, his neighbor and old friend.

"Matt, my boy. When they told me you was comin' home, I couldn't believe it. I figured I'd be dead and buried before you showed your face around here again." He propped the weed-whacker against the side of the house, then extended his thick hand. His smile melting into a serious expression, he stared deep into Matt's eyes. "How you been, boy?"

Matt grinned and took the offered hand, gripped it firmly, then shook it. "I'm fine, Sam, but what on earth are you doing?" He gestured around at the mowed lawn.

The older man adjusted the cap on his bald head. "Oh, you know Alma. Soon as she heard from Mildred Henderson that you was back, she insisted I come over and start gettin' the place tidied up for you." He glanced around at his handiwork. "Even though I had my doubts, Alma always said your roots were here and, when you got the itch outta your shoes, you'd make for home." He removed the cap, scratched his bald spot, shook his head, then set the cap back in place. "In over forty-six years, she's never been wrong. Makes a man damned uncomfortable to live with a woman who's right all the time."

He grinned, telling Matt what he already knew: Sam loved his wife and wouldn't change a hair on her head. A pang of envy coursed through Matt, then disappeared as quickly as it had come.

Content to let Sam talk, Matt allowed pleasant memories to wash over him, memories of sitting in Alma's fragrant kitchen on a cold day, drinking hot chocolate and eating her oatmeal cookies. Memories of the Thatchers' good-natured bickering. Memories of the love they shared with every glance.

The Thatchers had never had children and had more or less adopted every kid they came in contact with, no matter who. A couple of cookies and a glass of milk or a cup of hot chocolate had always been readily available at the Thatcher house. While the kid enjoyed the repast, Alma had handed out large doses of her wisdom and love.

Matt had spent a lot of hours at their kitchen table, wondering what his life would have been like if he'd been born to these gentle, loving people instead of to Lois and Kevin Logan. Now he wondered if he'd ever know the love and happiness the Thatchers shared.

"Greenhouse needs some glass replaced, but for the most part, it's just like your mama left it." Sam's voice cut through Matt's musings. "What do you plan on doin' with it?"

Matt's gaze drifted to the greenhouse. "I'm not sure. I've got a couple of ideas, but nothing definite yet."

Sam patted his arm. "Well, whatever it is, the missus and I are behind you all the way, and we just know you'll do good.''

Rather than making him feel good, Sam's confidence in Matt served to underline once more how little faith his own father had had in him.

''Matthew Logan! Bless my soul. Is that you?''

A woman's excited, high-pitched voice drew their attention. Hurrying through the overgrown grass separating Matt's house from the Thatchers', a woman in a pale pink dress and a matching pillbox hat headed toward them. He didn't need to see her face to know it was Alma Thatcher. She drew close, then stopped. Clutching her hands to her heaving breast, she stared up at Matt.

''My word, Matthew, but you did grow up nice.'' Then, before Matt could respond, she launched herself at him, wrapped her arms around his neck and planted a kiss on his cheek. Tears gathered in her sparkling blue eyes. ''Good to have you home. This house has been empty far too long. It needs a family in it.'' She stepped back a little and glanced around, as if looking for that family.

Grinning, Matt squeezed her hands. ''Well, the family part is going to have to wait a bit.'' Suddenly, an image of Honey and Danny filled his mind. He shook it away.

''Everything in good time.'' She turned to her husband. ''Sam, your lunch is ready, and I'm late for my book club meeting. You best get yourself over to the house before the cat eats your tuna sandwich.''

''No need nagging, woman, I'm going.'' Sam tempered his words with a kiss to his wife's rosy cheek, then turned to Matt. ''Nice to have you back, boy.

Now, don't forget to drop in on us, when you got the time. I'll be back later to finish up this yard for you.''

Knowing it wouldn't do any good to protest Sam's offer, Matt merely nodded. ''I'll do that, Sam, and thanks for doing the lawn.''

''Pshaw!'' Without turning back, Sam acknowledged Matt's words with a wave of his hand, then started across the yard, dragging the weed-whacker behind him.

''I'll be along in a minute, Sam,'' Alma called after him, then turned back to Matt and studied him for a moment.

Matt avoided the questions he saw in her face by moving his gaze back to the greenhouse. Alma came to stand beside him. The scent of Roses in May perfume drifted up to him on a soft breeze. He'd bought her a bottle of it for her birthday the year he'd left Bristol. The scent anchored him to this place more than anything else could have.

The silence stretched out, then Alma laid her hand on his arm. ''Anger's like a weed in a garden. If you let it grow, pretty soon it chokes out the love. If you're going to be settling here and you plan on being happy, Matthew, you must let go of the anger and the hurt.''

Frowning in confusion, he let his gaze rest for a few moments more on his mother's greenhouse. He turned to ask Alma what she meant, but her surprisingly quick step had already carried her across the lawn and out of earshot.

HONEY FOUND HERSELF driving down Thatcher Lane. That wasn't what the county maps called it, but everyone had known it as Thatcher Lane for so long, she wasn't sure anyone remembered the real name. She hadn't been in this part of town for a long time and, truth be known, she wasn't sure why she was here now.

Then she saw Matt's black truck parked in the driveway of his old house. Had she come here intentionally hoping to see him? She shook her head and started to push harder on the accelerator, determined to pass the house and head for home. But seemingly of its own free will, her foot hit the brake, slowing the car, allowing it to veer off the paved road and into the gravel drive, stopping within inches of Matt's back bumper.

Now, what?

Playing for time, she stared at Matt's house. Rundown and badly in need of some TLC, it hadn't really changed much. Nor had its effect on her. The warm feeling she'd known as a young girl came rushing back. For reasons she could never explain, the house had always called to her, beckoning with a warmth her own home had never offered.

She scanned the yard for signs of Matt, but he was nowhere to be seen. Then she glanced at the Thatcher house. Good people. It made a person question justice in this world when two people who loved kids so much couldn't have them, and then a man like her father, who could barely tolerated their existence, had been blessed with three. It wasn't fair, but then, what in life was?

If life were fair, Matt wouldn't have left her. If life were fair, she never would have agreed to marry Stan, and Danny would have known his real father from day one. If life were fair, Matt would still love her.

That thought jolted her from her reverie as little else could have.

Get a grip, Honey. You need a clear head to face Matt. Don't let your fantasies get the better of you. The last thing you need is Matt back in your life. If you were smart, you'd turn this car around while you still can.

Despite her warnings to herself, she opened the car door and slid from the seat. She needed to talk to Matt. Maybe if she talked to him, they could at least alleviate this tension between them, tension Danny would certainly pick up on, and which would only worsen his problems. She and Matt had to live in the same house for the next few weeks, and it would be better for all concerned, especially Danny, if they did it as amiably as possible.

Resolutely, she yanked the hem of her red T-shirt down over her denim clad hips. Absently, she wished she'd worn something less…less what?

Get real, she scolded herself. *This isn't a fashion show. You're simply going to talk with your son's father. Period.*

As she stepped to the side to close the car door, she noted that the corner of the backyard she could see was mowed. Matt? Taking a deep breath, she headed for the side of the house.

As she rounded the back corner, she noticed the door of the small greenhouse standing open. Slowly, she made her way toward it. Inside, she could see Matt, fingering a rusted hand trowel, his brow furrowed in thought. She could simply turn on her heel and leave, and he'd never know she'd even been there, never witnessed the slump of his proud shoulders or the droop of his head.

Something akin to compassion grew inside her. Something that made her feet stay rooted to the dirt floor. Something that made her speak.

"Matt?"

He never looked up. "I gave her a set of hand tools for Mother's Day the year before she died." His voice was low and lifeless. "She said it was the best present anyone had ever given her because I did odd jobs for a month for the money to buy it, so I wouldn't have to ask my father."

Honey didn't know what to say, so she remained silent, her heart going out to the little boy in Matt that still mourned the loss of his mother. The look on his face reminded her of the day the social worker had brought her brother, Jesse, to them after his mother died—a baby lost, alone and badly in need of a friend.

Suddenly, the antagonism between them dissolved, and she thought with the heart of a mother. "You loved her a great deal."

He nodded. "Yes. If it hadn't been for her, I would have left here as soon as I learned to walk."

Honey couldn't resist asking, "Why did you leave, Matt?"

He glanced at her, tossed the trowel he'd been fingering onto the rotted wooden planting table and turned away. He'd never shared this part of his life with anyone before, but the compassion in her eyes told him that Honey would understand the part about his father. As for the rest, the part that involved her, he could never see her understanding.

"I couldn't live with my father or my brother's memory." He picked up a clay flower pot. "I tried. God, how I tried, but I could never be what he wanted me to be."

"Which was?"

"Jamie. He wanted me to be my brother." Matt glanced at the ceiling, then tossed the pot on the table with the trowel. It hit another pot and broke into several large pieces. He stared down at the broken shards and chuckled without humor. "Par," he muttered, then turned to Honey. "My brother was the all-American kid, the kid who made the teams, won the awards, got straight As. But there was one thing he didn't do well—stay alive."

Honey took a step toward him. "How did Jamie die? Since he was so much older than us, I never knew him."

"One of his many accomplishments was learning to fly a plane. My father was so proud of him, he helped Jamie buy a plane for his eighteenth birthday..." Matt sighed and looked away "...in which Jamie immediately crashed and killed himself." Though his words sounded crisp and unemotional to his ears, the pain of his brother's death still had the power to cut a deep swath through his heart. "After that, my father tried to make me over in Jamie's image." He glanced at her. "Funny part was, the harder he tried, the worse I got."

"But you were so young then. What did that have to do with you leaving?"

He propped his hip on the edge of the wooden table. "Oh, it didn't stop there. The more I failed, the harder he tried. The harder he tried, the more possessed I became with filling Jamie's shoes and taking his place, and the more I failed. It was a vicious circle. Then, when my mother died, the buffer she'd provided between us died, too. We got so we could barely look at each other. We became strangers." He stood. "I finally decided that if I had to live with a stranger, it might as well be someone who didn't judge me every time he looked at me."

"So that's the reason you left?"

"That and a few more."

"Such as?"

Matt avoided her question. The other reasons were the ones he knew she'd never understand and ones that didn't matter now, anyway. "Don't you have to be home for Danny?"

Honey glanced at her watch. "Not for a couple of hours yet. Where did you go when you left here?"

"I knew two things well enough to get a job— horses and flowers. Since there wasn't any big call for landscaping in Texas, I joined a rodeo." He brushed past her on his way to the door, his limp somewhat more pronounced than it had been that morning.

She looked pointedly at his injured leg, then raised her gaze to meet his. "Rodeo? Isn't that dangerous?" Stan racing around a track in a car with an engine far too powerful for her peace of mind flashed across Honey's thoughts. Why did men feel that happiness meant risking their lives? Anger that Matt would have put himself in danger bubbled up in her.

"No more dangerous than walking across a busy street." He stared at her for a long minute. "Everything involves a risk, Honey."

Though his reply only made her angrier, she got the distinct feeling the comment was somehow directed at her. "What does that mean?"

He shrugged, then opened the greenhouse door. "Whatever you want it to, I guess."

He stepped outside, then headed for the back door

of the house. She made no move to follow. Instead, she stood very still, listening to the hum of the insects, the breeze rustling the trees and the birds singing, and tried to figure out what his words meant.

While she couldn't find an answer to that puzzle, she did draw one conclusion from their conversation that made her heart twist in pain. With all the unhappy memories this place held for Matt, he would never plan on staying here, or even in Bristol. She'd been a fool to even let that dim hope surface. And why would she want him around all the time, anyway? He was nothing to her, just Danny's father.

By his own admission, Matt had a history of running from his problems. The last thing that Honey needed was a man who couldn't face his problems and responsibilities head-on. She'd been down that road once, and once was more than enough.

MATT WORKED HARD most of the afternoon. As long as he kept busy, he could keep the look of compassion on Honey's face from haunting him, the look that told him that if he'd talked to her instead of running away, she might have understood him. Such a thought bordered on plain crazy. How could any woman understand that loving her more than anything in his life had scared the hell out of him? Scared him enough to make him run.

Not until this very minute had he ever wondered just who he'd been more afraid of disappointing—his father or Honey.

Chapter Five

At dinner that evening, Danny chattered on about his day at school, and as usual, Amanda hung on each word, encouraging him to tell her every last detail. Distracted by thoughts of Matt and their conversation that afternoon in the greenhouse, Honey half listened, nodded at the appropriate moments and offered mumbled replies when needed.

Her lack of attentiveness did not go unnoticed.

"Are you all right, dear?" Amanda's whisper jerked Honey from her deep thoughts and back to the cozy dining room and the roast beef dinner everyone but her seemed interested in eating.

A dull pain passed through her. *All right?* She'd never be all right and nothing would ever be the same in this house or her life again, at least not until Matt left—and he would, eventually. Contrarily, the thought of him going only served to drive her deeper into the pensive mood that had followed her home from Matt's house.

She roused herself long enough to satisfy Amanda with a reply. "I'm fine. Just a bit tired."

Amanda studied her for a moment longer, but when Honey forced a smile, her mother-in-law went back to being absorbed in her grandson's chatter about the school play.

A distant noise drew Honey's gaze to the dining room window overlooking the driveway. Outside, Matt's black pickup slid to a stop. He'd called earlier saying he'd be late and not to wait dinner for him. Honey had hoped against hope that "late" meant after she'd finished eating and had escaped to the upper regions of the house to help Danny get ready for bed. But as usual, fate threw her plans in her face.

At the same time, an odd sense of relief washed over her, almost as if she'd been waiting for Matt's return—which couldn't have been more absurd.

Heavens, but she had to get hold of herself. She concentrated on her food, trying to appear as if she didn't know who would walk through the door at any second.

A few minutes later, Matt hurried inside, called an apology for being late and disappeared up the stairs. Honey's heart assumed a normal rhythm, and she let out the breath she'd been unconsciously holding. She tried to quell the concern that Matt's more pronounced limp generated in her by concentrating on her son, who was using his fork to make small sculptures in his mashed potatoes.

"Danny, please stop playing with your food and eat your dinner. You have to get ready for bed soon." Hopefully, she could see at least part of her plan through to fruition and make a clean escape before Matt came down to eat.

"Aw, M-M-Mom. It's early y-y-yet. Gram p-p-promised we could w-w-watch a v-v-video before I go t-t-to bed."

Amanda threw her a questioningly look. Honey

glanced at the sunshine pouring through the window, then shrugged her shoulders and smiled weakly at Amanda.

"I guess it's all right. But no videos unless you finish your supper." In an attempt to ease the moment and distract her mother-in-law before she asked one of her probing questions, she added, "You know your grandson. If I don't remind him that the object of sitting down at a dinner table is to eat, he'd play with his food all night."

Amanda's gaze dropped pointedly to Honey's plate, and the unappealing mixture Honey had made of mashed potatoes, gravy, peas and pieces of roast beef. Then she looked back at Honey and raised one eyebrow. "It would seem that the acorn doesn't fall far from the tree, hmm?"

Honey avoided Amanda's interrogating gaze. How could she explain to her mother-in-law what was happening inside her, when she couldn't explain it to herself? She had no idea why, but she felt as if she were standing on the edge of a precipice, and the slightest move in any direction would plunge her over the side into a bottomless void. And not knowing why troubled her. Honey made a point of knowing the whys, wherefores and hows of her life. Not knowing had caused her to make one of the biggest mistakes she'd ever made—marrying Stan Logan.

What she did know for certain was the cause of this out-of-control feeling. Matt Logan. Every time he came into a room, her common sense flew out the closest window, with her good judgment right on its tail.

She stiffened her spine. The time had come for that to stop. She was taking back control of her life, her senses and her judgment, and Matt Logan could go to—

Amanda's hand on her arm interrupted her thoughts. "Are you sure there's nothing bothering you, dear? You seem so…distracted and tense."

To prove, both to herself and Amanda, that she was fine, Honey shook her head, then shoveled a forkful of food into her mouth. Honey's throat muscles worked to swallow.

Footsteps sounded just outside the dining room door. Matt entered the room. She nearly choked on the food.

He'd taken a quick shower and changed his clothes. The lights bounced off his wet hair, highlighting its blue-black sheen. A tiny droplet of water slipped down his muscular arm, left bare by a white T-shirt that molded itself to his muscular chest. Her fingers itched to reach out and catch the water droplet, then bring it to her lips to see if it tasted like him.

Danny's eyes lit up and his face broke into a wide grin. "Hi, Uncle M-M-Matt!"

"Hey, sport. What's up?" Matt rumpled Danny's hair, then took the seat next to him and directly across from Honey. "How did the rehearsals for the play go today?"

Honey didn't hear her son's answer. Until this very moment, as they sat side by side, she'd never totally realized just how much they looked alike. Danny had inherited that dimple in one cheek that always showed up when Matt's mood turned playful. Like his father, a lock of jet-black hair fell across Danny's forehead, almost obscuring one eye. Good grief! They even held their forks the same way. The resemblance exceeded uncanny; it was downright unnerving.

"Honey?"

She started at the sound of her name. Matt was staring at her expectantly.

"What?"

"When you come back from your daydreams, could you please pass the potatoes?"

She glared at him, then handed him the bowl of potatoes.

"M-M-Mom's tired, not d-d-daydreaming. She says that d-d-daydreaming is n-n-not a good thing to do."

"Oh, and why is that?" As he scooped two large spoonfuls of potatoes onto his plate, Matt's gaze bounced between Honey and the task at hand.

She tried to speak, but couldn't. The ripple of raw muscular power in his arms had made her throat go dry.

"Mom s-s-says that daydreamers get left b-be-hind in the world and t-t-that they live in a f-f-fantasy land of irre…irre…"

"Irresponsibility?"

"Yeah, t-t-that's it."

Honey smiled at hearing Danny repeat word-for-word what she'd told him over and over since he could understand. Matt's censuring look dampened her pride in her son and replaced it with a strange discomfort. Determinedly, she ignored him.

"Danny, slow down when you speak, sweetie, and think about your words before you say them. Now, finish up those peas." Honey avoided meeting Matt's gaze by rearranging the white napkin on her lap.

"Aw, M-M-Mom, p-p-peas are yucky. B-b-be-sides, Uncle M-M-Matt's not eating any."

Finally, Matt drew his gaze from her, then grinned

down at his son. "Nope. I never touch them. They rank right up there with liver." He mimed a shudder. "What do you say we stage a strike against eating anything small, round and green?" Matt picked up Danny's plate and scraped the peas into an empty serving dish.

Danny's face broke into a grin. "Okay." He held up his hand, then he and Matt slapped their palms together in a pledge of agreement. Both broke into gales of laughter.

Amanda joined in.

Honey did not find any of this amusing. How dare he undermine her authority right in front of her son?

"Well, I'm your mother, and I say you *will* eat those peas or you will not watch the video with your grandmother." Her tone surprised even her. She'd never spoken to Danny like that before.

"Oh, Honey, lighten up," Matt said. "Peas aren't the end of the world. After all, President Bush didn't like broccoli, and he managed to govern an entire country and hold onto his standing as the leader of the free world."

Honey glanced around the table, at the three sets of eyes boring into her. She refused to gratify Matt with an argument in front of Danny. After all, peas weren't the issue, and both she and Matt knew it. His insufferable interference was. He couldn't suddenly step into the child's life and take over. As Danny's mother, she would decide what was good for him. And, dammit, peas were good for him.

Silence thick enough to slice with a knife fell over the dining room. Amanda frowned in confusion. Matt scowled in disapproval. But the sheen of moisture gathering in her son's crystal blue eyes crushed

Honey's resolve. What mattered more, a few small, green vegetables or Danny? The fact that Matt had seen that first brought her anger to full boil.

"Very well. But this is the last time you get away with this, young man," she told her son sternly. Then she cast Matt a we'll-discuss-this-later glance. He answered with a count-on-it look.

Honey silently accepted his challenge, then stood and busied herself clearing away the dirty dishes.

MATT PROPPED HIS LEFT FOOT against the wooden railing, his knee bent to support the weight of his right leg. He massaged the aching flesh until it relaxed, cursing himself for doing too much that day. The pain gradually eased.

With a relieved sigh, he leaned back in the chair he'd dragged through the French doors to the balcony outside his bedroom, and breathed deeply of the balmy night air. He'd come upstairs with the idea of going to bed to get an early start in the morning, but the balmy summer night had seduced him. Having grown accustomed to rodeo dust filling his nostrils for so long, it took him a few minutes to sort out the smells that typified home.

From beyond the hedges came the perfume of Aunt Amanda's rose garden. Wafting up to him on a renegade breeze, the fragrance of Tess's fresh baked cookies made him smile. The scents of pine needles and freshly mowed grass put a finished signature to the night.

He leaned his head back and gazed up at the sky. Wispy clouds floated slowly past a full, lemon-colored moon, and stars peeked through the thin veil, as if playing hide and seek with him. In the distance, a dog bayed and a voice reprimanded the animal. Then all fell silent, except for the rhythmic chirp of crickets.

He closed his eyes and let the contentment of being in familiar surroundings wash over him. Why had he ever thought he could find this kind of peace anywhere else on earth?

The reappearance of the dull ache in his thigh disrupted his reverie and reminded him of the nightly task he had to take care of before he could retire. Resignedly, he heaved his tired body from the chair and limped back inside. He removed all of his clothes, then reached for a large plastic bag. Carefully, he wrapped it around his thigh, then secured it with a large rubber band at the top and bottom. Satisfied the wound and the bandage would remain dry, he headed for the bathroom.

His shower took no time, and he was soon back in the bedroom clothed only in clean Jockey shorts. Sitting on the edge of the bed, he deposited a box of large gauze pads, a roll of adhesive tape, a roll of gauze and a tube of prescription antibiotic ointment on the coverlet at his side.

Placing his foot on the chair he'd retrieved from the balcony, he carefully removed the plastic wrapper, then the bandage encasing most of his upper leg. Supporting his calf and foot on the seat of the chair, he bent his leg to the side, then examined his injury in the light from the bedside lamp.

Despite his worry that his jeans might have irritated the wound, the surface skin showed a healthy pink. Twelve stitches, at regular intervals, dissected a zig-zag scab running from about four inches below his crotch to just above his knee. The wound exhibited all the signs of healing without a problem.

The muscle, however, had sustained serious damage and would take much longer to become healthy and strong. The surgeon had warned him that the muscle pain would last long after the surface wound had healed, and that he might always walk with a limp.

Removing the cap from the tube of ointment, Matt squeezed a liberal amount on his fingertips. Slowly and gingerly, he slathered it on the wound, then covered it with several of the large gauze pads. Next came the fun part. From day one, he'd had trouble keeping the pads from slipping on the ointment while he wound the gauze strips around his thigh to anchor them in place.

Using his fingertips to secure the first pad, he began to unroll the gauze. But just as he made the first pass around his leg, the pad slipped free and dropped to the floor.

"Damn!" Grabbing a new pad and wishing he had an extra hand, he repeated the action, only to have another fall to the floor.

"May I?"

Matt's head jerked up.

Honey stood in the doorway, her face a soft pink, her gaze riveted on the roll of gauze. "That is, if you don't mind."

"Mind?" He handed her the gauze. "Be my guest. If there's one thing I've learned in the past few weeks, it's that nursing is definitely not a career option for me."

Honey laid the gauze aside, then squatted gingerly in front of him. She replaced the gauze pad that had fallen off with a clean one. Her warm fingers grazed his skin, bringing to mind other times her fingers had danced over his bare flesh. A tingle raced up Matt's leg and settled in his groin. He jumped with the force of the sensation.

Honey pulled back and looked at him in concern. "Did I hurt you?"

He shook his head, not trusting his voice.

"Hold this." She took his hand and placed his fingers on the corners of the pads.

Then she leaned forward again, barely grazing his upper thigh. The tingle came back. This time it coursed up his leg and fanned out over his entire lower belly. His breathing stopped. As nonchalantly as possible, he grabbed a pillow and placed it over his lap. Maybe this wasn't such a great idea.

As she began unrolling the gauze around his leg, he studied her bent head and sure movements. This whole thing didn't seem to be fazing her in the least. Then he detected a slight trembling in her hands.

Though she reminded herself that this was a task she'd done repeatedly when she worked in the hospital, she hadn't missed the move with the pillow and why it was necessary. Added to that, she found she could not separate her emotions from the vision of Matt maimed and in pain.

She'd seen enough wounds to know that this one could have meant the loss of his leg or worse. After all, she'd seen Stan's lifeless body being pried from the mangled piece of metal that had once been a race car.

Despite her anger at Stan's careless disregard for his life—and Matt's as well—her legs suddenly felt like cooked spaghetti.

Gathering her wits about her, she concentrated on keeping her hands steady, and centered her mind on her task. It helped to a degree. Then his other leg pressed against the back of her thighs, and the large bed Matt sat on took on a whole new significance. If she didn't find something to occupy her thoughts, this little scenario would end with far more than a neatly bandaged wound.

"When do you get the stitches out?" Honey hoped her voice didn't sound as unsteady as she felt.

"In a week or so."

"Instead of you going back to the doctor's, I can do it for you, if you'd like." Now why had she offered to do something that would once more place her in close proximity to Matt? Would she never learn that only distance, and lots of it, kept her safe from his charm?

"You've got a deal. Thanks." Matt's voice sounded strained, as if he feared she'd cause him pain.

"Don't worry, I won't hurt you. Dealing with Danny has made me very sensitive to treating wounds as painlessly as possible. I can even remove a splinter without as much as a squeak from my patient." She was babbling. She knew it, but how else could she keep her mind off Matt's body and on the task at hand? Better she look like a fool, than give in to the yearnings rushing at her from all sides and actually become one. "I've been told I have a very gentle touch."

"I remember," he said, his voice low and tight.

Her skin burned under his scrutiny. She fought off the memories and continued to keep her gaze centered on what she was doing. Quickly, she secured the end of the gauze with a strip of adhesive. "There. You're all set."

Unconsciously, she backed away a few steps and came up against something solid. Only when she heard the soft click of the door closing behind her did she realized she'd sealed off her only avenue of escape. Her gaze darted to him. She wished he would put something on, something besides that ridiculous pillow. Something that would cover the hard planes of his body, the deeply tanned skin, the—

Quickly, before she listened to the voice telling her to throw herself into this man's arms and never leave, she forced thoughts of what had brought her to Matt's room back into her mind. Danny. If she concentrated on her son, she'd be fine.

Matt hadn't moved since she'd stepped away. He stared at her, his eyes saying things that made concentrating on anything hard. Willing a vision of her son to her mind, Honey faced the man on the bed.

"Matt?"

Honey's voice roused him. He straightened, then lowered his foot slowly to the floor, all the time gazing at Honey. Hands folded at her waist, her eyes large and apprehensive, she looked like a schoolgirl waiting for a reprimand. He knew Honey. Control mattered to her, and right now she thought she had it in her grasp. But the rapid rise and fall of her chest told him otherwise. There was an emotional tug-of-war going on inside her, the same tug-of-war being waged inside him.

Taking a deep, cleansing breath, he dragged his gaze away from where the dim light from the bedside lamp silhouetted her body through the sheer cotton sundress, outlining every curve to taunt him. In a way, that unnerved him almost as much as her presence. Oddly, having her standing in his bedroom seemed to complete his vision of home and sharing a life and a bed with her.

Against his will, his lower body hardened more. He took in a lungful of the night air, threw the pillow aside, then reached for his discarded jeans. Standing and turning away from her, he pulled them on, leaving the zipper and the snap at the waistband undone. Replacing the chair against the wall, he gripped the back with rigid fingers, waiting for the desire to drain from his body.

When he finally had himself under control, he sat on the edge of the bed, then pointed at his injured leg. "Thanks."

"You're welcome," she said in a tone she'd probably learned in nurse's training.

She didn't make a move to leave. He glanced at her questioningly. "I know you didn't come here to play nurse, so what's on your mind?"

"We need to talk about Danny."

He nodded. "Yes, we do."

This wasn't something he'd been looking forward to, but the change in topic squelched his sexual urges more thoroughly than a bucket of cold water. An anxious silence filled the room.

He didn't need a degree in psychology to recognize that his interference at dinner had not sat well with Honey. But he couldn't stand by and let her stifle Danny's imagination or his right to make his own choices, even to what vegetable the kid preferred. Every human being deserved to be an individual. Matt's father had never understood that, but after their conversation in the greenhouse that afternoon, he'd thought Honey did. But this wasn't the first time he'd overestimated her, and it probably wouldn't be the last.

Honey remained standing rigidly near the door. "I'm not going to bite." He patted the coverlet at his side. "Sit." The mutinous line of Honey's mouth made him add, "Please."

Without a word, she moved to the bed, eyed it and him suspiciously, then sat. When she crossed her legs and folded her hands in her lap, as if they were at a church service, he smiled. Though he found her bearing humorous, he hated that this barrier of polite formality separated them. But, from her stiff demeanor, he guessed that the impending conversation troubled Honey as much as it did him. He took some comfort from that.

He searched his mind for a way to keep the tentative peace and to break down that wall that collected another brick of resentment every time they met. Despite the fact that he still couldn't forgive her for marrying Stan, and he didn't trust her in the least, for Danny's sake they had to find a middle ground.

"You had no right to undermine my authority with Danny." While spoken quietly, Honey's words held an edge that clearly told him she would give him a fight on this.

"I didn't mean to undermine your authority. I merely tried to make you see that you were being silly insisting that Danny eat peas." Matt swiveled to face her. Her profile remained stiff, her brows furrowed, her mouth set in a straight line. "He's an individual, Honey. He deserves the right to make choices and to dream dreams—his own dreams and his own choices." He touched her hand. "If he doesn't eat peas, he won't end up a serial killer."

"Don't be ridiculous. Peas are not the issue, and you know it." But what was? Was it that Danny stuttered less around Matt than he did around her? Was it the way their son had taken to Matt as if they'd always been buddies? Was she really making more of this than the situation warranted?

Honey pulled her hand away from Matt's warm grasp. Sitting this close and trying to think coherently had become nearly impossible. Having him touch her threw her mind into a whirlwind of thoughts that had nothing to do with Danny and everything to do with her and Matt. She had to stay centered or lose all control over her son's life.

"I *do* allow him to dream his dreams."

"How? By telling him that daydreams and fantasies are foolish nonsense and will get him nowhere? Think of where we'd be as a society if everyone felt that way."

"It's not like that." She could feel the threads of desperation slipping insidiously into her thoughts, tangling them and making it difficult to sort illusion from logic. She struggled to clear her mind. She had to make Matt see that she would not allow her son to become another Stan, with his head in the clouds and his feet buried in insubstantial dreams.

"Dreams need a base in reality, just like anything else. That's what I've tried to teach Danny." Why was she defending herself to this man? She took a deep, calming breath. "My relationship with Stan didn't have the best influence on Danny, and I want to make sure that changes."

Matt said nothing for a long time. He just looked

at her, long and hard. When he finally did speak, his words dug deep into her resolve to put the past behind her.

"Living with Stan couldn't have been that bad. You didn't have any problem sticking it out for six years. Tell me, Honey, if Stan hadn't died, would there still be a marriage?"

To Honey's dismay, once the dammed up memories had been breached by his words, they came pouring forth like a spring flood.

Chapter Six

The soft night air sifting through the open French doors into Matt's room had suddenly turned stifling. Honey opened her mouth to breath in large gulps. The floor seemed to tilt beneath her feet.

Matt's question about the stability of her marriage brought back the doubts that Honey had had to face after Stan's death. Had their talk of divorce been instrumental in Stan missing that turn and smashing into a wall at ninety miles per hour? Had he been preoccupied with his thoughts so much that he'd missed a turn he'd taken hundreds of times before?

She refused to give way to those doubts again. She'd come to terms with them long ago. Living on the edge as he did, Stan would have killed himself eventually, with or without her. But even with that admission, she refused to tell Matt that she and Stan had talked about divorce only a few weeks before the accident that killed him.

She pulled back from Matt's overwhelming presence and answered as honestly as she dared. "I don't know."

He didn't need to know that, when it came down to the wire, Stan had been as unhappy being married to her as she'd been, married to him, or that he had harbored some wild notion that she'd never gotten over Matt. As it turned out, she didn't need to tell Matt. Her expression must have given away her thoughts.

"So, you were thinking of leaving him?" Matt didn't know why, but her answer was very important to him. He waited.

"Don't be too quick to judge me. You don't know what it was like living with Stan. How could you? You'd run off to your safe place and left me to live with a man who spent more time chasing rainbows and death than he spent with his family."

"And whose fault was that, Honey?"

"Okay, so maybe it wasn't anyone's fault but mine. But if you'd stayed, we would have—"

"What? Married? Lived happily ever after? Hasn't it occurred to you that maybe I would have found another way to disappoint you?"

She didn't answer. She couldn't. To admit, even to herself, that she and Matt might have had a chance at a life together would bring back all the pain and anguish of his leaving.

Besides, now that they had started digging into the past, she couldn't stop the flow of her memories of Stan. "At first, I went along to Stan's races, thinking that Danny needed a father, and even from the grandstands, it was better than nothing. We sat there and watched Stan race around a track, daring death to stop him. Then one day, when the car skidded out of control, I saw Danny turn white. He had nightmares for weeks afterward. That was it. After that, I stayed home with my son while Stan chased his dreams. Until the last race."

She paused, gathering the strength to go back to the day Stan died. In the end, she couldn't bring herself to relive the screams of the crowd, the clash of metal, the blood, the looks of sympathy as they dragged the sheet over Stan's marred face. And the guilt.

She rose, then began pacing the length of the room, her footsteps muted by the carpeting. "I knew that being with Stan and sharing his crazy dream was only hurting Danny. Stan never objected when I refused to go with him because, by then, Danny had started school."

"Danny's not Stan, Honey."

She swung on him. "No! He's not, and if I can help it, he never will be. I want my son to be normal, to live life with sense and good judgment. To take on his responsibilities."

Matt stood and came toward her. "He will. Don't you see that if you leave him to make his own decisions, he will? He's a good kid, Honey. You've done a fine job with him...."

She didn't miss the unspoken *but*. Fueled by his obvious doubts about her, and by her own frustration, her anger rose anew, this time beyond her control. "Make decisions like you did?" She laughed derisively. "The poor kid doesn't have much going for him, does he? A mother with no backbone. A stepfather who played Russian roulette with his life, and a father who solves his problems by running from them."

Matt froze.

Honey couldn't believe she'd said that. After what he'd told her this afternoon, she knew that Matt had been running from an intolerable situation, a situation much like her own. They'd just handled it differently. He'd chosen to run, and she'd chosen to marry a man she didn't love. Were they really all that different? Her anger dissolved.

"I'm sorry, Matt."

He waved a hand to silence her, then turned away, his broad shoulders stiff. "We're not talking about me or you or Stan, dammit. We're talking about a little boy who shouldn't have to pay for anyone's mistakes but his own."

He either hadn't heard or chose to ignore her apology, and she'd be damned if she'd say it again. "No, we're never talking about you, are we?"

He sighed and scrubbed his hand over his face. "We have to stop this. Danny senses the tension between us and that's not helping him."

She raised her chin. "You're right, and the best way to do that is for you to stay out of my business and let me raise my son my way."

"*Our* son," he reminded her softly, but firmly. "And your way is not helping him."

Her defensive shield rose immediately. "I'm doing exactly what Dr. Thomas told me to do."

"And it's not working." Matt rose, then strode to her, stopping a few feet away. "Don't you see? Telling Danny to slow down and think about what he's saying is only frustrating him more. Those practices are as antiquated as Dr. Thomas. Good grief, Honey, the man is as old as Methuselah. As a nurse, you should know that medicine and psychology are changing all the time, that the methods are being improved and that they're finding what they thought worked doesn't."

"And exactly when did you get your medical degree?"

He cradled her shoulders in his hands. For a moment, she held herself as straight and unbending as a two-by-four, then he felt the stiffness drain from her.

"Trust me, I know a lot more about this than you think I do."

He wanted to tell her about the little boy who had started stuttering right after his mother died. About the father so wrapped up in his own grief that he couldn't help, and about the teacher who had helped Matt overcome it, not with frustration, but with patience.

Then Honey looked up at him with those clear, sensitive eyes. He could see her torment, feel her pain, understand her disappointment at not being able to help Danny. And it tore him apart.

She opened her mouth to speak, but the words never passed her lips. Instead, she just looked at him, reminding him of the Honey who had lain in his arms and whispered love words. Back then, her sad eyes had reflected her frustration. Matt had seen the young girl who had wanted her father's love as badly as Matt had wanted his own father's. Now he saw a woman who desperately wanted to help her child and didn't know how.

The beautiful woman before him filled his vision and his mind. He forgot that she had betrayed him by marrying his cousin. He forgot that she'd kept the birth of his son a secret. He forgot that he didn't love her anymore.

As he gazed down at her, her mouth opened the slightest bit. Nervously, she wet her lips with her tongue, until they glistened silver in the lamplight. He let go of her shoulder and cupped her cheek, then traced her bottom lip with the pad of his thumb. She groaned softly and leaned toward him.

Honey felt herself torn between the heaven of being in Matt's arms and the hell of never feeling him hold her again. She wasn't sure which would hurt worse.

Where Matt's hand lay on her bare shoulder, her skin burned as if singed by a raging fire. The years of loneliness fell away. The empty nights vanished beneath a rush of memories of all the nights Matt had held her close and made tender love to her. His thumb caressing her lips caused little pinpricks of heat to sting her everywhere.

She looked up at his mouth, the mouth that had brought her to a fever pitch of desire time after time, holding her there, then dropping her over the edge still clinging to him. She wanted that again—now.

She knew that what she longed for could destroy her, but she didn't have the strength to turn away. And, God help her, when his mouth slowly descended to hers, she could do nothing more than moan with the pleasure of finally coming home.

She threaded her fingers through the thick mass of hair at his nape, combing the silky, night-black strands as she'd wanted to do so many times. Half aware of the danger of what she was doing, she opened her lips and allowed him access. A groan started deep inside him and, as he tightened his embrace, escaped into her mouth. She could feel the open zipper of his jeans digging into her stomach, but she pressed closer, savoring the rigid proof of his arousal. He ran his hand up her rib cage, and her breath caught, waiting for the touch she knew would follow.

Slowly, he moved the back of his hand against the side of her breast, then turned it and cupped her fullness in his palm. Her nipples swelled painfully against the fabric of her dress. Dimly, she was aware of him slipping the strap down her arm. The cool night air coming through the open French doors caressed her bare flesh, then warmth followed as he covered her exposed skin with his hand.

When she could stand no more, when she began wanting things that she should never want, when she longed for the feel of Matt inside her, she did the one thing that she thought she never could. From deep inside she summoned the strength to deny them both. She pushed at his chest to be free. He let her go.

She glanced at his face. Flushed and filmed with a light sheen of perspiration, he looked as frightened as she felt. Without a word, she slowly backed away from him, then turned and fled to the safety of her room and the undeniable knowledge that ahead of her lay a long and wakeful night.

HONEY STEERED HER CAR into Emily's driveway. Beside her, Danny strained against the seat belt, craning his neck to see the horses frolicking around the corral. She knew his innate love of those four-legged beasts came from his Aunt Emily and his grandfather. She certainly had no affection for them.

Emily's foreman, Chuck Emerson, stood in the center of the corral watching them approach. He waved. She and Danny waved back, and she slowed the car.

"Is Emily home?"

"Inside feeding the girls lunch," he called.

Honey nodded, eased the car up the driveway to

the large white house at the end, then parked under one of the towering maples edging the front lawn. They both climbed out and Danny ran around to her side.

"C-c-can I go s-s-see the horses, M-M-Mom?"

Actually, she'd been hoping something would distract Danny while she spoke to Emily. "Sure, but make sure you do as Chuck tells you."

"T-t-thanks, Mom. I w-w-will." Danny scampered off toward the corral.

Honey watched him go, then turned toward the house, relieved that she could talk to her sister alone about Matt and their kiss. Maybe then she could end this feeling of wanting to run as far from Matt as she could, while at the same time wanting nothing more than to be back in his arms.

Honey needed to know how her sister's husband's first kiss, after he returned, had affected Emily. She dearly wanted to hear her sister say that Kat had left her cold and it hadn't made her realize she loved him. She needed it because she was afraid she'd stumbled into the same trap she had years ago—falling in love with Matt. If that were the case, she had to stop it now, before she got in too deep.

For the last few days, Honey had given Matt a wide berth. She wasn't ready to face what the incident in his bedroom had meant, and from his behavior, guessed that he wasn't, either. He was gone before she came down every morning, and returned home long after dinner had been served and the table cleared. He'd even disappeared for a full day to have the stitches removed from his leg, instead of asking her to do it as she'd offered. That suited her just fine.

Their kiss hadn't lasted for more than a breath of

time, but it had done untold damage to her emotions. She thought she'd be safe in her room, but the want, the need followed her and stayed beside her all night, taunting her with dreams she'd put away seven years ago.

She'd already knocked on Emily's door when her gaze swung to the barn and the black pickup parked in front of the open doors.

Matt. Damn! Why here? Why now?

"Come in. It's open," her sister called from inside the house.

As much as she wanted to leave before she saw Matt, Honey couldn't run now. She had to go in or face one of Emily's inquisitions. Slowly, she turned the knob and swung the door open.

"Em?"

"I'm in the kitchen," Emily called back.

Upon entering the warm, homey kitchen, Honey made a quick survey of the room. When she found only Emily sitting in front of two high chairs, feeding her twin daughters, she heaved a sigh of relief.

"Hi," Emily said, wiping a glob of peaches from Cat's cheek. "Have a seat. Rose had to run upstairs for a moment, but she'll be right back. I'll get her to make us some coffee." She looked around. "Where's my favorite nephew?"

"Outside with Chuck, looking at the horses, as usual."

"That kid is going be a great vet someday."

Honey kissed each of the chubby, dark-haired girls on the cheek, then flopped into a chair. "Danny isn't going to be a vet. He's decided on another career." She avoided Emily's gaze by brushing a wisp of baby fine hair off the forehead of the nearest twin.

"Danny decided or you decided?"

Hell's bells, now her own sister was getting in on the act. What was this, a conspiracy to make her feel as bad as she could about raising her son in a responsible way? "Danny decided, of course."

Emily eyed her skeptically, but let the subject drop. "I hope Chuck takes Danny to the barn and shows him Goldie's puppies. I don't suppose you're in the market for a pet, are you? We've got eight of them to find homes for." Emily shoveled another spoonful of peaches into each of the girls.

"No, the last thing I need is a dog."

"But these are purebred golden retrievers, and I wouldn't charge you full price. Maybe a night or two of baby-sitting, so Kat and I could live it up and go to a movie or something." Emily's face broke into a wide, encouraging grin.

"I don't care if you're giving them away. I do not need a dog to run after. And don't you dare mention it to Danny." Honey's voice came out much sharper than she'd meant it to be.

Emily clicked her tongue. "A bit touchy today, aren't we."

"Sorry. I have something on my mind."

Emily dipped her head and studied Honey's face. "Ah, this *something* wouldn't be named Matt Logan, would it?"

"He kissed me." She hadn't meant to just blurt it out, but the words left her lips before she could stop them.

Emily's eyes widened. Then a smile broke out across her face and she burst out laughing. Because their mommy was doing it, the twins joined in. "I love it! My staid, in-control sister, shaken to the soles of her size seven shoes. You never have a camera when you need one.''

Before Honey could answer the taunt, Emily's mother-in-law came into the kitchen.

''Well, Honey, what brings you here?''

''Hi, Rose.'' Honey and Emily locked gazes.

Rose stood just inside the doorway and looked from one sister to the other. ''Did I interrupt something?''

Honey sent Emily a speaking glance, hoping her sister wouldn't share with Rose what she'd just told her.

''No, we were just...gossiping.'' Emily stood and wiped the mouths of the twins, then turned back to Rose. ''Would you put them down for their nap so Honey and I can talk in peace and quiet?''

''I'd love to.'' Rose smiled warmly at her granddaughters and hoisted one to each hip. ''Give your mama and auntie a kiss.'' She leaned down so each got their kisses, and then went upstairs, the twins chattering away in their own language.

Sighing, Honey leaned back in her chair. ''Thanks for not saying anything.''

Emily grabbed two sodas from the fridge and returned to the table. She set one in front of Honey, the other in front of her, then propped her chin on her palms. ''I believe we left off at 'He kissed me'.''

Now that they were alone and the opportunity to talk about the kiss presented itself, Honey felt self-conscious. Embarrassment had never been a part of her makeup, but then there were a lot of things she'd been experiencing lately that she'd never felt or done before. How could one man throw her life into such turmoil?

Emily tapped her forefinger against her cheek. "I'm waiting."

Honey played nervously with the tab from the soda can. Never in her life had she admitted to another human being what she was about to tell Emily.

With an impatient grunt, Emily dropped her hands and stared hard at Honey. "Don't think for one minute that you're going to drop that bomb on me and not explain. If I have to barricade the windows and doors, you're not leaving here until you spill the beans."

There was no sense beating around the bush. "I'm scared."

The playfulness went out of Emily's expression. "Scared? Of what?"

"Matt." There, she'd finally said it. "I don't like what's happening to me, Em. I'm beginning to feel like I did seven years ago."

"And this is bad?"

Honey stared aghast at her sister's cat-ate-the-cream smile. "You're damned right it's bad."

"And you've come to this conclusion because...?"

Honey stood and began pacing the small kitchen. "Do I have to spell it out for you? It's bad because I don't want to be hurt again. Because I don't want Danny hurt. Because eventually, Matt will leave and I'm not sure I can go through that again." She sat and took her sister's hand in hers, squeezing until Emily winced and pulled away. "It took me six years to get my life back together and now—"

"—and now you've jumped to what you see as the only possible conclusion, right? What makes you think he'll leave?"

"It's complicated. There are...memories. Memories connected with his house, with the town, that are painful for him. Why would he want to stay and be reminded of that?''

''If these memories are so painful, then why is he here?''

''I don't know. I guess to pay the taxes on the house, to wait for his leg to heal....''

A knowing smile crept across Emily's face. ''Be careful. If you recall, I was the one jumping to conclusions when Kat returned, and look what happened. I couldn't have been more wrong.''

''But you were wrong because...'' Oh, hell, nothing was making sense anymore.

Logically, people wouldn't intentionally subject themselves to living with memories that hurt. Honey was a prime example of that. She hated this house. However, Emily cherished the old homestead enough to have married a man she wasn't sure loved her, and to have begged him to help her have a child. Had it been Honey's choice, she'd have let the house burn first. Not because of the man or the child, but simply because the place held too many painful memories. Wasn't it logical that Matt would feel the same about his home?

''Em, how did you feel the first time Kat kissed you...after he came home?''

A dreamy look came over Emily's face. ''It's hard to explain. My mind went blank and my body tingled—you know, like when you come into a warm cozy house after being out in the bitter cold. It was like coming home.''

Oh, hell. She was in big trouble. That was exactly how she'd felt in Matt's arms.

She started to speak, but just then the back door opened and Kat walked in. Behind him was Matt.

"Hey, squirt." Kat placed a kiss on Emily's lips, then smiled down at her, love brimming from his eyes. He glanced at Matt, then back to Honey, and waved his fingers in greeting. "I believe you two know each other."

Honey avoided looking directly at Matt and squelched a stab of envy at her sister's happiness. "Hello, Matt."

"Honey."

His cold greeting pierced her like an arrow. Was this the same man who'd kissed her with such passion just the other night? Feeling that hated self-consciousness creeping in, she stood. "I gotta get going."

"Don't run because of me," Matt said. His eyes were hard and unemotional.

"Don't flatter yourself. I'm leaving because I have to pick up Amanda's cleaning before the place closes." She waved to Emily and Kat. "See you."

The look Emily threw her couldn't be misread. *Coward.*

Maybe, Honey thought. *Maybe I am a coward. Maybe I'm running from my problems, just as I accused Matt of doing.*

But dare she stay? Dare she admit to what she felt for Matt? Dare she take a chance with her heart again? And what about Danny's? Could she risk her child's well-being on a man who could walk out of their lives as quickly as he'd walked back in?

Chapter Seven

Honey couldn't have been home for more than twenty minutes when Matt pulled into the driveway. She'd been sitting on the porch, trying to make sense of her reaction to him and her quick departure from Emily's house. Deep in her heart, she agreed with Emily's assessment. She'd run because of fear. Fear of that feeling returning, the one that always bombarded her when Matt entered a room. Fear that she'd give in to it as she very nearly had in his room.

"U-U-Uncle M-M-Matt." Danny came running from his swing set and catapulted into Matt's arms.

"Hey, sport." Matt hugged him close, and Honey had to turn away from the pain she saw in his eyes, pain at his son calling him uncle. Matt set Danny on the ground. "If you check the cab of my truck, I think there's someone in there waiting for you."

She watched Danny run to the truck and throw open the door. Instantly a ball of light gold fur jumped into her son's waiting arms.

"A p-p-puppy! Is it m-m-mine? What kind is it?"

"He's all yours and he's a golden retriever. One of Goldie's puppies," Matt said, avoiding Honey's censuring gaze.

Now she knew what he'd been doing at Emily's house. Once more he'd just barged ahead without consulting her. While she watched her son playing with the puppy, she fumed. This was the last straw.

"You might have asked," she nearly growled. "Amanda doesn't like animals."

"That's odd." His brows furrowed. "When I asked her, she didn't seem to object."

Honey bolted to her feet. Jamming her hands on her hips, she didn't even try to disguise her outrage. "You asked Amanda? Did it ever occur to you that I'm Danny's mother, and it might have been a good idea to ask me, too?"

"It occurred to me, but I figured you'd probably say no." Matt continued to watch his son and the new puppy. "I just hope it works."

Honey was suddenly swamped by another emotion, one she'd never felt before concerning her son—jealousy. Having been the center of Danny's young life, aside from Amanda, she was suddenly faced with sharing him with another human being, and it scared her half to death. That fear prompted words she never would have envisioned herself saying.

"It's unnecessary, you know."

He swung toward her, totally baffled at what she was getting at. "What?"

"Buying his affections. Danny gives his affections without bribery."

Matt had been prepared for any number of objections to his gift, but not this one. "I'm not trying to bribe Danny or buy his affections."

More than anything, he wanted his son healthy. He wanted to hear Danny call him Daddy. But to bribe him to accomplish his ends had never occurred to him. That she could think him capable of such a thing stung. But then, he reminded himself, Honey had a vivid imagination when it came to him.

"Then why this sudden gift? It's not his birthday. It's not any holiday."

Without asking her permission, Matt grabbed her hand. "Come on. If it does work, I want you to be there to hear it."

He lead her around a large bush next to where Danny and the puppy were rolling on the ground. His son's laughter filled the air, interspersed with the puppy's excited yips.

"Matt, I don't—"

Stationing them behind the bush and out of Danny's line of vision, he laid a finger on her lips. "Just listen." He parted the branches so they had a clear view of the boy and the dog.

Danny lay on his back. The puppy, sprawled on the boy's chest, exuberantly licked every inch of Danny's face.

"Hey, boy, I washed my face today." Danny giggled, then sat up and settled the puppy in his lap. "I need to give you a name. How about Rover?" He considered the name for a while, then shook his head. "Nah. Tommy Henderson's dog is named Rover and he can't even fetch a stick." His brows furrowed in thought, then his eyes came alive and he grinned. "I got it. I'll call you Buddy, 'cause you and me will be buddies forever and ever." Then he frowned again. "I gotta tell you that sometimes I talk funny." The dog stood on his hind legs, placed his paws on Danny's chest, then covered his face with wet, sloppy kisses. The boy giggled and fell backward, the dog standing on his chest. "I guess that means you don't mind, right?"

Honey stepped back. Her heart sang out at the fact that, for the first time in over a year, her son spoke without stuttering. It was as if she'd witnessed a miracle. Her gaze flew to Matt's. His face blurred through the mist of her joyful tears. "Why?"

"Because the dog is not judging him."

Grabbing at her midsection as if she'd been kicked, Honey stared at Matt. Had she been judging her son? Is that what Matt was trying to tell her? "But I—"

Matt gently took her arm and led her to the gazebo a few yards away from Danny, and out of earshot. When they were both seated on the bench inside, he turned to her. His face held an earnestness she'd never seen before.

"Before we get into that, I want to clean up any misconceptions you might have about why I did this. It wasn't to show you up or to win Danny's affections from you. The boy can love us both without becoming the pawn in a tug-of-war." Matt took her cold hands in his. "And contrary to what you believe, I am not trying to undermine you or your authority. I did, however, have very selfish reasons."

She frowned at him, waiting for the rest of his explanation.

"Every time Danny calls me Uncle Matt, I feel like a slice of my heart has been removed. The only nefarious reason I had for getting him that dog is that I want to hear my son call me Daddy. That can't happen until he's well. In the meantime, I will do whatever I have to reach that end, Honey. Even if it means going against your wishes."

"But how did you know the dog... I mean—"

Honey couldn't speak coherently. Her mind seemed filled with the fact that somehow she had failed Danny. Unable to stop them, she felt warm tears washing her cheeks.

Matt's heart twisted. Ignoring the possible consequences of his actions, he gathered Honey in his arms. "Don't beat yourself up over this. You did what you thought was right."

"I should have known...it wasn't working...when he didn't...get any better." Her tormented sobs sounded as if they were being torn from somewhere deep inside her.

He tightened his embrace, then kissed her hair and tried not to think of how right it felt to hold her like this, how he wished he'd been there to hold her through all those nights when Danny lay sick or when the world seemed too big for her to conquer on her own.

For the very first time since he'd walked out of Bristol, Matt wondered if he'd done the right thing.

Honey's sobs had quieted, but she didn't pull away. "How did you know what would cure him?"

Matt rested his chin on the top of her head and breathed deeply of the sweet scent of her shampoo. "First of all, Danny's not cured." When she tried to pull back, he again tightened his arms, unwilling to let her go just yet. "He's relaxed. He's not worrying that Buddy will tell him how to speak, or to slow down. That makes it easier for him to forget his problem and be himself.

"When he's around us, he'll still stutter, but if we let him know that we're not going to correct him or hold his speech problem up to him every time he opens his mouth, he'll eventually relax around us and forget about his problem.''

Honey tilted her head back to look up at him. ''How do you know all this?''

He grinned. ''Ever hear the saying 'Been there, done that'?''

She nodded.

Her silky hair brushed his skin, sending ripples of contentment through him. ''Well, I have and I did.''

She sat up, and this time he let her go, but it didn't make the feeling of emptiness inside him any easier to tolerate. He took her hand and rested it on his thigh. He felt her fingers curl around his, as if she were clinging to him for strength. He decided he liked that idea—too much. But he continued to hold her hand anyway.

''After my mother died, I developed a stutter. Not as bad as Danny's, but a stutter nonetheless, and noticeable enough to make my life at school a living hell. Thanks to a very patient teacher, Mrs. Clayton, who took me under her wing, I overcame it. She used to keep me after school, just to talk. It wasn't until I grew up that I realized our little chats had been designed not only to give the schoolyard bullies time to go home, but also the chance for me to talk with her without having to worry about being taunted or corrected.''

He leaned back, then glanced at Honey. Was that compassion he saw in her eyes? ''Anyway, when I got on the rodeo circuit, we used to do benefits on occasion. One time, we did one at a school for kids with learning disabilities. We were there for a few days and I started dating one of the teachers.''

Honey pulled her hand from his. He should have

been concerned, but the fact that she might be upset that he'd dated another woman brought him the strangest feeling of pleasure. He hid his smile and continued.

"She worked with kids with Danny's problem. By talking to her, I realized that the methods Mrs. Clayton employed, when I was a kid, were a crude form of what they were doing at this school." He glanced to where Danny and the puppy were wrestling in the grass. "Margo said they often employed animals to help with the therapy sessions."

Honey stood and walked to the filigreed white railing of the gazebo. She placed both hands on it before speaking.

"How could I have been so wrong?" She heard her voice emerge as a near whisper, but Matt must have heard. He came to stand behind her, putting his hands on her shoulders and squeezing reassuringly.

"How could you know? Dr. Thomas didn't know, and you were just following his instructions."

She shook her head, guilt still eating into her. "But I should have taken Danny to a specialist. Someone who knew all the latest methods."

Matt turned her to face him. "No more regrets. We're on the right track now and that's what counts."

Thanks to Matt, Honey felt much better about her son and hopeful as never before about the chances for his future progress. But something haunted her. Something that shouldn't have bothered her and wouldn't have, she was sure, if Matt hadn't kissed her.

She shifted her gaze to the front of his shirt. "This, er, Margo... Was she pretty?" She could have bitten off her tongue for voicing her thoughts.

He laughed softly. "No. She was beautiful."

Honey's heart fell to somewhere beneath the floor of the gazebo. She started to move away, but his strong hands held her fast.

Placing his finger beneath her chin, he raised her face to his. "She wasn't you, Honey."

She chanced a glance at him. His eyes were dark and filled with unspeakable invitation. What she'd intended to be just a peek at him became a mesmerized study of his handsome features.

The late afternoon sun etched sharp shadows across his cheekbones, making them even more prominent than usual. The lone dimple that had always fascinated her appeared in his cheek.

Then she made her second mistake. She reached up to brush back the wave of dark hair that had fallen across his forehead. He caught her hand and pressed his warm lips against her palm. Shivers of delight cascaded through her. She became aware of her body as she hadn't been in years.

Her thighs burned. Her breath labored for release from her lungs. Her lips felt as dry as a parched desert. Reflexively, she licked them.

"Not a good idea," Matt whispered, his head lowering.

She wasn't sure if he meant what she'd done or the fact that he wanted to kiss her. And he did. The desire shone in his eyes, in the muscle working in his jaw, in the way he gently eased her toward him.

She could have pulled away; his gentle grip told her that she had that option. But she didn't want to. God help her, she wanted to feel his lips on hers again, to know the security and warmth of his arms around her, to hide in his embrace. And she no longer questioned why; she just knew, with the same certainty that she knew that one day Danny would speak as clearly as she did.

Once again, she'd fallen in love with Matt Logan. Then again, maybe she'd never fallen out of love with him.

"LOOKS TO ME AS IF THINGS are moving along quite nicely." Tess turned from the window and smiled conspiratorially at Amanda. Then she frowned. "I just wish we could have done it without the animal." She cast a disdainful look at the puppy romping with Danny on the lawn outside the window. "I'm surprised you agreed to it."

Amanda had known Tess would not welcome a dog into her pristine house, but she hadn't cared. "Wiping up a few piddles from the puppy is a small price to pay to see them become the family they were meant to be. Don't you think?" She eyed Tess.

"I suppose so." Tess glanced back to the couple locked in each other's arms and then to the little boy. She smiled and the dimples in her rosy cheeks came into prominence. "Yes. Yes, indeed it is."

Amanda nodded. She'd been so relieved to see Honey and Matt kissing. For the first time since she'd arranged this meeting, she felt at ease about the outcome. Obviously to all but them, these two loved each other too much to let this second opportunity for happiness slip through their fingers. And if they showed signs of that happening, she and Tess would plug the holes and give the romance whatever gentle nudge it required.

She assessed the scene beyond the window. From the look of things, there would be no nudging needed.

It seemed, for the moment, at least, that they had things well in hand without any outside help.

She shifted her gaze to Danny and the new puppy. She'd been right to allow Matt to get Danny the puppy, even at the risk of incurring Honey's anger at both of them. After he'd explained how it might be just what Danny needed to get over his stutter, she could hardly say no. She sighed contentedly. "Who would have guessed a puppy could open a locked door?"

Tess giggled. "Who indeed?"

BARELY AWARE of the late sun beating down on his shoulders, Matt settled Honey more completely in his arms. He couldn't seem to get her close enough, get enough of her, feel enough of her. His body had been starved for the touch of hers, the sensation of her lush curves conforming to his.

Had he been waiting all this time for this? It seemed so. He knew one thing for sure—this woman in his arms was the reason no other woman had ever satisfied him. His embrace seemed to have been made with Honey in mind, and no one else could fill it, or him, as she could.

He deepened the kiss, as if he knew this couldn't last, that this might be the last time he ever held her, kissed her. To that end, he drank his fill. Her lips shaped to his like soft velvet. Except no velvet ever generated the heat coming from Honey. No velvet ever clung to him as she did. No velvet ever made him want to hold her forever. If only they could—

He pulled away, jarred out of the delirium in which he'd been immersed. Missing her already, he stared down at her face, washed by the late afternoon sun seeping through the bushes surrounding the gazebo. He wanted to continue. God knew he did, but logic told him he'd be a fool to trust her again, a fool to trust himself to be what she wanted.

Hadn't she hurt him enough already by keeping his son from him? By running off with Stan the minute he'd—

But did he have a right to hold that over her head? Hadn't she said she'd tried to find him to tell him about Danny? But could he believe her? And why had she married Stan? In this day and age, women didn't have to worry about being unwed mothers, that the stigma would ostracize them from society. Even in a backwater town like Bristol, she could have raised their son alone without marrying Matt's cousin.

Even as he made excuses, he knew, deep inside, that he had drawn back for the same reason he'd run all those years ago. Honey was beginning to get under his skin, and the idea of loving anyone scared him half to death. It only brought disappointment and heartache. Not from them, but from him.

In one way or another, he'd managed to disappoint everyone who had ever touched his life. Honey and Danny had suffered enough disappointments. They didn't need him complicating their lives and adding more.

He took one more look at the woman standing just out of reach, staring at him in confusion and waiting for an explanation. He had none to give her, none that would make sense and not hurt her more than he had already.

"I never should have come back here," he mumbled, and then walked away.

Honey watched him go, her heart tearing to shreds

in her chest. She wanted to run after him, to scream at him for making her love him again, when he obviously didn't want her love. She grasped the gazebo's railing, digging her nails into the painted wood.

No, she would not give him the satisfaction of letting him know how deeply he'd hurt her. Besides, she shouldered as much blame for it as he did. She had accepted the kiss, even begged with her lips and body for more. She knew all too well the price she would have to pay for her actions. It was a payment she'd been making one way or another for years.

"M-M-Mom, w-w-why are you c-c-crying?" Danny, his face flushed from playing with his new friend, looked up at her from just below the railing. He clutched Buddy close to his chest. "D-d-did Uncle M-M-Matt hurt you?"

Yes. She wanted to cry out, to share her pain with someone, but she didn't. Danny didn't need to know about this. He had his own problems.

Her son's returned stutter dealt one more blow to Honey's already bruised heart. When would this nightmare end? Unable to trust her voice, she shook her head.

Danny climbed the stairs into the gazebo, his face creased in concern. "Y-y-you wanna h-h-hold Buddy?"

Without a word, she nodded, then took the squirming animal. Cradling him in her arms, she sat heavily on the bench.

"I-i-isn't he g-g-great, Mom? Uncle M-M-Matt sure kn-kn-knows how to pick dogs." He gently stroked the puppy's head, then gazed up at her. Carefully, just as she'd done so many times for him, he wiped the tears from her cheeks. "If y-y-you tell m-m-me where it h-h-hurts, I'll kiss it f-f-for you, M-M-Mom."

Not until she heard her son's words did Honey realize that her tears were still falling. She put an arm around him and pulled him close.

Squeezing her eyes closed against the sharp pains piercing her heart, she let her tears flow freely. If only life were that easy. If only a child's kiss could repair her lacerated soul. If only she could hear her son say "Mom" without stuttering. If only Matt could love her as much as she did him. If only…

Chapter Eight

Honey wandered through the living room, thick with the smells of pine-scented furniture polish from Tess's recent cleaning and several vases of fragrant lilacs. Despite the pleasant, homey atmosphere of the eclectically furnished room, an unaccustomed restlessness dogged Honey's steps.

Aimlessly, she picked up the latest copy of her favorite magazine, sat on the sofa and fanned through the pages without seeing them. Minutes later, unread, the magazine fell into her lap. With her thoughts under siege by memories of the kiss she and Matt had shared in the gazebo, and all its implications, she gave up reading, tipped her head back and closed her eyes.

She could still feel the heat of his lips against hers and the strong outline of his body fitting into her curves, warming her through to her bones. It hadn't been nearly as hot and urgent as the kiss they'd shared in his room, but it had done infinitely more damage to her peace of mind. In his room, she'd felt passion. In the gazebo she'd felt contentment, security—safety.

Her eyes snapped open and her fingers curled into the material of the sofa arm, her nails biting into the soft, hunter-green damask fabric. Only half aware of her surroundings, she didn't notice when the magazine slipped from her lap to the floor.

Matt Logan had given her one more reason to hate him. He'd brought to life the burned out cinder that had been beating in her chest for seven long years, even though she knew it would once more be torn to shreds when he left.

Despite everything, she couldn't stop the love she felt for this man from growing inside her, like an out-of-control virus, a virus that could infect the life she'd made with her son. How had she let this happen? The answer was simple. Her love for Matt Logan had never died. It had lain dormant, waiting for the spark that would bring it surging back to life. The wound hadn't healed at all. Denial had just dulled the pain.

The loud roar of an engine coming from the garage interrupted her reverie and sent icy chills racing over her body. She knew the sound. She'd heard it often enough when Stan was alive. Slowly, she stood, then walked to the window to push the filmy curtain aside. Fear, cold and bitter, invaded her.

One of the garage doors stood open. Protruding from it was the front wheel of a black motorcycle. A chill raced up her spine. Of all Stan's toys, his motorcycle, with its total lack of protection for the rider, had frightened her the most, even more than the race car that had taken his life.

As if in a nightmare, she watched, unable to pull her gaze from the glitter of sunlight reflecting off its demon-black paint. The motorcycle eased froward, like a wild animal stalking its prey. Matt straddled the black leather seat with his muscled, denim-clad legs. His helmet's opaque mask concealed his face. He dropped one booted foot to the ground, revved the engine, then replaced his foot on the peg that would support it during the ride.

Then, with the high-pitched whine of a tortured soul, the motorcycle sprang from the garage. Honey froze in abject horror. Danny clung to Matt's waist, his face also concealed behind a helmet's mask. In helpless terror, she followed the motorcycle's progression down the driveway and out of sight.

She ran out the front door, but it was too late—the motorcycle had vanished. She could follow in her car, but once they reached the four-way stop, she'd never know which way they'd gone.

ACUTELY AWARE of his precious load, Matt carefully guided the motorcycle off the road, then stopped beneath a large, shady oak. Danny reluctantly let go of Matt's waist and climbed off the bike. He swept the helmet from his head and grinned up at Matt.

"Awesome." Following Matt's lead, he carefully hooked the chin strap of the helmet over the handlebars. "Why are we s-s-stopping?"

Matt smiled down at the boy, ruffled his hair and, without a word, began unloading the goodies he'd packed in the saddlebags. "I know you can probably make it to dinnertime, but I need a snack. I packed this stuff for me, but we can share it."

The boy's eyes brightened at the sight of a large bag of barbecue potato chips and a can of root beer, indulgences Matt had observed Honey did not often allow her son. He experienced a slight tug of his conscience, but shook it away, rationalizing that the boy needed to be indulged from time to time, and a guy-day with unauthorized snacks constituted one of those times.

This wasn't the first time his conscience had felt a nudge. When Danny had found him polishing the motorcycle and begged for a ride, Matt had hesitated. Then, seeing no harm in it, and pushing aside thoughts of what Honey might say, he'd agreed. He only planned on riding to the corner and back, then dropping Danny off and heading for the house to do some work. A ride just long enough to satisfy the boy.

Once they'd gotten on the road, Matt had realized this would be an opportunity for him and his son to have some time alone, something Honey had made very certain—until now—never occurred. Her constant presence reminded him of how little trust existed between them, and that she feared he'd tell Danny he was his father before she felt the boy should hear it.

Matt didn't expect she'd be too happy about this when they went back to the house, but by then it would be too late. He and Danny would have started the bonding process that he hoped would eventually lead to him telling Danny he was his real father.

Danny's progress since the arrival of Buddy had been remarkable. Matt figured it wouldn't be long before he could finally claim his son, and he found himself looking forward to it with eager anticipation. More than anything, he wanted to be the type of father his own dad had never been to him.

Danny took the bag of chips Matt handed him, followed him to the base of the oak tree and settled himself beside Matt. Opening the soda, Matt handed it to Danny. For a long time, backs propped against the gnarly tree trunk, they shared the drink and ate in companionable silence.

When the chips were gone and the soda can empty, Matt put them aside to take back to the house. He sighed, folded his hands behind his head and leaned back against the tree. Smiling, he watched as Danny followed suit. It occurred to him that this might be a good time to learn a little bit about his son.

"So, wanna talk?"

"W-w-what do you w-w-want to talk about?"

"I don't know. How about what you're going to be when you grow up?"

Danny sighed. "W-w-well, I really wanna be a vet like Uncle Kat, but M-M-Mom wants me to be somethin' else."

Matt came alert. "Like what?"

"Well, she says I should b-b-be a l-l-lawyer or a doctor, cuz it's safer."

The boy's reasoning sounded too adult for Matt's peace of mind. Had Honey put the words in his mouth? The idea angered him. "And you don't like that idea, huh?"

"Nah. I think it's d-d-dumb, but M-M-Mom says only f-f-fools live dangerously."

Matt's anger built to the point that he had to bite his tongue to keep from saying what he felt. The more Danny talked, the more Matt became convinced that Honey had brainwashed the kid into believing this tripe. Kids should at least have the right to chose what they wanted to be for the rest of their lives. Eating peas was one thing. Career choice was something else again—something Danny should be able to decide, not her.

"Uncle M-M-Matt? Do you have a d-d-dad?"

Danny's question jolted Matt from his angry thoughts. "Yes, but he passed away awhile ago," he said, speaking very slowly, hoping Danny would imitate his speech as easily as he did his movements.

Thoughtful silence followed.

"Was he a g-g-good dad?"

The silence stretched again while Matt searched for an answer. Had his dad been a good father? No, Matt didn't believe he had been, but he didn't want to tell Danny that.

"Why don't we talk about something else?" he said, hoping to put an end to the discussion.

Danny turned and positioned himself on his knees at Matt's side. His youthful face held a serious expression that conveyed to Matt the importance that Danny put on this conversation. "No! Please, Uncle Matt? I really, really n-n-need to know."

He wasn't going to let this go. He clutched Matt's shirtsleeve, his little fingers biting into the material. Matt was sure the boy was so intent on an answer that he hadn't realized his stutter had all but disappeared.

This seemed so very important to Danny that Matt delved deep into his memory, searching for something to tell his son. "Well…" Out of nowhere an incident surfaced in Matt's mind "…I remember a time when we went swimming, and I almost drowned, and he dived in and saved me. I guess that makes him a good dad."

He'd stopped talking, but the memory kept coming. One image after another surfaced, bringing back an event in his life that, until now, Matt had completely forgotten. As if watching a movie, the whole episode unfolded before him: his father's face etched with lines of worry after he'd gotten Matt to shore, tears streaking his ruddy cheeks. A sob had caught in his throat as he'd called Matt's name. When Matt opened his eyes, his father had hugged him so tightly Matt almost couldn't breathe, then had whispered his name over and over.

"Uncle Matt?" Danny tugged on his sleeve.

The unbidden memory had hit Matt like a punch to the gut, and it took him a moment to recover. "Yes?"

"Do you miss him lots?"

"Yes. Yes I do." Oddly enough, Matt realized he had spoken the truth. Despite everything, he did miss his father.

"Were you a good boy? Did you always do what he told you to?"

"I tried to be, but sometimes I wasn't. It's hard to always be good. Sometimes you forget."

Danny's face screwed up, his bottom lip began to quiver and a tear rolled down his cheek. "I knew it was my fault."

"What?"

"That my d-d-daddy died. I was b-b-bad, just like y-y-y-you. Your d-d-daddy died 'c-c-cause you were b-b-bad and so d-d-did m-m-mine."

Matt's heart broke as he watched the boy beat himself up for something he had nothing to do with. He gathered him close and held him until his sobs faded into hiccups.

"You're wrong, Danny. People get sick or they have accidents or they just get old. But that's nobody's fault. No one causes it." He held the boy away, then gently wiped the tears from his cheeks. "Understand?"

Danny nodded, but Matt felt sure that he didn't get it.

BY THE TIME the motorcycle roared up the driveway, Honey had been stationed outside the garage door for an hour. Buddy sat at her feet, his tongue hanging out the side of his mouth. If Matt thought she'd been mad the other night, he had a big surprise coming. While she'd waited for their return, her fury had built to its peak. She wanted to shake him until his teeth rattled.

The motorcycle headed directly at her, but Honey held her ground. She'd given in to Matt's irresponsible behavior one time too many. This time she planned on asserting herself with all the fury of a mother who had spent the last two hours pacing and worrying.

The bike came to a stop, the front tire mere inches from her. While Buddy dashed to greet Danny, she never so much as flinched. Her hands planted firmly on her hips, she glared at Matt, waiting patiently until he and her son had climbed off the bike and removed the helmets that hid their faces.

"Exactly what were you thinking, putting Danny on this death trap?"

Never looking in her direction, Danny bent to scratch Buddy's ears. "A-a-aw, Mom, it w-w-was fun. Uncle M-M-Matt was real c-c-careful."

Never taking her gaze off Matt, she put her hand on the small of Danny's back and gently pushed him in the direction of the house. "Go inside and wash up for dinner. I'll be there in a minute. I want to talk to your uncle."

Danny glanced first at her, then at Matt, as if waiting for his okay. That only served to intensify Honey's fury.

"Do as your mom says, sport."

Both adults watched in silence as Danny and

Buddy made their way up the porch steps. Then, casting a questioning look over his shoulder, Danny shrugged and the two disappeared inside the house.

"Well?" Honey demanded.

"Well what?"

Matt's casual attitude did nothing to calm the fear that still clutched at her heart. "What do you have to say for yourself? Why did you take Danny on that thing?" She pointed an accusing finger at the motorcycle.

Hanging his helmet on the handlebars, Matt turned to her. "Because he asked and because I wanted to spend some time with my son."

"Damn you, Matt, you could have taken him for a walk or gone fishing or..." She took a deep breath and swallowed the tears of relief rising in her throat. "How dare you make me worry that the two of you would end up in some ditch? Dammit, how dare you risk your son's life!" An instant later, another reprimand formed in her mind. *How dare you risk your own life?*

She lost the battle to suppress the tears, and her voice trailed off on a choking sob.

Not until her mind played out the words in her head had Honey realized that what she'd thought was anger had been stark fear—and not just for her son. If anything had happened to Matt....

She avoided looking at him, not wanting him to see what she was afraid of was clearly written in her eyes. "I want your word that you'll never, ever take Danny on that thing again." Again she pointed at the motorcycle. When she saw that her hand trembled, she quickly buried it in the folds of her sundress.

"Aren't you going to ask what we did, what we

talked about?'' His tone, calm and holding not a trace
of anger, only served to unsettle her more.

"As long as you didn't tell him who you are, I
don't give a rat's patootie what you talked about or
where you went.''

Matt sighed and glanced toward the upper branches
of the tall maple beside the driveway, then back to
her. "No, I didn't tell him. I wouldn't do that without
talking to you first.''

"Why not?'' she cried, his easy answer causing her
to lose the precarious hold she'd had on her emotions.
"You've never thought you needed to talk to me
about anything else. You never asked me if I'd care
if you walked out on me and your son. You never
asked if I would worry that you put Danny's life in
danger. You never—''

She was saying things she'd never meant to say,
but she couldn't seem to stop the flow of words. That
is, until, to her utter horror, she felt the stinging tears
overflow and slip silently down her flushed cheeks.

Hearing the raw terror in Honey's voice and seeing
her tears made Matt fully understand what he'd put
her through by taking Danny for a ride on the motorcycle. The woman was terrified to the point of near
hysterics.

"Honey, it was just a ride,'' he said, trying to make
light of it to calm her down.

She wiped angrily at her tears and glared at him.
"No, Matt, it wasn't *just* a ride. It was you flaunting
my authority again. It was you encouraging Danny to
do something I don't approve of.''

Matt felt the hairs on his neck rise. "He's my son,
too. As such, I should be able to make decisions for
him.''

"Not when it endangers his life," she hissed. "Not when it's an introduction to the kind of life Stan led. Not when I have done everything in my power to make sure Stan was the very last person in this world that Danny might pattern his life after."

Matt dragged his fingers through his hair, frustration eating at his insides. "So, we're back to that, are we?"

"Yes, we're back to that, and we'll keep coming back to that as long as you keep interfering where you have no right to butt in."

Fury boiled up inside of Matt. Before he could say anything, he noticed Danny standing on the porch watching them. His little-boy face was distorted in confusion, and even from a distance, Matt could make out the quiver of the boy's bottom lip. They were tearing their son apart with their quarrels. Matt recalled all too vividly listening to his own parents arguing about him. He could not and would not put his son through that. It had to stop and there could be no better time than now.

He lowered his voice so Danny couldn't hear. "We can't talk here, and obviously, we have plenty to say to each other."

"We have nothing more to say to each other," Honey snapped. She'd caught sight of Danny as well and adjusted her tone accordingly. Glowering at Matt, she turned to leave.

Matt caught her arm and began walking toward his truck. "I think we do, and it's past time that we got this sorted out and stopped pulling Danny in two different directions."

"What do you think you're doing?" She worked to twist her arm free of his grasp. "Let me go!"

"No. You're coming with me, and we're going to end this once and for all." Matt put her firmly into the passenger seat, then leaned down and said assertively, "Stay put, I'll be right back." Quickly, he ran inside and asked Amanda to look after Danny. Once he'd secured her okay, Matt returned to the car. Surprised to find Honey still there, he climbed into the driver's seat, then turned to her. "We're going to my house, and you're going to tell me what's really eating you."

THE RIDE WAS SILENT and tension filled. Honey stared mutinously out the windshield, and Matt gripped the steering wheel with white-knuckled fingers. Neither said a word.

When they got to his house, Matt had no idea how he would approach Honey about her strict upbringing of Danny, but he did know that it had to be said. His mind kept replaying the look on Danny's face when he'd come back out on the porch and found them yelling at each other. If they kept going this way, the boy would never get over his stutter and—Matt would never hear his child call him Daddy.

But that was inconsequential compared to Danny's well-being. Someone had to stop Honey before she ruined his life completely with rules and restrictions that hampered his natural development. Someone had to make her see that she had to let Danny make his own choices. They could be there to guide him, but in the end, Danny should be what he wanted to be, even if it was a race car driver like Stan.

Glancing at the mutinous set of her mouth, Matt concluded that no matter how he approached the subject, this was not going to be an easy task. Honey had lived through a marriage that had forced her to take control of her life and Danny's, and Matt couldn't expect to change that in a few hours or days.

Honey could feel Matt's gaze resting on her from time to time, but she continued to stare straight ahead. She was all too aware of how Matt's charm could soften her, and Danny's life was too important to allow that to happen.

The residue of her fear and anger clung to her. She welcomed it. As long as just a little of it remained, she'd feel better about having a defense against Matt and his ideas of child rearing.

What did he know about little boys? Did he realize that the old saying "As the twig is bent, so grows the tree" was never more true than in the case of a young, impressionable boy? She knew what was right for her son, and nothing Matt Logan could say or do would change that. He could bat his long lashes and smile his dimpled smile until the cows came home, and she would hold her ground.

The truck made the last turn into Matt's driveway. He shut off the motor, then climbed out and came around to her door. Opening it, he took her arm.

"Come on. We can talk inside."

Though she knew it was fruitless, she balked. "We can talk out here." The last thing she needed, considering the tingles of pleasure racing up her arm from his touch, was to be alone with Matt inside that house.

"Inside." He firmly removed her from the truck and aimed her toward the front steps to his house.

Given that he hadn't offered her a choice and was much stronger than her, Honey reluctantly went, mentally arming herself against the magnetic man at her side.

Once inside, he took her to the kitchen. An old kitchen table from the fifties reigned supreme in the middle of the cracked linoleum floor. Four dark green, vinyl-covered chairs surrounded the gray-topped table. One chair sat askew, and the outline in the dust on the seat showed that someone had sat there not long ago. A white plastic lid and a paper cup with dark liquid in the bottom were the only things on the table.

Honey sat down, trying not to think about the dust that would cling to her clothes. She had more important worries at the moment. Matt sat across from her and pushed aside the cup and lid.

''Honey—''

She held up her hand to stop him. ''Matt, you just don't understand, and coming here is not going to make anything any clearer.''

''I understand that you're going to ruin Danny's childhood, just like your father did yours and my father did mine. Is that what you want for him? Do you want Danny to end up hating you?''

Honey bristled at his words. ''You know nothing of what my childhood was like.''

''Then suppose you tell me.''

Honey wet her lips, then glanced at Matt. How could she tell him that not only did she feel Stan hadn't been a good role model for their son, but now she strongly doubted that Matt was either? And was he right? Would Danny end up hating her the way she'd always hated her father?

Chapter Nine

Matt settled deeper into the uncomfortable vinyl kitchen chair. Leaning back, he put one ankle over the other. He looked at Honey, then crossed his arms over his chest.

"Well? Tell me about your childhood." He frowned for a second, then gave a short laugh. "Seems strange that we knew each other for so long, but never *really* knew each other." He laughed again, but this time with real humor. "I guess we had other things to do."

Honey could feel the color rising to her cheeks. Damn him for being right. What little time they could steal together had most often been spent in each other's arms. They'd spoken little and loved often. Neither of them had felt a need for words. What had to be said, they'd expressed with their bodies and hearts. Unfortunately, she'd been the only one speaking the truth.

"Honey? Your childhood?"

She shook herself free of the sensuous memories running rampant through her mind. Why couldn't she stay focused? She had only to glance at the man across the table from her to find an answer. No matter how angry she was with Matt, he still had the power to turn her bones to jelly and her mind to a blank slate.

Quickly, she tore her gaze away from him and centered it on the sun glinting off the roof of Matt's mother's greenhouse. The smell of neglect wafted to her from the unused room. Deliberately, and maybe because the pain of remembering would help her find her center of balance again, she delved deep into her memory for the explanation he wanted.

"My childhood was about the farthest thing from idyllic that a kid could get. My mother died when I was fairly young. My father never should have had children, at least not the kind with feelings and a need to be loved." She glanced at Matt. "You see, my father had no idea how to love. He pampered Emily because she was the one who loved horses. He tolerated Jesse, who came to live with us after Jesse's mother died, and me...well, let's just say that—"

"No. No skipping over anything. What about you?"

She thought for a time, trying to give definition to the relationship she'd had with her father. "We lived in the same house. That about covers it."

"So, what you're saying is that he pretty much ignored all of you?" Matt leaned forward to rest his forearms on the table.

"Oh, no." She rolled her eyes. "Ignore is not what my father did with anyone. He told us what to do, when to do it and how to do it. He wasn't happy unless he was running our lives." She gave a derisive laugh. "Do you know why Emily and Kat got married?"

He shook his head.

"Because my father left a codicil in his will saying that Emily had to have a baby before her thirtieth birthday or the farm would go to charity. She asked Kat to help her because she couldn't bear the thought of losing the place she loved. Kat refused unless they got married. Lucky for them, it worked out.

"That's the way my father looked at his children. We were like vassals in an old medieval castle. His property." She sighed heavily and looked back at the greenhouse. "Not all of us were as lucky as Kat and Emily."

"Meaning?"

She glanced at him. He wasn't going to let this go until he had it all. Well, why the hell not? What harm could it do now? "After you left and I found out I was pregnant, my father arranged for me to marry Stan, because he didn't want the Logan name smeared with the dirt of an illegitimate child. I didn't love Stan, and I didn't know if he loved me. I just knew that I didn't want to stay there, and I didn't have you anymore, and I didn't care what happened to me. So I married Stan. Needless to say, my marriage was not the resounding success that Emily's was. Jess is the smart one. He took off before my father had a chance to screw up his life."

Again she laughed. "When I look back on it now, I wonder if it was so much his fault. He might have thought he was doing what was best for all of us. But even in my most benevolent moments, I find holes in that argument." She looked at Matt. "You know why?"

He shook his head.

"Because he never even tried to love us." Honey stood and walked to the window over the sink. She absently traced her forefinger in the dust covering the white porcelain. "If he had just tried. If he'd just once shown one small glimmer of affection, things might have been different."

Matt studied her. He could feel her pain as if it were his own, because it came so close to what he'd suffered as a child. However, he at least had had the love of his mother to buffer his father's cold, demanding personality. Honey had not even had that. Then to be almost sold to Stan for the price of respectability... No wonder she felt this almost tangible need to hang on to control of her life and Danny's. Between her father and Stan, she'd been robbed of that for too long.

What baffled Matt was that she had no idea that she was doing to Danny exactly what her father had done to her. She was running his life, making his choices for him. How did Matt tell her that?

Quietly, he stood, then moved behind her at the sink. He placed his hands on her shoulders and gently turned her to face him. To his surprise, her cheeks were stained with moisture. Gently, he wiped the tears away with the pad of his thumb, and to his further surprise, she let him.

"What I'm about to say is not going to be easy to hear, but please let me finish before you say anything." He tipped her chin up so their gazes met. "Okay?"

She nodded, then moved around him and went back to the table.

Matt started to turn, then stopped. The markings she'd made in the dust on the sink caught his eye. She'd drawn a heart and inside it had sketched "HL loves?" The pain gathering in his heart nearly took his breath away. Even though the last thing he wanted or needed in his life was for Honey to love him, it killed him, seeing this visible signature of her loneliness.

Tearing his gaze away and wiping his hand through the dust to erase the words, he walked slowly to the table. He sat, then took her cold fingers in his. "Honey, what you're doing to Danny, no matter how well-intended, is exactly what your father did to you." When she would have spoken, he raised his hand to stop her. "Let me finish." She closed her mouth and looked away. "I know you don't want to believe that, but from where I'm sitting, it sure looks the same. Your father made your choices, decided your life, determined what path you would take. Aren't you doing that for Danny in a way?

"I know you want him safe, and you don't want him to end up like Stan, and that's wonderful. God knows, I want that for him, too. But in the end, when you can no longer influence him, he'll do what he wants, anyway."

She swung to face him. "Are you suggesting I just let him run wild?"

He shook his head. "Of course not. He's a little boy. He'll make some bad choices until he learns differently. We—you and I—need to be there to make sure he doesn't get hurt by those choices, and to show him why they are bad. But even then, the final decision will still be his. We can only pray we teach him to use his head."

"You and I?" She searched his face.

"Yes, both of us. His parents." He leaned closer. "Don't you see? You are no longer alone. I'm here now."

For how long? she wondered. But she didn't say it because she didn't want to know the answer. Not knowing hurt less.

Even that admission brought fresh pain. Her feelings for Matt were intensifying, no matter how hard she fought to keep them under control.

Even worse, Danny's affections for this man were also growing. That meant that she wouldn't be the only one hurting when Matt walked away again. And he would. Maybe he didn't plan to, but as soon as things got too rough for him to handle, he'd do what he'd always done—run.

Then an outrageous thought struck her. If Matt would eventually leave again, why shouldn't she at least take advantage of the time with him that remained? Her heart was already invested. What more could she give? What more could she lose? She could protect Danny, but not herself. The damage was already done. The time for her to turn back had long passed, if there ever had been a time when she could have. She loved Matt and it seemed she would forever.

"Will you at least think about what I said?"

She wanted to laugh. She'd probably think of nothing else. The idea that she had been treating Danny as her father had treated her made Honey hurt in a way she hadn't since she'd lost Matt. For now, though, she pushed it from her mind. Later. She'd think about it later, when Matt's breath wasn't fanning her cheeks. When Matt's eyes weren't boring into her. When she could think.

She nodded and pulled her hands from his, no longer able to tolerate his touch. "Yes. I'll think about it."

Then he did the strangest thing. He just sat there and looked at her, as if memorizing her features. A flame grew in his eyes. She could feel its warmth all the way across the table.

Abruptly, she stood. "So, what have you done to the house so far?"

He swallowed hard, then stood. "Not much. Some cleaning. I want to get the furnishings this week, and new curtains." He didn't add that getting new things was part of his plan to vanquish the ghosts of his childhood, or that he hadn't been able to bring himself to enter the room at the top of the stairs that had been his father's.

Even though Honey had told him about herself, he still couldn't bring himself to tell her about the little boy who had lived here and yearned for a love that never came, because he just wasn't good enough to be loved.

"Hey. Wanna help me measure the windows?" he asked abruptly.

Just then a knock sounded on the front door, surprising both of them. Matt hurried to see who it was. Honey lagged behind, then stood at the end of the hall near the kitchen. He threw open the door to find a man on the porch, his waist encircled by a weighty tool belt, the writing across the pocket of his blue work shirt declaring him to be from the telephone company.

"Damn! I forgot that I called to have a phone installed today." He opened the door wider. "Come on in." The man entered and looked around. "I'd like the phone in the kitchen hooked up. The rest can wait until I decide where I want the jacks."

Matt led the man past Honey to the back of the

house. He felt a surge of disappointment that he and Honey were no longer alone. She glanced at him and he saw the same disappointment in her eyes.

BY THE TIME the telephone man had left and a shiny new, white phone adorned Matt's kitchen wall, Honey checked her watch and realized that Tess would soon be putting dinner on the table.

While they'd waited for the telephone man, Matt and she had measured all but two of the upstairs bedroom windows for curtains and blinds. All the time, both were aware of something happening between them, something neither acknowledged, but was nevertheless there. Like a magnetic field, it kept intensifying and drawing them like two steel splinters toward the core.

"We can do the two rooms we missed now." Matt came up unexpectedly behind her.

His breath brushed her bare neck, causing gooseflesh to blossom on her skin. She grabbed the tape measure and climbed the stairs, acutely aware of Matt close on her heels. She'd really enjoyed the last two hours and had all but forgotten the motorcycle incident. Matt had seemed so contrite about upsetting her that she took him at his word that it wouldn't happen again, and dismissed it from her thoughts. Now, something else preyed on her mind.

"To your right," Matt instructed from behind her.

She hesitated for a breath of time, then stepped over the threshold and looked around. Even in its state of disrepair and need of cleaning, the room made Honey's eyes widen. As she'd seen downstairs, white dustcovers draped several pieces of furniture scattered about the room. Something told her it had been Matt's bedroom, and she could safely assume that the ghostly disguises concealed a bed, a dresser and a night table.

While not overly large, the room, situated at the front corner of the house, boasted a large bay window. A window seat stretched along its width, exactly as she had always imagined it.

"This is a wonderful room," she said.

Walking to the bay window, she kicked off her shoes, then dropped onto the bench seat and curled her feet beneath her. She looked out at the front yard. The newly mowed grass, thanks to Sam Thatcher, lay dappled with late afternoon sunlight.

While she checked out her surroundings, it hadn't escaped her notice that Matt had remained quietly in the background. The pregnant silence between them hummed with expectancy.

"You just *have* to put white, organdy tie-backs on this window, Matt. It just cries out for them," she said, hoping to ease the tension and dispel the thick emotions that seemed to fill every corner of the room.

Still not a sound came from Matt.

Every nerve in her body, every muscle knew he hadn't left; every instinct in her sensed his presence. Curiosity getting the better of her, she turned to face him. His expression told her something had changed between them in the few minutes it had taken to climb the stairs, something so powerful that she wanted to run, but she couldn't, because—at the same time— she wanted even more to stay.

He stood just outside the door, blocking her escape, his hip leaning against the door frame, his gaze centered on her. Still he said nothing. Honey squirmed beneath his intense scrutiny. Finally, he took a step into the room, but his devilish blue gaze never left her, never stopped speaking to her in ways that she couldn't resist heeding.

"This is my old room." He looked around, then focused his gaze back on her. When he spoke again, his voice was low, soft, seductive. "You know, I used to envision you sitting there, the sunlight dancing off your hair, your eyes begging me to make love to you."

"Really?" The only word she could force from her lips sounded weak and breathy. She wondered if he had any idea what he was doing to her. Or did he? She blinked, hoping to dissipate any emotion revealed in her eyes.

"Really." Matt resumed his slow approach, as if measuring every footstep carefully before taking it. His gaze burned into her with a question she didn't want to answer.

When he got within a few inches of her, he caressed her cheek with his callused fingertips. "On the nights we made love, I'd come back here, sit right where you are and relive every moment we'd spent together. The way your skin felt on mine. The way you made those pleasure noises. The way your hair brushed over my skin like a breath of air. The way—"

"Stop!" Honey swallowed hard and drew back, searching for a bit of space that would allow her to breathe. "Please." Was that her voice sounding so desperate?

She glanced away, looking around as if she could actually see the cloud of sensuality cutting off her air.

Everything, right down to her teeth, ached with the need to throw herself into his arms and beg him to relive those memories with her—for real—right now on the dusty floor of his old room. She fought to withstand them, even as she knew that, more than anything in the world, she wanted to comply, to sink into his warmth and to give herself over to him. Even though she knew it would be this once and never again.

"Why stop, Honey? Why not give in to what we both want? Don't try to tell me you don't want it, too. I've seen it in your eyes, felt it in your kiss, in your response to me." He moved closer to the window seat and took her hand, pulling her to her feet and into his arms.

"But I—"

"No. We owe ourselves this much. The last seven years have been the loneliest of my life, and I suspect yours, too. Why shouldn't we steal an afternoon for us?"

"But dinner—"

He lowered his head, his lips a breath away. "I'll feed you, Honey. I'll feed you the only food either of us needs."

His minty breath was like an aphrodisiac to her senses. And the touch of his lips wiped her mind clear of rational thought, leaving only him.

Matt knew deep inside that he should stop now, while he could, but he brushed the thought aside. He'd waited seven long years for this to be something other than just a dream from which he'd awaken, unsatisfied and still wanting Honey. If he'd never done anything else right in his life, he knew that making love to Honey was—the one thing that *was* right— and to hell with the pain that would come later.

Their labored breathing filled the musty silence in

Matt's childhood bedroom. So much time had passed since he had last experienced anything like this…this total absorption of his identity by another human being. The last time had been with Honey. The admission sent his senses reeling.

Then Honey made a sound that had lived on in his memory for all these years. That low, catlike purr that came from somewhere deep inside, where her passion resided, buffeted him with recollections of other loving times they'd shared. In response, something that had lain dormant inside him, deep inside, stirred to life.

At that instant, if someone had held a gun to his head, he couldn't have turned back.

The essence of the woman in his arms seemed to fill his senses, blocking out everything else, including the ever-weakening voice warning him of the danger of seeing this to its inevitable end. Like a man with an addiction, he craved Honey, and there was no denying that need.

Shoving all else aside, he concentrated his whole being on fully experiencing the woman in his arms. The flowery fragrance of her hair, as he buried his face in its luxuriant thickness, engulfed him. The smooth silkiness of her skin under his questing hands made him hungry for more. The sweet honey taste of her lips was like a drug.

As his blood throbbed, quick and hot, through his veins, he fought for a small measure of control. Drawing on every bit of his strength, he pulled back far enough to look into her face. To his intense pleasure, her eyes, their blue depths darkened with burning need, reflected his own passion. Still, he needed to give her the chance to back away.

"Do you want to stop?" Holding his breath, he waited for her answer.

She shook her head.

He exhaled and smiled down at her. "Good. Neither do I." Tenderly, he brushed her hair from her cheek with the back of his fingers. "I want to love you until neither of us has enough strength to walk away again."

Honey laid her fingers across his lips. He kissed them. "No conditions. No expectations." Her voice, low and husky, held the thickness of sexual longing. "Just love me…now."

Matt needed no further encouragement. He hauled her back into his arms and kissed her. The kiss, long, deep and hot, contained years of unfulfilled need. He dipped his tongue into her mouth and tasted the sweetness that he remembered being a part of her.

When she imitated his action, his insides twisted with an agonizingly pleasurable ache. Finally, he released her mouth. She sagged against him. He tightened his grip to prevent her from slipping to the dusty floor.

Matt's kiss had not only drained all the strength from Honey's body, it had also erased all logic from her mind. She wanted Matt and nothing—not Danny, not regrets, not old pains—could prevent her from taking what he offered…one rapturous afternoon. An afternoon in Matt's arms might never come again, and she wasn't about to let this one go. She had no illusions that there would be more than this. She closed her eyes, blocking out everything except Matt.

"It seems so right that we should do this here, where it all began."

Honey almost didn't hear Matt, but then the words

sank in. Silently, she agreed. That they should end it where it had begun all those years ago, on a sultry summer night while the world slept, seemed apt. Matt's room had not been the scene of their first lovemaking, but his home had.

The July night had been unusually warm, and they'd decided to swim naked in his family's aboveground pool. It had escalated from there, into one of the most wonderful nights of Honey's life. The pool had long since been torn down and discarded—just like their love—but the memories remained intact.

Now she would have another memory to add to that, another memory to warm her on those long, lonely nights after Matt left again. But she couldn't, wouldn't think of that now. Now she only wanted to think about the way Matt's hands skimmed her bare thigh beneath her dress. The way his fingers played over her skin, enticing, exciting her until she couldn't manage a single coherent thought.

Suddenly, he stopped. She opened her eyes in surprise.

His gaze scanned the room. His breath, forced from his lungs, allowed only one word to escape. "Where?"

She glanced toward the sheet-draped outline of a narrow single bed.

He shook his head. "Wait here. I'll be right back." He hurried toward the door, then stopped and looked back at her. "You won't change your mind while I'm gone, will you?"

She shook her head. "Not a chance." Then she flashed him a sexy grin. "Hurry."

He smiled, then disappeared into the hallway. She could hear him racing down the stairs and out the front door.

Chapter Ten

Moments later, Matt reappeared in the small bedroom, a navy blue sleeping bag clasped in his arms. He tore the dustcover from the bed, unzipped the sleeping bag and spread it over the bare mattress.

He kicked off his sneakers, took her hand and led her to the bed. Slowly, they sank to their knees in the center of the mattress, their gazes locked in heated invitation.

Haltingly, agonizingly, he unzipped her dress. With a whisper, it slipped off her shoulders, then fell slowly to her waist, its downward progress stopped only by the swell of her hips. Trailing his fingertips tantalizingly over the quivering flesh threatening to spill from the cups of her bra, he stared deep into her eyes.

Matt's touch was new, yet familiar. The same, yet different. She stilled beneath it, unconsciously studying the changes. Calluses. Not the smooth fingertips of the young man who'd made love to her in the family pool.

But his touch… Ah, his touch. Mature, knowing, confident, yet tender, ever sensitive to her needs. He relentlessly explored the places on her body that had longed for his attention. She stiffened with the effort to keep from crying out.

Suddenly, when his roughened skin caught on the fine lace of her bra, Matt pulled his hand away. "My hands are too rough."

She caught his fingers and laid them on her partially exposed breast. "Your hands are just right."

His fingers contracted, kneading her softness, then he buried his face in her midriff. His warm breath feathered over her sensitized skin. She gasped. He kissed her quivering flesh. When he moved his face, the cool air hit her moistened middle and sent tingles of erotic pleasure dancing over her.

He inhaled deeply, then stood and locked his gaze with hers. "I always loved the way you smell. I didn't realize until now how much I missed it." Sadness invaded his eyes. "It's been so long, Honey."

Although she agreed and wanted to add "too long," she couldn't find the strength to form the words and force them from her lips. Instead, she dropped her hands to his hips, then burrowed them beneath the hem of his T-shirt. With the same tantalizing slowness he'd employed removing her dress, she inched the material up his chest, the backs of her hands lightly skimming his bare flesh.

By the time she approached his underarms, his patience had reached its limit. He grabbed the shirt from her trembling hands, then ripped it over his head. He threw it to the floor and turned his attention to her bra. For a moment, he fumbled clumsily with the delicate catch. Then, as if the memory flooded back to him, with one deft twist of his fingers he popped it open. The lacy garment slid down her arms and off her hands, to fall forgotten between them.

She knelt before him, fully exposed to his hungry gaze. A sudden bout of shyness accosted her and she reached to cover herself with her hands. "A woman's body changes after childbirth," she explained, when he looked at her in question.

He sighed deeply, then gently removed her hands, his gaze remaining locked with hers. "I want to look at you." Seeing the resistance slowly fade from her eyes, he let his gaze drift down her body.

She'd been right. Birthing their child had changed her. Her breasts held a fullness they hadn't had before. Her hips, while molded to perfection, had altered, gotten more curvaceous, more enticing. Her skin glowed like burnished bronze. The girl he had loved seven years ago had become a woman in the truest sense of the word.

"Beautiful," he murmured, totally mesmerized by the sight of her.

Matt couldn't get enough of her, see enough of her, hold enough of her. But he held back, taking it slow, savoring every moment, every curve and dip of her luscious skin.

Tenderly, he sketched her collarbone with the tip of his finger, then the swell of creamy flesh below it. He looked at her, locking their gazes, then outlined the rosy circle pouting from the center of her breast.

She shivered.

He glanced at her arms for signs of gooseflesh, then smiled knowingly. The shiver had not been born of a chill, but the surge of desire running as hotly through her as it was through him.

"Matt, I—"

"No." He laid his finger across her lips, caressing their slick smoothness as he spoke. "Don't talk,

Honey. Just feel. Feel what my touch is doing to you. Feel the way it builds inside you. Just feel, babe.''

Obeying him, she closed her eyes and threw her head back, exposing her white throat to his ravaging kisses. "Mmm."

Dimly, he was aware of her hands fumbling insistently at his belt buckle, and when the leather and metal finally gave way, she moved on to the button at the waist of his jeans. Seconds later, the soft rasp of the zipper being lowered could to be heard despite their heavy breathing, and cool air assaulted his hot skin through his shorts. Matt dragged in a tortured breath. When he felt the caress of her fingers on his hardened flesh, he buried his face in her neck and nibbled at her fragrant skin, trying not to lose it completely, and just throw her to the bed and love her senseless. He wanted this to be slow. Slow, hot and unforgettable. He wanted this time with Honey to be a memory he would carry with him to his grave, because deep inside, he knew there would be no more. He closed his eyes and let the moment claim him. Almost as if he were afraid she'd vanished in that short time span, he slowly opened his eyes.

"Stand up," he said.

She slid to the end of the bed, then stood, placing her hands on his broad shoulders. The muscles bunched and relaxed under her fingers. Deliberately, he grabbed the sides of her dress, then slid it over her hips to let it pool at her feet. Only sheer, white, lacy bikini panties concealed Honey from him. Hooking his fingers in the elastic, with a swift downward pull he removed them as well.

When he looked up, he drew in his breath and held it. She stood before him, bathed from head to toe in the dying sunlight. The muted rays kissed her skin with all the golden hues of her namesake. Her eyelids drooped with passion. Her mouth glistened with moisture from their kisses. From between her open lips came that purr that never failed to weaken his knees.

He rained kisses on her skin, starting at her rib cage, then the underside of her breasts. She tasted like some candy he'd loved as a kid. Moving his mouth to the hardened tip of her breast, he engulfed one engorged nipple. She started, as if he'd hurt her. He felt the vibration of a moan building deep within her, bursting out in a sigh of pure pleasure. She buried her fingers in his hair.

Like a hungry child, he suckled first one pouty nipple, then the other, unable to get enough of their sweetness, while he kneaded the surrounding softness. Again she moaned and tightened her hold on his hair, pressing his mouth closer. The scent of her, which had always intoxicated him, reached out to blanket him, enveloping him in a heady mist of sensuality so thick he felt he might never escape.

Blindly, led only by touch, he continued a trail of kisses up her collarbone and her neck, then around to her mouth. He pulled her against him and gasped with unbearable pleasure when her naked breasts crushed against his chest. Fire coursed through him.

They still fit together like two halves of a whole, one incomplete without the other. But then, even in his earliest memory of her, Honey had always been the other part of his soul.

Quickly, he levered her gently from his embrace, then divested himself of his jeans and shorts in one swift movement. They stood face-to-face, clad only in their desire for each other.

"What about your leg?" she asked, glancing at the long white bandage on his upper thigh.

"What leg?" he said, nuzzling her throat.

Bending her head, Honey kissed his collarbone. With the tips of her fingers, she explored his flesh, relearning the body of the man who had fathered her son, and filled her dreams, the man whose gaze now asked her to give the final measure of herself to him.

Matt groaned as if in exquisite pain. "Oh, babe, you're really testing my control."

In answer, she stepped back, then lowered herself to the sleeping bag on the bed. Stretching out, she opened her arms in silent invitation. Moments later, Matt's warm, naked body covered hers, his hot hardness nestled between her open thighs. She closed her eyes to savor the intimacy, then raised her hips to bring him even closer.

For the first time in seven years, Honey trusted him. Opening herself to him, she waited. With a groan, Matt fit himself to her, then pushed forward, burying himself inside.

The frantic pace he set took her breath away. It was as if they were trying to make up for all the lost years. Then, feeling his control slipping, Matt slowed, deliberately stretching it out, waiting for Honey to catch up to him. He wanted to share the final moment with her. Wanted them to ride together on the cresting waves of passion that broke around them.

The drowning sensation washing over him reminded Matt that making love to Honey was like a kind of rebirth, like surrendering his breath for all time, then having life restored, but in a new and glorious way. Then all thought faded in a red haze of desire.

Honey arched her spine and opened herself to his hardness, accepting him as part of her, preparing to ride out the hurricane of their lovemaking.

Like a gathering storm, love swelled inside her. She wrapped her legs around him, trapping him against her heat. Silently, she took the lead, showing him with the rhythmic movements of her body that she wanted him—*all* of him.

Their lovemaking once again took on a frantic pace, each fighting to get closer, to feel more, to squeeze every last drop of ecstasy from their coupling. Her heart throbbed in her ears and battered at her chest, as if trying to escape sensations that were too much for her to bear. Torrential emotions rained through her, swamping her in their intensity, coating her skin with a slick moisture that only added to her awareness of the man above her.

Matt's heartbeat joined hers in a frenzied pounding. The pressure of impending release built low in her belly, then climbed and reached for the pinnacle of pleasure. Finally, lightning slashed through her, gripping her in electric spasms of fulfillment. She curled her fingers on the mattress edge, but it wasn't enough. She wanted to feel Matt. When she clutched his sweat-soaked skin, a shudder passed through them, again and again. Then they lay still, the only sounds in the room from their efforts to fill their starving lungs.

When reality returned, she had only the strength to hold on to Matt and wait for the impact of what they'd done to hit her. And it would, she was sure. But for now, she clung to him, as if not letting go would ensure a future for them, as if she wouldn't wake one morning to find him gone again.

Matt stirred, raising himself on his elbows to look down at the woman who had just turned his world upside down. Her hair lay in golden tangles around her flushed face. Her eyes, as blue as a summer sky, looked up at him drowsily from beneath lashes tipped in gold. In their depths, he could see not the regret he'd expected, but a profound sadness.

In that instant, looking down at her, Matt realized something he'd been lying to himself about for too long.

He loved Honey.

He loved her more than he had seven years ago when he'd walked away. He loved her more than he ever thought he could love again. While the realization brought him joy, it also brought him the most excruciating pain he had ever known. He had disappointed everyone he'd ever loved in one way or another, hurting them without meaning to. He could not do that to this woman. Not again.

HONEY STARED BLINDLY out the windshield of Matt's truck. She couldn't believe she'd been so stupid again. Why hadn't she insisted on protection? Hadn't she been the one who'd lectured Emily on not indulging in sex with Kat until she made sure it was safe? But then, Honey had had no way of knowing how frantic their first encounter would be.

"Matt, maybe we should have used protection…?"

"Don't worry. When I got injured, they had to do a blood transfusion. They tested me for anything and everything. I'm clean."

"I didn't mean to suggest—"

He turned to her and frowned. "It's a little rough to make love with a gash in your leg, Honey. You're

the first since the accident." Turning his gaze back
to the road, he added, "Do you think I would have
endangered you? That I would have done this if I
hadn't been absolutely sure there was no danger of
infecting you with some social disease?" His voice
held a tint of sadness that she would think him so
callous, so irresponsible. "You lucked out this time.
Better be more careful the next."

Next time? What was that supposed to mean? Did
he think she went around hopping in and out of beds?
Or…did he mean a next time with him? Her heart
speeded up at the possibility.

She thought about voicing her question and pointing out that he hadn't seemed to have any problem
making love with the leg injury a little while ago.
However, considering his testy attitude, she remained
silent.

From the corner of her eye, she studied him. His
fingers gripped the steering wheel so tightly that his
knuckles were white. He glared straight ahead. What
was he thinking? Why was he so angry? Was he re-
gretting what they'd done? Was he already planning
his departure from Bristol and her life, and that of
their son? Had she, while selfishly making memories
to sustain her, given him the excuse he needed to
leave again?

And while she was asking questions, she might as
well aim a few at herself. She trusted Matt, when he
assured her that his health was fine, but what about
pregnancy? Neither one of them, it seemed, had given
a thought to that eventuality. Could she face raising
another child without Matt?

When they pulled into Amanda's driveway, the silent question hung between them like a concrete wall.

MATT HUNG the For Sale sign on the handlebars of the motorcycle and wheeled the bike to the edge of the lawn bordering the street. He couldn't do much else to make up for the pain and anguish he'd caused Honey when he'd taken Danny for a ride the day before, but he could ensure it would never happen again. He just wished to God he could find a way to make it up to her for his carelessness that afternoon in his bedroom.

He'd asked her to trust him and she had, but only to guard her against disease, not against pregnancy. Now there existed a very good chance he'd repeated the same mistake he'd made seven years ago. Honey might be pregnant. The only saving grace was that this time he'd be here to help her through it.

He thought about Honey's flat stomach ripe with his child. As lovely as she was now, he knew with an innate certainty that she'd be even lovelier then. Of all his regrets, and he had many, not seeing Honey carrying their son remained at the top of his list.

His groin tightened at the thought of making a child with her. Just what he needed. He'd lain awake the entire night hard and ready for a replay of their afternoon in his old childhood bed. In his mind, he'd relived every second, every emotion, every touch of their bodies. Now here he was, in broad daylight, doing it all over again.

"Damn!"

"U-U-Uncle Matt?"

Matt stiffened, then moved around the bike so that the sign blocked the lower half of his anatomy. "Hey, sport!" He'd been so absorbed in thought he hadn't even heard Danny's school bus drive up and let him out. "How was school?" Buddy came bounding across the lawn to Danny.

Danny's gaze never moved from the For Sale sign. "Why are y-y-you selling the bike?" Absently he rubbed behind Buddy's ear. "Hi, boy."

Since Buddy had come into his son's life, Matt could see a big improvement in Danny's speech. Getting him the dog may have incurred Honey's temper, but even she couldn't deny that Danny was on the road to recovery. Matt had finally done something right, and as a result, he'd soon have the pleasure of hearing his son call him Daddy.

"Because it's best."

"But why's it b-b-best?"

Matt took Danny's books and then ushered the boy to the stone wall at the bottom of the driveway. He placed the books on the wall, then hoisted Danny up beside them and stood in front of him. Buddy flopped at their feet, content to wait for his afternoon playtime with Danny.

"Sometimes things we do, even things we really, really like doing, cause other people—people we love—to worry about us. Understand?" He waited for Danny to nod before going on. "When you and I went out on the bike yesterday, your mom was very worried that we'd get hurt."

"But we didn't." Danny's forehead creased in a deep frown.

"No, we didn't. But she was afraid that we would and that's what upset her. Now, even though we like the bike, do you think it's fair to worry your mom about us riding it again?"

Danny thought for a moment, then shook his head.

"Okay. Then I'm selling my bike so she never has to worry about it again. Do you understand?"

A hesitation followed before Danny raised his gaze to Matt's. "If we promise to be careful, and we don't go fast, won't that be just as good? Then you can keep the bike."

It was Matt's turn to shake his head. "Nope. You see, even if she never sees us on it or never knows we went for a ride, she'll still worry that we will. Every time she can't find us, she'll think we're out on the bike. It's a reminder that the bad thing, the thing that makes her sad, is there." He waited for Danny to absorb what he'd said. "Now do you understand?"

For a moment Danny remained silent, obviously deep in thought. Then he raised his gaze to Matt's, his eyes bright with an idea. Jumping down from the wall, he grabbed his books. "Come on, Buddy. We gotta go. See you later, Uncle Matt," he called over his shoulder.

Matt watched boy and dog race across the yard and into the house. Laughing, he shook his head in wonder at the child's mind.

He hated selling the bike as much as Danny did, but he hated more the terror he'd seen in Honey's eyes when he and Danny had pulled into the driveway after their ride. In his gut, he knew it had something to do with Stan. She'd said as much.

Even though he hadn't been there, Matt knew in his heart that he'd put that same look in her eyes once before—of fear for herself and her unborn child. He swore he'd never cause her that kind of pain and anguish again. The bike had to go. And should their afternoon of lovemaking have consequences…he'd have to face that eventuality when it came.

He smiled. The thought of having another child with Honey warmed him in places that had been cold for way too long, and that scared him half to death. He couldn't afford to start thinking about a permanent relationship with her. After all, hadn't he just sworn never to hurt her again? But no matter how much he tried to convince his head, his heart kept saying something different.

Chapter Eleven

Later that day, Honey stood just inside the door to Danny's room. On his bed was a For Sale sign, fashioned from a torn piece of cardboard and crudely printed in bright red and blue crayon. In a shallow box nearby sat his collection of race cars arranged in neat rows.

"Honey."

She spun around, clutching a hand to her heaving chest. Behind her, Matt leaned against the door frame, his gaze drifting past her to the box of race cars.

"Sorry, I didn't mean to scare you," he said, taking one step into the room.

She exhaled a deep breath. "That's okay. I just wasn't expecting anyone."

"What's that all about?" He motioned toward the box of race cars.

She glanced away from him and back to the array of items on Danny's bed. "I have no idea."

Before Matt could even venture a guess, Danny rushed into the room. "M-M-Mom, you shouldn't be looking at this s-s-stuff."

"Why on earth not? And what's this all about?"

Danny took the quilt at the foot of his bed and

spread it carefully over the box of cars. "I'm s-s-selling my car collection to Jimmy F-F-Fletcher."

"Why?" Matt and Honey asked in unison.

Danny shuffled his feet, glanced at Matt, then to his mother. "'Cause sometimes you have to do th-things that you don't wanna, 'cause it m-makes people unhappy if you don't."

Honey glanced at Matt. He nodded in Danny's direction and gave him a thumbs-up. At the sign of his approval, Danny's face broke into a wide grin.

So Matt knew more than he was admitting. Honey had an idea as to what was behind her son's sudden decision to part with his treasured collection.

"Uh, Matt, may I see you outside?"

He followed her from the room. To ensure her son would not hear the conversation, she closed the door, then motioned for Matt to move farther down the hall. When he turned to face her, her breath caught.

His eyes sparkled with an energy she hadn't seen in them since he'd come home. His full lips curved up on both sides into a smile, coaxing out the dimples that always robbed her of coherent thought. She blinked and moved her gaze to break the invisible thread that held her both motionless and speechless.

"Does that scene in there have anything to do with what's at the end of the driveway?" she asked, carefully watching the play of emotions on his face.

She'd seen the motorcycle and the For Sale sign when she'd brought Amanda home from her checkup with Dr. Thomas. Although Honey had experienced a surge of happiness and relief, she'd wondered out loud what had prompted Matt's sudden decision to sell his bike.

"Well, it appears to me as if Matthew took you

seriously when you told him you didn't want Danny on the bike again,'' Amanda had commented as they drove slowly past the motorcycle. ''If the bike's not here, then Danny won't ever be on it again.''

''I never intended for Matt to—''

''Maybe not, but it seems he took it that way. Then again, there may be more behind it than allaying your fear for your son.'' Amanda had smiled knowingly, confusing Honey even more.

''Honey?''

Startled from her memories of the exchange between her and her mother-in-law, Honey jumped nervously at the sound of her name. ''I'm sorry. What did you say?''

''I asked, what makes you think my bike being for sale has anything to do with Danny selling his cars?'' Matt's grin deepened and so did those damned dimples.

She leaned against the wall, hoping he wouldn't think she needed to support her weakened knees. He might not be aware of his male magnetism, but she certainly was. However, he didn't need to know that.

She cleared her throat. ''If for no other reason than this last week, if you think something's pink, Danny says it's pink. If you walk left, Danny walks left.'' She brushed a lock of hair off her cheek. ''In short, Matt, our son emulates every move you make and every thought you think.''

To her total astonishment, she no longer felt that slight jolt of jealousy at sharing Danny with his father. In fact, the idea of them as a family produced a warmth that encompassed her entire being—even if she knew her dreams were just that, dreams. The tension seeped out of her body.

Her calm stance and relaxed attitude must have communicated itself to Matt. He leaned his shoulder against the wall beside her, crossed his arms over his chest, then looked deep into her eyes.

"Do you realize," he said, his voice tight with emotion, "that that's the first time you've referred to Danny as *our* son?"

Honey dropped her gaze to the blue-and-gold Oriental runner stretching the length of the upstairs hall. "I'm sure I've—"

"No." Matt touched her hand. His fingertips were as warm as his voice. "Not the way you just did, like you've finally accepted it."

Despite their personal differences, Honey would have had to be blind not to see the attachment growing between Matt and their son. She'd be lying to herself if she didn't admit that Matt was having a positive effect on Danny, in a way Stan never had. And if she was right, his decision to sell his cars proved it.

But something more than that bothered her. Something she had to talk to Matt about. Every time he did something that impacted Danny in some way, she felt a desperation in the act, something she wasn't sure Matt even knew existed in him.

Deep inside, she'd come to believe that, unconsciously, Matt thought he had to win Danny's love with gifts and favors—rides on motorcycles, Buddy, getting him out of eating those hated peas. How could she explain that Danny gave his love unconditionally, without bribes? How did she tell him that he did not have to buy Danny's love—or hers? All he had to do was earn it by being there, always, for them.

She hesitated to bring it up, since last time they'd

argued bitterly about it, and she was reluctant to disturb this middle ground they seemed to have found, about both Danny and themselves.

"I've *always* accepted that Danny is *our* son," she said softly. "He loves us both," she added tentatively.

Matt's face froze. His expression took on a coldness that sent a chill up her spine. "I don't want him to love me. I just want to be a good father to him." He turned and stalked down the hall.

Unwilling to let this go without discussing it, Honey followed him. She felt the rush of the cool night air before she got to the bottom of the steps, then the screen door slammed. As she passed through the downstairs hall, Amanda came to the doorway of the sitting room.

"Anything wrong, dear?"

Honey didn't answer. She hurried to the door in time to see Matt's truck disappear down the driveway. By the time she made it to her car, he'd be long gone. *Damn!*

"Honey?"

She started, then turned toward her mother-in-law.

"Is there something wrong, dear?"

Seeing no reason to involve Amanda in this, she shook her head. "No, what makes you think that?"

"Well, Matthew doesn't normally leave in such a hurry or with the exuberance with which he just drove down the drive." Amanda studied her face. "But if you're sure everything is all right..." The elderly woman turned her wheelchair back into the sitting room. "Why don't you join me for a cup of tea?"

Honey sighed and followed her mother-in-law. She really didn't want to talk about this right now, nor did she want to socialize over a cup of tea. What she wanted was time to think about Matt's extraordinary statement about not wanting Danny's love.

Amanda rolled her wheelchair to a stop beside the rich dark mahogany side table where Tess had laid out the teapot, cups and a plate of very dark brown cookies. Amanda chuckled softly. If the idea that charcoal could be a wonderful digestive aid were true, she had the best digestive tract in town. She pushed the plate aside and poured three cups of tea.

"Three?" Honey asked.

"Yes, I wanted some company, and Tess said she'd join me." A friend as well as a housekeeper, Tess often joined Amanda for a late night snack, filling the time with catching up and planning meals. However, Amanda decided silently, it looked as though tonight they would be discussing something quite a bit different.

Honey nodded and took the offered cup, then moved to the seat at Amanda's side. Even if Matthew hadn't just slammed out of the house by the expression on her daughter-in-law's face, Amanda could tell all was not going well with the couple.

"Perhaps if we talked about it, we could remove those awful frown lines from your lovely face." She offered Honey an understanding smile, then leaned back in her wheelchair and hoped Honey would confide in her. "Hmm?"

Glancing up at Amanda over the rim of the cup, Honey took a sip, then set the cup and saucer back on the tea tray. She hesitated, obviously deciding whether to talk about what troubled her or not. Then her expression cleared, and she flashed Amanda a very weak imitation of a smile.

"Matt just made the most ridiculous statement." She crossed her legs and tugged the hem of her dress down over her knee.

Amanda raised an eyebrow in silent inquiry. Now that she'd gotten Honey to open up, she didn't want to disturb her train of thought.

"He said he didn't want Danny's love."

Amanda set her cup beside Honey's. "What?"

"My reaction exactly. Why would a father not want his son's love?"

"'Tis as plain as the nose on your face," Tess offered, ambling into the room, then seating herself tiredly in the third chair. Amanda and Honey turned questioning eyes on the housekeeper. "The lad's afraid."

Amanda stared at Tess, digesting her words. Tess picked up a cookie, bit into it, then chewed thoughtfully, obviously waiting for someone to ask her what she meant. Before Amanda could get the words out, Honey asked, "Afraid of his son?"

Tess laughed. "Glory be, no. Not afraid of the little tyke. Afraid of love."

Not certain if it was Tess's statement that caused it or the cool night air coming through the sheer curtains at the window behind her back, Amanda shivered.

Without comment, Tess rose and went to the window, pushing it down to a mere slit. "Fresh air's good for you," she said in explanation of not closing it all the way.

She reached for a rose-colored afghan, draped it around Amanda's shoulders, then resumed her seat and picked up her cup and saucer. Warmth coiled around Amanda's chilled body.

"Tess, what do you mean, my nephew is afraid of love? He's always been loved. His father, mother, his brother, me. Why should he be afraid of it now?"

Tess added another squeeze of fresh lemon to her tea. The pungent smell drifted through the air and Amanda wrinkled her nose.

Holding up her forefinger, Tess put her cup down and leaned toward the other two women. Her voice, when she spoke, had lowered to just above a whisper. "Ah, and you're right. But in most cases, that love has hurt him in some way or another. 'Tis no wonder the lad is not wantin' to be loved." She pursed her lips and sat back. "If he's not loved, then he can't be hurt."

"Hurt?" Honey stared at Tess, her mouth open in shock.

"Yes. Hurt. His mother died when he was but a wee boy. That tore the heart right out of him. His father all but forgot the child existed. The brother he loved and admired died suddenly, leaving him to contend with a bitter old man. Then you married his cousin when you were pregnant with Matt's child." She looked from one to the other. "Wouldn't you say that hurt him? The only love he ever knew that didn't hurt him was right here, from you and me." She pointed her finger at Amanda. "And even we failed him by not going to that wretched old man and telling him that he had a grandson and the boy needed his dad."

Tess's admission that she, too, had guessed who Danny's real father was didn't shock Amanda, but it obviously took Honey aback.

"Not knowing, that hurt him more than anything, lass."

"But I didn't mean to hurt him, and Danny would never hurt him."

Shaking her head, Tess reached for one of Honey's hands. "Ah, but that doesn't make it easier for him to accept. 'Tis like sticking your finger in a mousetrap. Once or twice you might be able to stand the pain. But after a few times, you don't want to try it again."

Amanda could not suppress the smile that Tess's homespun analogy brought to her lips. "But what if he's shown that the trap won't hurt this time?"

Tess grinned at Amanda. "Ah, now you're thinkin'."

Both women turned to Honey.

"How can I do that?"

"You love him, don't you?" Amanda asked, knowing the answer before she even heard it. Honey's love for Matt, whether she knew it or not, shone from her like a beacon in the night.

Honey hesitated, then said softly, "Yes. Yes, I love him."

"And Danny?" Tess asked.

"Yes, I think Danny loves him, too, although he's never said so."

"There you go," Amanda and Tess said in unison.

"Now, what are you going to do about it?" Amanda waited hopefully for Honey's answer.

Taking another cookie, looking at it skeptically, then placing it back on the plate, Tess poured herself more tea and added lemon and sugar, before leaning back to wait with Amanda.

Honey looked from one woman to the other. Her mind swirled with the information Tess had imparted. Were they right? Had Matt been hurt so many times that he didn't want to chance it again? How could she undo damage that had been years in the making? And what about her? She'd been hurt by love, too, and no one was going to any great lengths to prove that she wouldn't be hurt again.

Obviously, from the looks on their faces, both women considered her capable of performing this miracle. But how?

"I don't know," she finally said.

Tess huffed impatiently, and Amanda sighed.

"Glory be, girl, do we need to lay it out for you in black and white?" Tess grabbed her hand again and squeezed. "Go to him. Tell him how you feel."

"But he doesn't want that. He made that perfectly clear before he left. He does not want to be loved. And if he doesn't want love from his own son, how will he accept it from me?"

Amanda covered Tess's hand with hers and both women looked at Honey. "He wants it. He just has no idea how to accept it. You need to help him. You need to show him that your love and Danny's is not going to hurt him." She paused and looked deep into Honey's eyes. "Is it?"

"I would never hurt Matt."

"Then go to him." Amanda and Tess released her and leaned back, watching her, waiting for her to make the move that could change her life, Danny's and Matt's forever. "Convince him that loving and being loved doesn't have to hurt."

MATT LOOKED DOWN from the upstairs window at Honey's car. He'd seen the swipe of light across the ceiling of his old bedroom and knew someone had pulled into his driveway. When he checked to see who was there, the last person he'd expected to find sitting in his driveway was Honey.

Why didn't she get out of the car? No sooner had he thought it than the dome light came on and the door swung open. Honey stepped out into the dark yard, then raised her gaze to his window. Matt moved behind the frame, unwilling for her to see him.

After he'd made the remark about not wanting Danny's love, then stalked from the house, he'd had time to think. His thoughts had confused him. He loved both Danny and Honey, yet he didn't want that love returned.

It had taken awhile, but he'd finally figured out the logic of it all. If their hearts weren't at risk, then he wouldn't have to worry about hurting them.

Simply saying he loved someone wasn't enough; he had to be prepared to back up his emotions with actions. But he wasn't. He didn't know how. When Matt was a kid, he'd tried to show his father how much he loved him, but had failed. He'd tried to love Honey seven years ago and ended up walking out on her because he knew, in the end, he'd been afraid he'd fail her as well. Things hadn't changed. He was still the same guy who had left town all those years ago.

He couldn't and wouldn't risk Danny's or Honey's happiness again. He never should have come back. Why couldn't he have left well enough alone?

The front door squeaked.

"Matt?"

He held his breath, hoping she'd leave.

"Matt. I know you're here."

Her voice was closer. He could hear her climbing the stairs. One of the treads squeaked loudly under her weight. The soft click of the light switch sounded just outside the room, and light flooded under the door.

Please, Honey, go away. I don't want to hurt you, and if you come in here, I will.

The door opened slowly, sending blinding light into all the dark corners. Honey stepped into the open doorway.

"Matt, we need to talk."

"If it's about what I said before, I've said all I plan to on the subject. Now, go home, Honey."

She took another step into the room, then switched on the overhead light. Matt blinked. "I'm not going home until we talk," she said. "And you're wrong. I think you have a lot more to say on the subject of love."

Turning away from her, Matt stared out the window into the darkness, hoping it would reach in and swallow him up so he didn't have to reach into his own darkness and pull out the memories that Honey wanted him to bring into the light.

"Matt, talk to me."

Suddenly, he felt anger rising in him like a flood tide. "What good will talking do? Will it change the past? Will it make the unhappiness of a lonely little boy disappear? Will it make my father accept me for who I was and not who he wanted me to be?"

"No. We can't change the past." She came to stand beside him. He felt the warmth of her touch on his arm. "But it could help you to understand it better and help you build a future."

Unable to bear her nearness, but even less, her pity and her sympathy, he shook off her hold, then stalked to the door. "Understand it? Oh, I understood it a long time ago. I don't think I could stand to have it made any clearer than it is.'' He stared at her for a long moment, the muscles in his jaw working frantically as he ground his teeth. ''Leave it alone, Honey. Just leave it alone. I don't want to hurt you or Danny, and if we continue this conversation, I will.'' He turned to leave.

Suddenly afraid that if she let him go, she'd never see him again, Honey dashed across the room and grabbed his arm. If she couldn't make him understand with words that love didn't have to hurt, maybe she could show him.

With all her strength, she turned him to her, then threw herself into his arms. Pressing her lips against his, she said a silent prayer that she still had enough power over him to prove that he was wrong, very wrong—that love only hurt when it wasn't returned.

At first he remained stiff and unresponsive. Then, like a snowbank assaulted by hot spring winds, he melted into her, wrapping his arms around her and returning her kiss with equal fervor.

As they had a few days ago, their kisses held a heated urgency, but this time the pleasure made Honey's heart twist in pain. This time she felt not the joining of two people who had waited years for this moment, but the desperation of knowing something was about to end. Matt was saying goodbye.

Honey refused to allow that to happen again. This time she'd fight for herself and for Danny—and for Matt.

The lips broke apart and she gasped for air. ''Matt, you can't just walk away again. Running didn't solve the problems before and it won't this time. Running isn't the answer.'' When he didn't speak, she leaned back and looked at his face. "Stay and fight for your life. I'll be here to help. Danny will be here."

Matt smiled and outlined her face with his fingertips. "There's nothing to fight for." To her surprise, his cheeks were damp with tears. "And even if there was, you couldn't help."

"Let me try." She grasped the front of his shirt. "Please, let me try."

"It's too late to try." He pushed her from him and turned away. "I couldn't be what my father wanted and I can't be what you want."

"What did he want? Tell me."

He swung back to her. "He wanted me to be my dead brother. He wanted me to be Jamie."

Honey swallowed. "And me? What do you think I want?"

For a long moment, he just stared at her, and she wondered if he'd answer. "A man who can live up to his responsibilities. A man who isn't your father or Stan." He shook his head. "Don't you see? I'm not sure I can be any better for you than either of them were."

She shook her head in vehement denial of his words. "Stan and my father are dead."

"Only in the physical sense, Honey. Because you let them continue to dictate your life, they will never be truly dead for you. You'll always be comparing other men to them, measuring them, distrusting them. As long as you do that, you'll never be as independent as you think you are."

He took her shoulders in his hands and stared hard at her. "I have a long history of disappointing people, Honey, and I can't give you any guarantees that I won't turn out like Stan or like your father. Or that I won't disappoint you and Danny.''

His words hit Honey like a fist to the stomach, knocking the wind out of her, stunning her, robbing her of the power of speech. She felt his hands slide from her shoulders. Then she was alone.

Matt had walked away—again—just as she'd known he would. The worst of it was, she wondered if he was right.

Chapter Twelve

Her bedroom lay in shadows, as dark as Honey's thoughts. Everyone slept soundly but her. She glanced at the bedside table clock: 3:27 a.m. Just then, the glowing red seven changed to an eight. Time passed, yet her life seemed to always be on hold, waiting. Waiting for what? Waiting for someone else to make a decision that would affect her.

She'd waited first for her father to notice her, to acknowledge that she made up a small part of his life. But he never did. Then it was Stan. She'd waited and prayed that one day he would give up racing cars and motorcycles and risking his life, and settle down to build a home with her and Danny. But that never came, either.

Finally, she'd waited for Danny's stutter to go away. So far, that hadn't come to pass, either, although she had to admit that, since Matt had come, Danny's speech had improved a great deal.

Now she waited for Matt. But then, she'd always been waiting for Matt in one way or another.

She rolled to her side and stared off into the night. Maybe Stan had been right all along. She'd never gotten over Matt and never would. He was a part of her that completed who she was, and although she'd proved she could live without him, she didn't want to. However, after tonight, it looked as though the choice had been taken out of her hands. Matt didn't want her or Danny, at least not in the way they wanted him.

She recalled his accusation that she would never be truly free of either Stan or her father as long as she allowed them any small measure of control over her life. Even thinking about it made her laugh. Both her father and Stan were dead. Since the day she'd stood next to Stan's grave, she'd sworn that neither he nor any man would hold the reins of her life, and she'd lived by that motto ever since. *She* made the decisions. *She* decided what was best for her and her son.

She rolled to her back and kicked the sheet off her bare legs. The honeysuckle-scented air caressed her, cooling her skin, but her mind continued its heated analysis of her conversation with Matt.

He'd said she compared all men to her father and her dead husband. That she had compared him with them. Utterly ridiculous. There was no comparison. Matt had come back to make a home. Matt took a great interest in their son and his well-being. Matt cared about what happened to her and Danny, and that they were happy. Matt...

Matt ran from his problems. Suddenly she knew that as long as her last thought held true, she and Matt could never have a relationship. No matter how many times she told herself that she would be happy with her memories after Matt left, she knew in her core that it wasn't true. She knew that he'd leave her heart in shreds once again. This time, however, he'd also leave a little boy's heart in shreds. She could not let that happen.

Above all else, she had to protect Danny from any more pain.

EMILY SAT DOWN in the rocker on Amanda's front porch. "I can't stay long. Rose has a dentist appointment later this afternoon. I promised I'd be back to take over with the twins before then." Her gaze drifted to where Danny and Buddy played on the lawn.

"He sure loves that dog, doesn't he?"

Honey nodded. "It was the best thing we could have done for him."

"We? As I recall, you were not exactly keen on the idea of Danny having a dog."

Honey glanced at her sister's raised eyebrows. "Okay. The best thing Matt could have done for him."

"Speaking of Matt, where is he?"

Honey looked away and watched the stray orange cat creep along the wall, its attention centered on Danny and Buddy. "He's working at his house."

"Is it about done?"

"I don't know. I haven't been over there for a few days."

Actually, she hadn't been there since the night she'd gone after Matt, nearly a week ago. Nor had she seen Matt. He'd once more begun the ritual of getting up before her every morning and coming home well after the rest of the house had retired for the night. It was just as well, she told herself. She didn't need a daily reminder that very soon Matt would be out of her life again.

Her gaze drifted to her son. And if Matt wasn't here as a constant fixture in Danny's life, it would be easier to sever the bond that had been growing between them. She ignored the axiom that Tess had spouted this morning when Honey had asked if Matt had left already.

"Absence makes the heart grow fonder," the housekeeper had purred, then winked.

Just then, Danny screamed her name. "Mom!"

Honey and Emily shot to their feet. Buddy had noticed the stray cat and had taken off after it at a dead run. The cat darted back and forth, trying to outmaneuver the dog with its fancy footwork, but Buddy stayed on its trail. Behind Buddy, Danny ran frantically, trying to stop his dog and calling his name.

Honey and Emily ran down the stairs and took up the chase, neither of them sure who they were trying to catch.

The cat veered right and scampered under some shrubs. Buddy followed. Honey held her breath. A split second later, the cat emerged on the other side, Buddy hot on its heels, and took off like a shot across the open lawn.

"Buddy," Danny called. "You leave that cat alone. Bad dog!"

Buddy paid no head. He was closing in on the cat.

"You go that way," Honey told Emily, pointing toward a big clump of lilac bushes. "I'll go the other way and maybe we can catch one of them."

Emily circled the lilacs and Honey went in the opposite direction. She barely felt the brush of the cat's fur as it scooted between her legs and headed for the big old maple tree on the edge of Amanda's rose garden.

"Hell's bells," she mumbled, sidestepping Buddy as he emerged right behind the cat. "They're over here," she called to Emily.

Heading after the animals, Honey stopped when she saw the cat scramble up the tree trunk and disappear among the branches. Emily and Danny arrived on the scene shortly after. Amid the high-pitched yipping of a frustrated Buddy and their own gasps for air, she managed to tell them where the cat was.

Danny immediately began to cry. "Fred will be stuck up there, Mom. You have to get him down."

"Fred?"

"That's what I named him. I know he's scared, Mom. We have to get him." Danny started forward as if to climb the tree.

"No!" Honey grabbed the seat of his pants and held him back. "I don't want you climbing that tree and falling out."

"But, Mom…" Danny's plea drifted off on a wail that made Buddy bark louder.

"I'll do it." She looked around as if trying to figure out who'd said that. Surely it hadn't been her. However, the look of total shock on Emily's face told her differently.

"You? My God, Honey, you're scared of heights. You can't climb that tree. Just leave the cat. He'll come down on his own."

Danny's wail intensified.

Looking from her son to her sister, Honey smiled hopefully. "You want to do it?"

Emily held a hand to her chest. "Me? I'm more scared of heights than you are." She shook her head and backed away. "Uh-uh. Not me."

"Mom, he's gonna fall. You gotta get him. Now!"

"He's not going to fall, Danny." Emily smiled at her sister. "Your mom will get him down."

Honey threw Emily a you-will-pay-for-this look, took off her shoes, drew in a deep breath and then approached the tree. She looked up and could just make the cat out. Fred was clinging to a branch nearly ten feet above her head, and she had to admit he looked terrified. His ears were laid back, his eyes large, and his fur stood in a spiked row down his back.

Swallowing hard, she thought about getting the ladder, then recalled Matt leaving the house with it in the back of his truck last week. She'd seen it in her headlights, leaning against the side of his house, the night she'd gone to talk to him.

"Mom!" Danny's cry broke through her thoughts.

"I'm going," she announced, trying to sound more confident than she felt.

Putting all her strength into it, she jumped for the lowest limb, grabbed it and then swung one leg up. Sitting on the branch, she avoided looking down, and reached for the branch above her. One branch at a time, she made her way higher and higher, all the time aware that the ground was dropping farther and farther away.

When she was within touching distance of the cat, Fred gave a mighty leap and hit the ground running.

"It's okay, Mom. He got down by hisself," Danny announced from below. "You can come down now."

Honey looked down and froze. Looking away quickly, she buried her face in the tree's rough bark. "No, I can't," she whispered to the tree limb.

"Mom?"

"Honey? Are you all right?" Emily's voice drifted up to her, but Honey couldn't answer. She could only cling to the branch with all her might.

"Aunt Emily, is Mom stuck now?"

Honey noted that her son's voice didn't seem to hold the same degree of concern for her as it had for Fred.

"I hope not. If she is, I don't know how we'll get her down."

"Thanks, Em," Honey whispered to her sister. Sweat had broken out on her forehead and palms. Her stomach pitched every time she tried to look down. Her only salvation at the moment was that the old gypsy who'd told her fortune at the fair last year had mentioned nothing about her spending her remaining years high in a tree.

"Honey?"

Matt? Oh great, just what she needed now. She tried to glance down, hoping she'd been mistaken about that deep voice. Taking a breath, she shifted her gaze for a lightning-fast glimpse of the ground below.

"What's she doing up there?" Matt's voice held just a hint of laughter, which didn't improve Honey's mood.

"She went up to rescue Fred," Danny offered.

"Fred?"

"The stray cat," Emily said. "I told her not to, but Danny was screaming and—"

"I wasn't either."

"Then who did I hear yelling 'Mom, you have to get him down'?"

"It was me, but I wasn't either screaming. Girls scream. Guys yell."

"Okay, you were yelling," Emily conceded.

"Uh, excuse me." Honey's voice, while a squeak, came out a little louder. When the argument continued below her, she tried again, louder this time. "Excuse me."

"Yes, Honey?" Matt asked.

"Can someone get me down?"

"I'll be right up."

For a moment there was silence, and she wondered if they'd all left her to hang there indefinitely. Then the rustle of branches below her and Matt's soft grunts as he pulled himself up told her rescue was on the way.

"Give me your hand," he said from below her.

As hard as she tried, she could not loosen the viselike grip she had on the limb. "I can't."

"Yes, you can. Just let go one hand at a time. Come on, babe, you can do it."

Honey tried, but her fingers didn't seem to want to bend. "No, I can't."

"Okay. Hang on."

The branches rustled again, then she felt his warm body behind her. His arms slipped around her and, one finger at a time, he pried her grip loose from the branch. Slowly, he turned her toward him. She snaked her arms around his neck and buried her face in his shirtfront. Tears welled up inside her. She couldn't stop the sobs that burst forth.

He raised her chin with his finger. His smile eased her fear. "No time for snuggling now. We still have to get your feet back on the ground." He kissed her lightly on the tip of her nose. "I'll go first, you come right after me. I promise I won't let you fall." He grinned down at her. "Trust me?"

She knew he meant to get her out of the tree, but when she nodded, she meant a whole lot more. "Yes. I trust you."

The air around them stilled. Matt stared at her for a long time, as if he couldn't believe what she'd said.

She reached up and stroked his cheek with her fingers. "Shouldn't we be getting down?"

As if coming out of a dream, he nodded. "Ah, yes. Let's go."

He stepped to the limb below them, then held his arms out for Honey to follow. Without hesitation, she did. One branch at a time, they made their way back to the ground. Once there, he let go and stepped back.

Emily, white-faced and shaking, let out a sigh of relief.

Danny flew to her side and wrapped his arms around her legs. "Uncle Matt's a hero, Mom. He rescued you, just like you rescued Fred."

For an instant, Honey wondered if Danny's stutter was completely gone or had it just disappeared in the excitement of the moment?

"Yes, I guess he is," Honey said, gazing at Matt over Danny's head. "Thank you."

"My pleasure," he replied, his mouth breaking into a grin, those damned dimples eating holes in his cheeks and turning her stomach to mush. "It's not every day a man gets to rescue a damsel in distress."

"My teacher says that when you rescue somebody, you're respon...resp..."

"Responsible," Emily interjected.

"Yeah, responsible for their life after that. Is Uncle Matt gonna be responsible for you now, Mom? Is he your hero?"

She looked at Danny, then at Matt. "Maybe you can both be my heroes."

"A woman needs only one hero, and it looks like you've got yours already." Matt backed away, then turned and strode toward the house.

"What the hell did that mean?" Emily asked, her gaze going from Honey to Matt, then back to Honey.

"It means that Matt doesn't want to be my hero." Honey leaned down to hug Danny so her sister wouldn't see the tears gathering in her eyes.

MATT PUT THE glass cutter in the tool box, then turned to admire his work. All the broken panes had been replaced in the greenhouse and tomorrow, he'd call to have some seedling plants delivered. He hadn't made up his mind if he wanted to make a business out of the greenhouse yet, but he was anxious to see it flourishing with growth as it had been when his mother was alive.

Since he'd made up his mind to steer clear of Honey, he'd been spending all his time working on the house and it showed. He walked outside and couldn't help but notice the bright new coat of white paint on the house and the dark green shutters.

Inside, a new living room set occupied the majority of new wall-to-wall creamy white carpeting and brick-red tiles had replaced the cracked kitchen linoleum. He hadn't the heart to get rid of the kitchen set, so he had it recovered in creamy beige vinyl. Once he finished painting the kitchen cabinets, he'd be done. Except...

He had avoided the one room at the top of the stairs that his father and mother had shared, then his father had used after his mother's death. He'd lost count of the times he'd gone upstairs determined to go in there and once or twice actually had his hand on the door-knob. But he'd always turned away.

Because of that room and his avoidance of it, he'd gone back to Amanda's early, looking forward to a hot shower and some clean clothes. Then he'd found Honey stuck in the tree. It had been humorous until he'd gone up to get her. Then the feel of her clinging to him and her fear-filled eyes telling him she trusted him had nearly undone all the good he'd done by staying away from her and Danny.

Even worse was when Danny had designated him a hero for saving his mother. If there ever was anyone who didn't deserve hero status, it was Matt Logan.

He picked up his toolbox, then walked from the greenhouse and rounded the corner of the house to go to his truck. He'd just turned the corner onto the front lawn, when he saw a car pull up. He breathed a sigh of half relief and half regret that it wasn't Honey. As it turned out, it was nearly as bad.

Emily stepped from the car and studied him for a long moment. "Want to talk about that little scene back at Honey's?"

"No."

Emily strolled slowly toward him. Her hand clutched the strap of her brown leather purse to keep it from falling off her shoulder. The sun twinkled off her engagement ring and wedding band. It reminded Matt how alone he was. He averted his gaze.

She stopped a few feet from him. "Your son thinks you're a hero for saving his mother."

"We all make mistakes."

She glanced toward the house. "How's it coming?"

"Almost done."

Swiveling on one foot, she faced the building head-on. "Shame."

He looked at her, his eyebrows raised in question. "I'll bite. What's a shame?"

"This house. You. The work you've put into it. All for nothing."

He followed her gaze. "I'd hardly say it was for nothing. I do plan on living here, you know."

She turned back to him, her eyes serious, her mouth set. "For how long, Matt?" She took one step toward him. "Until you hit another snag in the road? Then will you pack up and move on again?"

He couldn't answer her. He honestly didn't know. No one had to remind him that he had a reputation for running when things got to be more than he could handle. No one had to tell him that it usually didn't solve anything, either. Would he do it again? He didn't plan on it, but he hadn't planned on taking off seven years ago either.

"That's what I thought." She looked away, exasperation written on her face. "You have a little boy who loves you." Matt started to say something, but she shook her head. "No, let me finish. Danny thinks you're the greatest thing since fire. Honey isn't sure who or what you are, but she's willing to risk her happiness and Danny's to find out. Don't you think you owe them something? An explanation? Something?"

He felt a stab of guilt in his gut. "Stay out of it, Emily."

"No. I can't do that, Matt. You see I love those two people, and I know Honey would have me drawn and quartered if she even thought I was here talking to you. But, dammit, someone has to. You're about to throw away the best thing that ever came down the pike for you. Doesn't that scare you just a little?''

Matt laughed. ''A little? Hell, it scares me more than anything else in this world.''

''Then do something about it. Talk to her. I can speak from experience when I say that the not knowing is the worst. You see, it puts your imagination to work overtime and all kinds of things come to mind. Insane, stupid, outrageous things. Things you know aren't even close to being real. But you go right on wondering and imagining. And until someone tells you what is for real, you live on those crazy thoughts until they overwhelm you.'' She took a step closer and touched his arm. ''Don't do that to her and Danny. Don't do it to yourself.''

Matt watched as Emily waved goodbye, then drove away. Her words rang in his head like the bells in a cathedral, driving everything else out.

Didn't she know, didn't everyone know that the last thing he wanted to do was hurt Honey or Danny? Didn't they know that the reason he had done everything was to keep from hurting them?

He slammed the tool box in the back of the truck, then made a fist and pounded the fender until a small dent appeared and his hand began to throb. He raked his fingers through his hair and looked around him at the fresh paint, the mowed lawn, the trimmed shrubs.

What the hell was he doing? He'd come back here, naively thinking he could vanquish the demons of his childhood with a coat of paint and some new carpeting. Emily had hit the nail right on the head. He'd made a house and had no one to share it with. With no one to share it, it would always be a house and never a home.

Who was he kidding. As long as he allowed them to, the ghosts would live here and no matter what he did, he would not exorcize them from his house until he exorcized them from his heart. But how did he go about doing what he hadn't been able to do for seven years?

Chapter Thirteen

That evening, Honey went to tuck Danny in. He and Buddy were sitting in the middle of his bed playing tug-o'-war with a sock. For a moment, she stood in the doorway watching them. The Superman quilt half on and half off the bed.

Danny's black hair, wet from his shower, hadn't been combed and a wavy lock hung over his forehead, just like Matt's did. His rosy pink cheeks displayed his father's dimples. The tiny pictures of superheroes scattered over his pajamas made her think of when Matt had pulled her from the tree that afternoon, after Fred's aborted rescue. But the recollection hurt too much, so she pushed it to the back of her mind.

"Come on, boy, get the sock." Danny dangled the sock in front of Buddy's nose, then jerked it back, just as the dog lunged for it. "Come on," he coaxed. "You can get it." The puppy lunged again and this time caught it in his sharp baby teeth. The sound of ripping material told Honey that that particular pair of socks had bit the dust.

"Good boy," Danny said, patting the dog on the head, then stroking his back with long leisurely swipes. "You're a good dog, Buddy."

Not until this very moment had she realized that not once during the entire time from when Buddy took off after Fred and she got out of the tree had Danny stuttered. Nor was he stuttering now. Was he cured? Her heart thumped. She said a silent prayer.

"Danny?"

He looked up, his father's blue eyes sparkling up at her with delight. "Hi, M-M-Mom."

The hope that had seeped into her heart drained away. Why? Was it her? And if he loved Matt so much, why hadn't that love helped him overcome the trauma of Stan's death? Had Matt been right about her? Was it not Stan's death at all, but something she was doing to perpetuate the boy's problem? She took a deep breath.

She concentrated on speaking slowly as Matt had instructed. "It's bedtime."

"Aw, M-M-Mom. Do I have t-t-to?"

Buddy stood up and looked at Honey. His ears perked up, and his tail beat out a steady rhythm in the air above his fluffy golden body. He barked, as if he too objected to the interruption of their play.

"Sorry, guys, it's late." She scratched Buddy behind one of his floppy ears. He pushed his head into her palm, obviously happy to give up the playtime for more scratches.

"C-c-can Buddy sleep in m-m-my room tonight?" Danny's little face held an expression of expectation that she found hard to ignore.

Honey looked at the dog, and his large brown, soulful eyes also seemed to plead for her okay. She didn't have the heart to deny either of them. "I guess so."

"All right!" Without further argument, Danny grabbed Buddy, slipped under the covers, tucked the blanket under the dog's protruding black nose, then laid back, Buddy's chin resting on his chest. "M-M-M-Mom, can Uncle Matt be my n-n-new daddy?"

Honey felt as if a large, cold hand had reached out and squeezed her heart. Like an out-of-control kaleidoscope, images of them as a family whizzed through her mind of them playing, laughing, eating, loving together. The room spun around her. She grabbed the bed post to stabilize herself. Mentally, she fought to hang onto reality, the reality that Matt would never be a part of their lives.

Taking a deep breath, she closed her eyes, then opened them. "I don't know," she whispered, afraid to say more.

"I'd really like that. S-s-so would B-Buddy. R-r-right, boy?" Buddy barked. The covers moved where his tail wagged vigorously. "S-s-see, Mom?"

Slowly, Honey's equilibrium returned, and her breath came somewhat evenly. Gathering what was left of her wits about her, she stiffened her spine and smiled down at her son. "It's very late, Danny. We'll talk about this tomorrow."

"Aw, Mom. W-w-when you say t-t-that, it always means n-n-no. U-U-Uncle Matt would like it. I saw him k-k-kiss you in the tree. Howie H-H-Hawkins says p-p-people who love each other d-d-do that m-m-mushy stuff all the time. He says that's how you m-m-make babies."

Leaning down to kiss Danny's forehead, she forced a smile. "Howie Hawkins needs to check his research." Silently, she congratulated herself for holding onto her composure. She tucked the blankets around Danny, then patted Buddy's furry head.

"Well, c-c-can he, Mom? Can U-U-Uncle Matt be my dad?"

"We'll see." She straightened.

Walking to the door, she switched off the light, then glanced back at her child. The light from the hall illuminated his precious face. She knew her son well enough to be certain he would not let this go until he had an answer.

"I love h-h-him, you know," Danny called. "And heroes m-m-make really good d-d-dads. Right, Buddy?" Buddy whined in response. "Aw, I love you, too, Buddy."

She eased the door closed, fighting the tears threatening to spill from her burning eyes. She didn't need to be reminded that the only hero she had in her life was cuddled up with his dog inside that room. That's the way it always had been and always would be.

Despite her efforts to forget the conversation with her son, Danny's words kept echoing through her mind.

Why did you have to come back here, Matt Logan? We were doing just fine without you. Why did you have to come back and make us fall in love with you again?

She clenched her fists and closed her eyes. Leaning against the wall, she let the tears fall. How could she shatter Danny's dreams? How could she tell him that his Uncle Matt was his father, but that he might be gone soon and break her little boy's heart as surely as hers was breaking now?

All her questions remained unanswered, as they always had. Matt didn't trust her enough to give her the answers seven years ago and nothing had changed, nothing. Deep in her heart, no matter how much she hoped and prayed otherwise, she knew as long as Matt was afraid to love and be loved, they would all live in a hell without an escape.

The following morning, when Honey walked into the dining room, Matt had nearly finished eating breakfast. She looked like hell. Dark circles stood out beneath her eyes. Her skin lacked the rich honey hue it normally had. Though he hated to even think it, he knew a big part of what had kept her awake was due to him.

"Mornin'," she mumbled. Pouring herself a cup of coffee, she sipped at it on her way to the table, avoiding his eyes. She set down the cup and glanced around the room, as if looking for something or someone. "Did Danny make the school bus on time?"

"It's Saturday. He's outside playing with Buddy," he replied. She may look like hell, but there was something about her sleepy appearance that made him want to kiss her senseless, then drag her back to bed—and not to sleep. He looked down at his nearly empty coffee cup and reached for a half-eaten slice of buttered toast. He had to stop thinking like that. Despite the reprimand to himself, his gaze was drawn back to her.

She rubbed her eyes with the back of her hands. "Damn. I slept through my alarm. What time is it?"

He checked his watch. "Almost nine o'clock."

As if it suddenly dawned on her that he was there, she stared at him. "What are you still doing here?"

"I was waiting for you." Her shocked expression dug deep into his conscience. He replaced the half-eaten slice of toast on the china plate, then pushed it away from him.

"Why?"

"Danny said you and he had a talk last night."

Her hand stopped with her cup half way to her mouth. She wet her lips, then replaced the cup in the saucer with a loud thunk. "Did he tell you what we talked about?" She glanced at him from beneath her lashes.

"He said he asked you if I could be his dad." The idea made his stomach drop and his heart beat faster. The idea of being Danny's dad still frightened and excited him.

She gave a short embarrassed laugh and fussed with the napkin on her lap. "You know how little boys are. They get an idea in their heads and—"

For most of the time since Danny had slipped outside to play, Matt had been giving serious thought to what he said next. "Honey, I think it's time we told him who I am."

A thick, all-enveloping silence fell over the room. The grandfather clock in the corner ticked out the heartbeat of the old house. Outside a bird trilled. Buddy barked. Probably after Fred again. Faint sounds drifted to them from the kitchen, along with the aroma of freshly brewed coffee.

"I don't know. I'm not sure he's gotten over Stan's death yet." She glance up at him. "We agreed that until his stutter was better, we wouldn't add to that trauma."

Matt sighed. "His stutter is much better. Sometimes these things take longer than we'd like. Sometimes we need to hurry them along."

"Hurry them along? Why would we want to do that? There's no rush." She stared hard at him for a long uncomfortable moment, as if reading his mind.

He couldn't continue to meet her gaze. "Or is there? Are you planning on going somewhere, Matt?"

"I—" His explanation was cut short by an ear-splitting squeal of tires on asphalt, followed by Danny's scream.

Both of them jumped from their chairs, then dashed toward the front door. Matt didn't recall touching the stairs as he vaulted off the front porch. With Honey keeping pace at his side, they headed toward the road, like two marathon runners on the last leg of the race.

His heart beat out a mantra. Please, not Danny. Please, not Danny. Not my son. Not until he saw the boy kneeling in the road, did he chance breathing. Standing next to Danny's bent form was Buddy, his tail ominously unmoving. Danny's arm was slung around the dog, his face buried in the dog's golden fur, while his free hand lay on something at his feet.

"It's okay, Buddy. It wasn't your fault. It was an accident. Fred didn't look both ways."

Not until he stooped at Danny's side did he see the casualty produced by the gray van parked a few feet down the road. Fred lay motionless on his side. His orange fur was ruffled and askew, but thankfully not bloody. When Matt looked closely, he could see the faint rise and fall of Fred's ribs. The cat was alive.

"Get your car," Matt told Honey. Without another word, she bolted for the garage.

"I didn't even see them. The cat came racing out from behind those bushes and the dog was right behind them. It's a miracle I didn't hit both of them." A man in a pest control company uniform stood near Danny, wringing his hands. "I never hit an animal in my life before."

Matt went to him and laid a hand on his arm. "It's

okay. The cat's not dead. He doesn't appear to be badly injured. We'll take him to the vet. Thanks for hanging around.''

The man touched the edge of his hat. "If I can do anything—pay the vet bill, whatever—here's my card." He handed Matt a business card, then glanced at Danny. "Son, I have animals of my own and I would never hurt them on purpose. I am so sorry."

Danny nodded. "Fred shoulda looked both ways."

Honey pulled her car up at the end of the driveway, jumped out, then threw open the back door. Matt scooped Fred's body up. Gently, he laid him on the back seat. When he stepped back, Danny started to climb in with Buddy.

"No, Danny, you wait here. Uncle Matt and I will take Fred to see Uncle Kat."

"But, Mom!" Danny's face screwed up. He looked at Fred and started to cry. "I wanna go with Fred. He'll be scared without me."

"Let him come along." Matt motioned for Honey to get into the passenger's seat, then took her place behind the wheel of the car.

"But what if—" Honey began.

"Fred will be fine." Matt threw her a look that precluded any more conversation. "Fred will be fine," he repeated, hoping he wasn't setting Danny up for a fall. He put the car in gear and careened out of the driveway.

As they drove through town, Matt could hear Danny talking to Fred. "It's okay, Fred. I'm right here. You're gonna be okay. Buddy didn't mean to be bad. He's real sorry and he wants you to get all better." A loud sniff followed. "Don't die, Fred. You can't die.'' Danny sobbed softly the rest of the way to the vet's.

A few minutes later, they pulled into the parking lot outside Kat's veterinary clinic. Matt jumped out, opened the back door and lifted Fred carefully in his arms. He checked the seat, pleased to see that no bloodstains remained behind on the beige upholstery. He hoped that meant Fred's injuries were not serious.

Sobbing, Danny followed, Buddy clutched close in his arms. ''It's okay, Buddy. Uncle Kat will fix Fred. He'll be good as new. You'll see.'' He looked at Matt for reassurance. ''Right, Uncle Matt?''

What could he say that wouldn't build up the boy's hopes? What if he was wrong and Fred had some serious internal injuries? Matt did the only thing he could think of. He smiled down at his son.

Kat stood in the outer office when they came through the door. He looked as if he was expecting them. Either Amanda or Tess must have called ahead. Without asking a question, Kat took Fred and then went into a back room that, when the door swung closed, gushed antiseptic odors into the waiting room.

Honey sat next to Danny on the bench. She slipped her arm around his slight shoulders. ''Fred will be fine.''

''I wanna...go with him,'' Danny sobbed, starting to stand up.

Stopping him with a hand to his arm, Matt eased him back onto the bench. ''Your mom's a nurse, sport. Suppose we let her go in? I'll stay out here with you and Buddy.'' He looked to Honey for her consent. She nodded and stood.

Kissing Danny's cheek, she held his chin for a second. ''I'll make sure Uncle Kat takes good care of

Fred, and then I'll report right back here to you, okay?''

Danny glanced at the closed door, then nodded. "Okay. But make...sure Fred knows Buddy and I are...out here. Then he...won't get too scared.'' Tears continued to cascade down his cheeks.

Tenderly, Honey wiped them away with a tissue she pulled from her purse. "I'll do that. I'm sure he'll be happy to know that he's not alone.''

Danny and Matt watched Honey disappear through the door where Kat had carried Fred. Danny turned to Matt and buried his face in his side. "Buddy...didn't mean it,'' he sobbed. "They were playing. It...wasn't his fault.''

Matt looked down at his son's bent head. "These things happen, Danny. Remember I told you that sometimes people get hurt and there's no one to blame? Well, the same is true with animals. Dogs chase cats because it's fun. Sometimes fun things lead to bad things happening. Like moms getting stuck in trees and cats running in front of cars. It's no one's fault. They just happen, and no matter what we do, we can't stop them.''

Danny's sobs died down. He raised his head. Stray tears continued to roll down his cheeks, but his eyes were bright. He sniffed loudly, then wiped the tissue Honey had left for him across his nose. He gazed at Matt for a long moment before he spoke. "Like my daddy's accident?''

He recalled what Danny had said the day of the motorcycle ride.

I knew it was my fault.

"Was it like that?'' Danny asked again.

Matt nodded. "Exactly like that. Buddy was a bad

dog for chasing Fred again, but that still doesn't mean the accident was his fault. Buddy just happened to be there. In the case of your daddy, he was a grown man. He made his decisions about what he did or didn't do. Your mom tried to stop him and he wouldn't listen. He probably wouldn't have listened to you, either. Right?''

Danny nodded.

"That makes it nobody's fault but his. Just like Fred could have run across the lawn like he did yesterday, but instead he ran into the road. That wasn't Buddy's fault. Fred chose which way to run." Matt studied the boy's face, and this time he saw comprehension there. He wrapped his arm around him and hugged him.

"I love you, Uncle Matt."

Matt froze. Before he could say anything, Honey and Kat emerged from the back room.

"How's Fred, Uncle Kat?"

Kat leaned down and heaved Danny up into his arms. "Fred's gonna be okay. I want to keep him here overnight. He can come home tomorrow, and he'll probably be playing with you and Buddy in no time." He smiled at Danny. "He has a really bad headache right now and a broken rib or two, but nothing serious."

Danny turned to the dog, who was now standing on the bench making vain attempts to follow Danny to his elevated position. Finally, he gave up and sat with a whine.

"Hey, Buddy, Fred's okay." He grinned down at his mother. "Did you hear that, Mom? Fred's okay."

Honey's heart skipped a beat. Her son had spoken

to her without stuttering. She cast a sidelong glance at Matt. His smile answered hers.

"Did ya hear me, Mom?"

She wiped at the tears gathering in her eyes and smiled up at her son. "Yes, sweetie, I heard you." How could she not have heard? Her son's words were engraved on her heart.

LATER, in Tess's kitchen over coffee with Amanda, Honey asked Matt a question that she'd been wondering about since they left Kat's office. "Do you think the stutter is gone for good?"

Matt shook his head. "I can't say. No one can. We'll have to wait and see."

"Whatever happened to make him stop so suddenly? Was it the accident with the cat?" Amanda looked from one to the other.

Honey shrugged and waited to see what Matt would say.

He added sugar to his cup, then stirred. Slowly, he told them about his conversation with Danny when they went for the motorcycle ride, and then later, in Kat's waiting room. "He's been obviously blaming himself for Stan's death."

Amanda leaned back in her wheelchair and gazed out the kitchen window. "My word. That poor child."

The afghan covering her legs slid to the floor, unnoticed by her. Honey gathered it up and, in stunned silence, spread it over her mother-in-law's lap. "I don't understand how he could have come to such an outrageous conclusion."

Shrugging, Matt avoided Honey's gaze. "Some

things are better left unexplored. Sometimes exploring them only hurts everyone more.''

She stared down at his bent head. ''Sometimes, bringing them out in the open helps all of us to better understand.''

He stared at her. The silence in the room became deafening. She knew, and so did Matt, that they were no longer talking about Danny.

''Sometimes bringing it out in the open only causes more pain for everyone concerned.'' He stood, then turned abruptly toward the door. ''I think I'll go over to the house and see if I can get some work done.'' He stopped, grabbed a piece of paper and a pencil lying on the counter, and wrote something down, then handed it to Honey. ''If you need me, here's my phone number.''

Honey held the paper in numb fingers. She watched him leave, then continued to stare at the swinging kitchen door as it oscillated back and forth, then stopped. If only solving their problems was as easy as dialing a phone. If only she could assuage this gnawing, aching emptiness inside her just by calling him on the phone and telling him she needed him.

Buddy's shrill bark brought her back to earth. Feeling Amanda's questioning stare, and unwilling and unable to explain, Honey placed the paper on the table and walked from the room. She might as well get used to the idea of getting along without Matt's help, because she knew in her heart it would not be long before he would leave.

Chapter Fourteen

Matt stood solemnly in the front hall of his house, his gaze fixed on the closed bedroom door upstairs. He knew that behind it resided the last of the ghosts of his childhood, the ones that had the power to cut him to his knees. He also knew that before he could truly make this house his, he had to exorcize them.

Not sure if it was just plain cowardice that caused it, or a desire to again put off the inevitable, he lowered his gaze and proceeded down the long hall. Without stopping to admire the completely renewed kitchen, he walked through it, then out the back door and straight to his mother's greenhouse.

Even with the house full of new furnishings and fresh paint, this was the one place in his old home where he was at peace with himself. In sharp contrast to the house, out here he'd taken special pains to make sure nothing was disturbed. Other than the new glass, it remained exactly as it had the day his mother walked out of it for the last time.

He felt certain his father hadn't touched it. The old man hated this place. Over the years, because of Matt's love for flowers and working in here with his mother, it had become a symbol of all Kevin Logan hated in his youngest son, all that Matt would never be. To Matt it had become a refuge, the one place his dad's expectations and coldness could not reach him. The place where Matt could sort through his problems.

His gaze wandered around the building, taking in every corner of it. The peace he'd expected to find eluded him. Instead, he noted the musty odor of decaying vegetation and dirt, broken pots, dead flowers and rotted wooden tables—the forgotten remains of a good woman's life.

He sighed heavily and looked through the sparkling glass at the sinking sun. In the distance, he could see the outline of the Thatchers' roof just beyond the old maple tree. Like a warm refuge, it beckoned to him.

He covered the distance between the houses in no time at all and found himself knocking on the Thatchers' back door. Hanging at eye level on the white door, a blue board dangling from a dried flower wreath proclaimed Welcome in large white letters. He smiled. How typical of Sam and Alma.

The door swung open. Alma greeted him with her cheery face and perpetual smile. Her brightly flowered housedress, almost obscured by the full, white bib apron she'd wrapped around herself to keep it clean, reminded him sharply of other times when he'd fled here for comfort. Flour powdered her salt-and-pepper hair and smudged her forehead.

"Matthew, how nice of you to drop by. Come in." She pushed the screen open and the smell of cinnamon rushed out to envelop him. She patted her hair and dusted off her apron. "It's baking day," she said in explanation.

"Hello, Alma. If you're busy, I can—"

"Sakes alive, since when am I too busy for you, dear? Now, get in here. I'm about to take some of the cinnamon bread that Sam loves from the oven." She grinned merrily. "As I recall, you were partial to it as well."

Her words brought the first genuine smile to his lips that he'd experienced in a long time. "Your recollection is exactly on target…"

"Well, then, get in here and make yourself to home. I'll have a piece for you before you can say Jack Robinson."

He entered the kitchen, recalling that she'd said something similar to him more times than he could remember, and it still brought a warm feeling gushing over him. Here Matt was welcome. Here he didn't have to live up to anyone's expectations. He could be himself.

While she busied herself getting his promised bread, Matt looked around.

Her kitchen appeared much the same as the last time he'd visited Alma and Sam. The curtains were still white and ruffled, with little strips that held them back from the windows. What had Honey called them? Oh yeah, tie-backs. The little niche shelves tucked between the window frame and the cabinets held Alma's teapot collection, bringing color to the work area around the sink. A small pine table and four chairs, their worn, scratched wood attesting to the frequency with which this room was used, occupied a bay window overlooking her flower garden.

He found himself a seat at the table and waited for the promised treat. In what seemed like no time, a large slab of hot cinnamon bread, dotted with plump raisins and slathered in melted butter, accompanied by a cup of steaming hot chocolate adorned with a spire of white whipped cream, sat on the table before him. Alma took a chair opposite him and waited expectantly for his first sampling of her fare.

He bit into the bread. Butter ran down his fingers and chin. "Umm. You haven't lost your touch, Alma. No one makes cinnamon bread like you do." He wiped at the dripping butter, then chewed in pure delight. "If heaven has a taste, then surely it tastes like your cinnamon bread."

Alma grinned. "Filling the stomach is always a sight easier than filling the soul," she said. Her grin faded. She stared straight at Matt with those all-seeing eyes he remembered from his childhood. "It appears to me like you're carrying a heavy burden these days. Is it your boy?"

Matt's hand stopped in the process of wiping more butter off his chin.

"Oh, I know Danny's your son. The whole town knows, Matthew. If you'd bothered letting anyone know where you went, you'd have known sooner, I'm sure. I don't see Honey as the type who would keep a boy from his rightful daddy." She wiped invisible dirt from the tabletop with a swish of her palm.

"Course, after you left, Kevin just closed himself off from the world. Got to be a genuine hermit." She glanced at Matt. "I think you broke his heart by running off that way."

Matt sidestepped the remark about his father. Something that wasn't there to start with couldn't be broken. "The whole town knows about Danny?"

The salt-and-pepper bangs framing Alma's face bounced as she nodded. "Course, they all kept it under their hats. No one knew for absolute sure and no one was about to speculate out loud and have the wrath of Frank Kingston come down around their ears. He always had folks in this town scared right out of their socks. His kids, too.'' She clucked her tongue. ''Never knew a man who put such store in the reputation of a family name as him. Must have just tore him up when Honey got pregnant without being married.''

Matt flinched.

Alma touched his hand. ''I didn't mean that to hurt you. Neither of you got a thing on God's earth to be ashamed of. He's a good boy, that Danny. A son to be proud of. Honey did a good job raising him.'' She shook her head sadly. ''Stan tried, God rest his soul, but being a daddy just wasn't in him. I sometimes think he'd have been happier being the child and having everyone leave him alone to play with his toys.''

Matt nodded. He couldn't dispute that. Nor could he dispute Alma's appraisal of Honey as a mother. She'd made her mistakes, but all parents did. On the whole, Danny had turned out to be a son any man would be proud to claim.

Alma moved to the sink and started washing her baking dishes. She looked up through the window at Matt's house. ''House is shaping up. When are you planning on moving in for good?''

Matt didn't answer. He was no longer sure he ever would move into that house, or any house in Bristol. With every day that passed, he questioned more and more the wisdom of coming back here. It seemed he'd done nothing but disrupt people's lives.

''I'm not sure yet.''

''Danny needs his own house. Not that Amanda isn't a good grandma, mind you. Lord knows, she's

done more than her share for Honey and that boy."
She took a terry dish towel from a cabinet drawer and
began drying the dishes she'd washed. "A boy needs
roots. A place that he knows is home. A place to
come back to, when he's all grown up." She eyed
Matt closely and then stacked a loaf pan inside the
cabinet closest to her. "A place that holds good memories that will take the chill from his bones and his
heart."

Matt looked at her, then finished the last of his hot
chocolate. "What are you trying to tell me, Alma? I
never was much good at reading between the lines."
He smiled at her warm expression.

Alma stopped drying dishes and placed the towel
on the countertop. "I'm trying to say that there are
some bad memories in that old house, Matthew. Bad
enough to make you want to run away again, but did
running away help the last time?"

He stared at her for a while, then shook his head.

"Right. Every last one of them was waiting for you
when you got back here." She sat in the chair at his
side and placed a warm hand on his shoulder.
"There's good ones here, too, Matthew. You just
gotta look for them. Sometimes all those bad memories stand in the way and block your view. Push
them outta the way, and when you do, you'll see
what's been there all the time, just like a good piece
of wood that shines after you wipe it with a clean
dustcloth."

Then she did what she'd done when he was a kid—
she kissed his cheek and went to another part of the
house. She'd always said it was to give him "thinking
room."

Matt stared down into the dark dregs in the bottom

of his cup. What was Alma saying? That he'd been intentionally trying to remember only the bad things that had filled his childhood?

Suddenly he recalled his conversation with Danny, and the memory of his father saving his life that had popped into his mind. Was he really pushing other good memories aside?

He glanced at the window that faced his house. The closed door at the top of the stairs materialized in his mind. Maybe it was time. He stood.

"Thanks for the hot chocolate and bread, Alma," he called. "I gotta run. I have things to do at the house." He started to walk toward the door and stopped. "Thanks...for everything," he added over his shoulder.

"Anytime, Matthew. My door's always open," Alma called back. He could hear the smile in her voice.

Matt covered the distance back from the Thatchers' in half the time it had taken to go. Maybe it was what Alma had said, maybe he was finally ready to face his demons. Whatever the reason, he suddenly couldn't get back there fast enough.

He bolted up the back steps, threw open the door and raced through the house and up the stairs. In no time, he stood before the closed door to his father's room. He stared at the knob, not quite so sure as he had been moments before. Tentatively, he placed his hand on it. The cold metal sent shivers through him. Once he opened it, there would be no going back. He knew the memories would be worse here than anywhere else in the house.

Holding his breath, he turned the knob and pushed the door open. Dust filled his nostrils. He coughed and sneezed. Rushing to the windows, he threw them open, one by one, until the room filled with fresh air and what was left of the sunshine.

Then he turned to do battle with the ghosts. A leak in the roof had turned one corner of the ceiling a sickly brown. Beneath it, a strip of the rose-colored wallpaper his mother had chosen and put up herself hung halfway to the floor, loosened by the moisture from the leak. The dark mahogany bedroom set, which had glowed a rich, deep sable under his mother's loving hand, now looked pale and old under layers of accumulated dust.

On the dresser, Kevin Logan's toiletries still sat, as if waiting for his return. Matt glowered at them, then impulsively swiped his arm across the lot, sending them crashing to the floor. The top popped off the aftershave bottle, and suddenly, he was engulfed with his father's memory.

He stalked from the room and headed toward the linen closet where he'd thrown empty boxes. Grabbing the biggest, he hurried back to his father's room and began throwing things into it with one purpose in mind.

He would banish the ghosts. He would remove every trace of Kevin Logan from this room and his life.

HONEY SAT ON THE PORCH watching Danny and Buddy play for a long time before she could summon the courage to do what she knew she must. From their conversation just before Fred got hit, she knew in her heart Matt was about to tell her he was leaving. Now, she had to prepare her son.

"Danny?"

Her son looked up, his dark hair picking up the dying rays of the sun. "Yeah, Mom?"

She smiled, pleased to hear that his stutter hadn't returned since they came home from the vet's. She had no idea what Matt had said to him, but whatever he'd said, it had worked miracles, and she did not question miracles.

"Come here for a minute. I want to talk to you."

Reluctance showing in every step, Danny came toward her, hauling behind him the stick he'd been using to play fetch with Buddy. The tip of the stick left rutted wounds in the long grass, just like the wounds that scarred Honey's heart.

Danny stopped in front of her. "Yeah?" Buddy sat patiently at the boy's feet.

"Sit by me," she said, patting the porch step.

Danny flopped down. "Can you make this fast, Mom? Buddy and I are playing."

"I see that, and I'll try not to keep you from your game." She took a deep breath and started. "Do you remember what you asked me the other night?"

Eyebrows furrowed, her son looked up at her. "You mean 'bout Uncle Matt being my new dad?"

Honey nodded, not trusting herself to speak. She swallowed the tears that threatened and went on. "Well, I think the answer is going to have to be no."

Danny bolted from the step to face her. "Why?"

Now came the hardest part.

You can do it. You've done worse than this.

When? she asked herself. When had she broken her son's heart and not known how to fix it because hers was breaking just as badly?

"Why, Mom? Why can't he be my new dad?"

She placed a hand on each of Danny's small shoulders. They were so frail to hold such a huge burden. "Because I don't think Uncle Matt will be staying long."

Danny's face broke into a grin. "I know that. He'll be moving to his new house. But we can live with him. Gamma won't mind. I'll come to visit her all the time." He started to turn away, but she stopped him.

"No, Danny. Uncle Matt won't be living in his new house. He's going to go away from Bristol."

For a moment, Danny looked at her blankly, then something happened that almost tore Honey's heart from her chest. For the first time in his life, Danny glared at her with contempt shining from his blue eyes.

"You made him go away," he yelled. "It's 'cause of you. You were always yelling at him 'cause he let me do stuff you wouldn't let me do." Tears filled his eyes and he swiped angrily at them.

"No, that's not—"

"Yes it is. It is t-t-too." He jerked away from her touch. "He even s-s-s-old his m-m-m-motorcycle 'cause y-y-you hated it."

The sound of Danny's returned stutter stopped Honey cold. What had she done? She'd only tried to prepare him for Matt's leaving, and instead, she'd brought back the very problem that Matt had been so instrumental in solving.

"Danny—" She reached for him again, wanting only to hold him and erase that look from his eyes, make him understand.

He yanked free of her hands. "No, I don't want you to touch me anymore. I hate you."

He turned and ran, his stubby legs carrying him

over the grass and into the trees at the edge of the lawn. Buddy followed, wagging his tail fiercely, obviously thinking this was a new game.

"It's no game, Buddy boy. I wish it was." She stood to follow Danny, but she stopped when she saw him lying under a tree, his face buried in the grass. Maybe if she left him alone, he'd feel better. Maybe she'd feel better.

Hell's bells, who was she kidding? She doubted either of them would ever feel any better.

MATT HAD CLEARED OUT every trace of his father from the room. He'd carried three boxes of his things down and stacked them with the trash. All he had left to clean out was the closet.

He found another large box and set it down outside the door. When he opened the closet, he froze. Inside, his father's clothes hung in a neat row. This would be harder. Clearing out bottles and brushes and newspapers hadn't hit such a personal note as clothes and shoes.

Matt hesitated. He felt almost as if he was about to throw his father bodily from the house. Foolishness, he told himself. Still he hesitated. Giving himself a mental kick, he stepped over the threshold. He'd come this far. He might as well finish it.

He plunged deeper into the closet and began pulling suits, shirts and pants from hangers and throwing them into the box. Shoes followed, then contents of the top shelf. Old hats, a baseball glove, a sweater with holes in the elbows, a battered suitcase all ended up in the box.

In a far corner of the shelf a pile of magazines were stacked, and atop them a white cardboard gift box.

Matt grabbed the box, then tossed it toward the pile. It hit the floor on end, dislodging the top and spilling the contents out over the bedroom floor.

"Damn!"

Ignoring the mess, he grabbed for the pile of magazines and slid them toward him. As he lifted them, the title of the top magazine caught his eye. He had to be dreaming. What would his father be doing hoarding copies of *Rodeo Review?* Fanning quickly through them, Matt checked the dates of publications. His father had every copy from the time Matt first started riding in the rodeo until the month of the old man's death. The pages were dog-eared from frequent turning.

He couldn't believe his eyes. Weakly, he sank down on the bare mattress and stared at the magazines. Numbly, he let the pile slide from his hands and cascade at his feet.

"What the hell does this mean, old man?"

Then he spotted something else that drew his attention—the box that had fallen open and spewed its contents on the floor. He reached for some of the papers that lay closest to him. Newspaper clippings. Each article was about a rodeo event.

Matt scanned the articles and found that each time his name was mentioned, his father had highlighted it in yellow.

Slowly, the significance of his find began to sink in. Kevin Logan had been proud of him, proud enough to keep track of his career and hoard the evidence in a box in the top of his closet. Proud enough to keep every magazine that mentioned his name.

Pain shot through Matt, sharp and fierce. He threw the papers on the floor and stalked from the room.

How could he stay in this house now? Somehow, living here with the ghost of a man he'd hated seemed infinitely easier than living here with the ghost of a man he loved and who had loved him in return, but had never told him so.

DANNY PRECEDED HONEY into the house. They'd brought Fred home and made him comfortable in the garage, but Danny hadn't spoken a word. In fact, since their talk on the porch, he'd been as quiet and stiff as a little tin soldier. Even when Buddy begged for his attention, Danny merely patted his head, then ignored him.

When he'd come in from beneath the tree, his eyes had been swollen and red from crying, but Honey couldn't find the words to heal the breach between them. If she touched him, he pulled away. If she talked to him, he listened politely, nodded, then walked away.

Now, he climbed the stairs and disappeared into his room without even being told it was late and time for him to go to bed. How could she undo the damage that she'd done? In all fairness, she told herself, the damage would have been far greater if he woke up one morning and found Matt gone, with no explanation whatsoever.

Then anger rose in her like a spring flood. How dare he leave her to do the cleanup again? How dare he! Who did he think he was that he could march in here and make them fall in love with him, then slip out a side door?

Well, this time he could clean up his own trash. She'd done her share for the last seven years. His coming home and ingratiating himself with Danny had created this problem, and his leaving had exacerbated it. Now he could just walk into that little boy's room and explain it to him. Maybe he could make Danny understand why he had to leave. Maybe he could make *her* understand.

As she rounded the newel post at the foot of the stairs, Honey glanced outside. His truck was still parked where it had been. Quickly, before her nerve deserted her, she climbed the stairs, then headed straight for the spare room. Without knocking, she barged in.

"I knew it," she said, taking in the suitcase open on the bed. Matt was placing a shirt inside.

"I planned on talking to you, but you were gone when I got here." He looked at her with large, sad eyes. "I wouldn't have left without telling you this time."

She swallowed her tears. She would not let him see her cry, damn him. "And Danny? What about him?"

He tossed another shirt into the open suitcase. "I would have talked to him, too."

"Well, you better come and do it now. I talked to him earlier about you leaving, and he didn't take it well." She paused. "The stutter came back."

Matt uttered a curse word, then turned fully to face her. "How did you—"

A derisive laugh broke from Honey's lips. "Déjà vu." She glanced at the suitcase, then him. "When we talked earlier, before Fred's accident, I knew. Nothing you said, just what you didn't say."

He held an imploring hand out to her. "I have to do this. There are things I need to think about."

"What things?" She took a step closer to him. "Matt, please talk to me. Maybe I can help."

He raked his hand through his hair and looked at the ceiling. "How are you at raising the dead?"

She frowned. What in God's name was he talking about? She almost asked him, but he put up his hand to stop her.

"Never mind. There's no sense talking about it." He looked past her in the direction of his son's room. "I might as well get this over with. Let's go see Danny."

Together they walked down the hall and into Danny's room. His bedside lamp glowed, but Danny wasn't there. Then Honey saw the piece of yellow construction paper on his bed and the green words scrawled in his childish printing glaring back at her.

me and budy run away
yur sun Daniel Logan

Chapter Fifteen

Matt and Honey rushed to Danny's bed. The bottom of Matt's stomach gave way as she snatched up the construction paper note and stared down at it as if it was her obituary.

She read the words aloud. "Me and Buddy ran away, your son, Daniel Logan." She turned to Matt, her eyes large and full of fear. "He's only six years old. Where would he go?" Her voice held all the anguish Matt felt building inside him.

He shook his head. "I don't know." He felt as if a bull had gored him again, but this time in his heart. His child, his only son, was out there somewhere, running from the two people who loved him most in the world. "When did you see him last?"

Honey closed her eyes to think. "About an hour and a half ago, when he came up to get ready for bed."

"That's not too long, and it gives us a better chance of finding him. He hasn't had time to go far." Although he said the words to comfort Honey, Matt still had to fight back the panic that threatened to take over his mind.

"My God, what have I done?" Honey's hollow

voice echoed his anguish. Her hand began to shake and the paper dropped from her fingers to the floor.

Matt glanced out the window at the gathering darkness. "There's no time for pointing fingers of blame. It's getting dark. We have to find Danny." The tortured rasp that emerged from his own throat hardly resembled his usual deep tones. "Come with me. I'll need your help." He turned to flee from the room. At the door, he glanced over his shoulder to make sure Honey had heard him.

As if rousing from a dream, Honey clenched her fists at her side, then followed him.

"I'll call the police," Matt told her, hitting the hall floor at a run and heading for the phone. "You check outside to see if you can spot him."

His fingers shook as he tried to hit the right numbers on the keypad. Not sure if he'd been correct, he pressed the button to disconnect. Taking a deep breath, he started again. Carefully this time, he forced himself to slowly go through the correct sequence: 9-1-1.

TWENTY MINUTES LATER, Matt hung up the phone just as Honey came hurrying breathlessly through the front door. She looked at him with wide, frightened eyes and shook her head. "He's nowhere outside. I even checked the garage. I thought he might have decided to bunk with Fred."

"The police will be here as soon as possible." What pitiful consolation to give a mother whose child had run off.

Helplessness settled over him. A father was supposed to protect his family and make sure things like this didn't happen to them. Why hadn't he done that?

Why hadn't he seen this coming? Because he'd been so absorbed in his own life, he'd failed to see that a little boy needed him and his love.

"Here." She handed him his keys off the hall table.

He knew what she wanted, but he shook his head. "No. We can't leave."

"No? What do you mean, no? We have to go look for him. He's just a little boy."

Her desperation tore at his insides like a sharp claw. God knew, he wanted to run to his car and start scouring every road in the vicinity, too. But they couldn't. Not yet, at least.

"The police asked us to stay put. They said that very often, when young children get outside in the dark, they'll get scared, change their minds and head back home. They said that, if he decides to come back, we should be here."

Please let that be the case.

The thought of Danny out there alone in the dark, with no one but a small puppy to protect him, made Matt physically sick. He raked his hands through his hair and looked around, as if somewhere on the walls he'd find the answer to his son's whereabouts. As if somewhere he'd find the answer to how he'd failed Danny.

Like a discarded rag doll, Honey dropped to the chair near the phone. "I never should have told him. I was just trying to…" She sighed heavily and shook her head. "Oh hell, I don't know what I was trying to do. It's my fault."

"What's your fault?" Amanda asked. She rolled her wheelchair over the threshold of the small sitting room and brought it to a stop beside her daughter-in-law, then glanced from her to Matt.

Honey looked up. "Danny's run away."

Amanda paled. "Oh, my Lord."

Matt found himself thankful for the wheelchair beneath his aunt. Otherwise, he'd have surely been scooping her off the floor. She turned to him, and he confirmed Honey's words with a nod.

Amanda gasped. "When? Where?"

"We aren't really sure about either. But we think he left sometime within the last hour and a half. The police are on the way." Matt moved beside her and laid his hand on her shoulder. "Why don't we all go into the sitting room and wait for them?"

Honey resembled a sleepwalker. Without a word, she rose stiffly, then walked into the room and sat on the rose sofa. Matt guided Amanda's wheelchair in and placed it at the end of the coffee table, then took a seat across from Honey in the matching love seat.

"Did you call Emily?" Amanda's voice was strained and unsteady. "He'd go there first."

Absently, Matt shook his head. "I tried her. She hasn't seen him. I also called the Fletcher kid. Nothing." Matt leaned forward, his elbows on his knees. A second later, he stood. Unable to remain still, he paced the length of the room. He looked first at his watch, then at the big grandfather clock. "Where the hell are the police?"

The sound of a small bell tinkling drew Matt's attention.

"I'm going to have Tess make us some coffee," Amanda explained, her voice as unsteady as her hands. She replaced the small silver bell she used to summon Tess. Tess appeared in the doorway. "Please make us a pot of strong coffee."

Tess's gaze scanned the occupants of the room. "What's wrong?"

"Danny has run away," Matt said.

"Lord above." Tess clasped her hand over her heart. Instantly, tears filled her eyes. "That poor wee lad." She hurried from the room, wiping at her eyes with the hem of her apron. "Oh, that poor wee lad."

Car headlights fanned the walls of the small room. "The police are here," Matt said, and went to let them in.

TWO HOURS HAD PASSED since Honey and Matt had found Danny's note. In that time the police had arrived, taken down all the information: Danny's description, Buddy's description, what Danny had been wearing, what he'd taken with him and where they thought he might have gone.

The last drew a blank. Where would a six-year-old and his dog go at this hour of the night? Sheriff Jack Dawson, an old friend of Amanda's, had reassured them that they'd do all they could to find Danny, and then left.

The silence in the room was suffocating. All of them had cocooned themselves in their own thoughts.

Tess had kept a steady supply of coffee coming. Not that anyone drank any, but it seemed to help her to keep making it, so no one objected. Amanda did something Matt could never recall his aunt doing before: sat silently staring out the window while fat tears rolled down her cheeks. Amanda Logan had always been the strong one with answers. This time, she had none, and her strength had almost visibly drained from her.

Honey worried him the most, however. In that two-

and-a-half hour stretch, she had become more and more withdrawn. Her eyes remained dry. She said nothing. Her hands, folded tightly in her lap, trembled from time to time—the only outward reaction she displayed. The one word he could think of to describe her was *brittle,* as if she would shatter into a million pieces if anyone touched her.

Matt sat beside her and pulled her head onto his shoulder. It was like cradling a board. Helplessness set in again. Now that he'd done all he could do, he could only hold Honey and hope their son was found soon. He hated that she had to go through this, but at least he was here for her.

Suddenly, it hit him that this must have been what she'd been like when he left seven years ago. The pain of the realization nearly doubled him over. Selfishly, when he'd taken off, he'd thought only of himself—the pain he'd endured in his home and the pain he would not be able to endure if Honey also turned on him with disappointment written on her face. He'd never once thought of those he'd left behind or the pain they would experience from his leaving.

And now he'd taught his son that the answer to any problem was to run from it.

The phone rang. Matt jumped up and grabbed it.

"Matt?"

He let out a sigh of disappointment. "I don't mean to be rude, Emily, but we need to keep this line open for the police."

"He's here. He got here about twenty minutes ago."

Tears stung Matt's eyes. He felt as if a two-ton weight had been lifted from his chest.

Emily lowered her voice. "I had to swear not to

call you, but I put myself in your shoes and figured he'd forgive me for breaking my word this one time.''

Matt swung to face Honey and Amanda. ''Danny's at Emily's,'' he relayed, unconcerned that tears had overflowed his lashes. Both women lost their glazed look and stared at him imploringly, as if wanting him to confirm what they thought they'd heard. He nodded. ''How did he get there?''

''He walked.''

''Walked? It's almost a mile to your house.''

''I know. I was amazed, too. Determined little boy you have here. Reminds me of his mother.'' She laughed lightly. ''He's asleep now. Poor kid was exhausted.''

''We'll be right over.'' Matt started to hang up, but Emily's voice stopped him.

''No. I put him to bed in the spare room. Let him sleep. I'll bring him home tomorrow morning, first thing. He'll be fine with us. I promise.''

Selfishly, Matt's first thought was that he wanted his son here, where he could see for himself that he was okay. Emily's words cleared his mind of that. He had to think of Danny now. Danny needed to sleep. Things would look better for all of them in the morning.

''All right. Let him sleep. See you tomorrow. And, Emily? Thanks.'' He hung up.

AMANDA AND TESS HAD GONE to bed. The events of the night had taken their toll on both the older women. But Honey couldn't sleep. How could she sleep with guilt gouging large holes in her peace of mind?

She'd wandered out to the porch and sat curled up

in a rocker, staring blindly out into the impenetrable darkness. The mountain air chilled her skin, but she took no notice. The coldness wrapped around her heart held far more discomfort.

Over and over she asked herself why she'd really told Danny about his father leaving. Had it been to spite Matt? To get to Danny first? To somehow ensure her place in her son's heart? Or had it been, as she'd first told herself, out of a mother's need to protect her son, to soften the blow?

The first thought sickened her. The second made her wonder just what kind of a mother she'd been to Danny. Had she been as right as she'd always thought? Or had she been doing what Matt had accused her of—trying so hard to not be her father that she had turned into a controlling mother who forced her *better judgment* on her child, just as her father had done to her? Was she still allowing Stan and her father to control her life, even from the grave?

She searched her mind for incidents of when Danny had wanted to do something and she'd stepped in to stop it. Too many came to mind. The race car collection she let him have, but not play with. Why? Because she'd been terrified that one day he might grow up and want a real one. One that raced around a dirt track at frightening speeds. One that would perhaps throw him into a wall. One that would bring him to his end just like Stan.

And what about his aspirations for himself? When he'd told her he wanted to be a vet like Kat, she'd done her best to talk him out of it. She'd always known about his love of animals, and being a vet would be a natural for him, but she had pushed for something better—a lawyer or doctor or a corporate leader. A career Danny would hate each and every day he had to do his job. But he would do it because she'd talked him into it.

Then there was the motorcycle incident. Had she really believed Matt would endanger his son's life by being careless? Or was it her own fear that had made her react so strongly? In her heart she knew Matt would never do anything that might hurt Danny. Had her reasoning truly been in her son's best interest or had she been using Stan as a yardstick by which to measure Matt?

The vast difference between the two men yawned like a great canyon. In almost every way, Matt was a strong, mature man with a level head on his shoulders. A man who put his son's welfare before his own. Stan never could have handled Danny's disappearance with the calmness that Matt had. Until the day he died, Stan had been a self-centered child. Had he lived to be as old as the mountains, he still would have been a child in an adult world. A Peter Pan looking for his never-never land.

Matt Logan was a good man. A fine man. Danny carried his father's genes. Their son had every chance of growing into the same kind of man, if she would just let him.

Those conclusions opened the door for Honey to take a good long look at who she was and who she wanted to be. The latter took no thought: she wanted to be a good mother and a good person.

But was that who Honey Kingston-Logan *was?*

She treated children and animals with kindness. She respected her elders. She loved her son with every breath in her body. But…

Honesty, she told herself. *If you're going to get*

anywhere with this self-analysis stuff, you have to be totally honest with yourself, no matter how much it hurts. Your son's happiness is at stake.

Biting the bullet, she looked at herself through candid eyes for the first time in years. Though she believed it was in his best interests, *she* made Danny's choices. *She* told him what to do and how to do it, what he liked and didn't like, what he could aspire to and not aspire to. In short, *she* was Frank Logan.

The naked truth made her sit up straight. She chuckled sardonically. Each of the Kingston kids had handled the residue of their father's relationship with them differently.

Emily had bowed to her father's wishes, and thankfully, it had worked out fine. Her sister had a happy life with a man she adored and two beautiful children.

Jesse… Well, Jesse chose to hide in the mountains and pretend none of it existed. He connected with the family from time to time, but essentially, kept his life separate from the Kingstons of Bristol, New York.

And Honey had taken refuge in the strangest way of all—by becoming exactly like the man she least wanted to emulate. The admission made her look at her father through different eyes. And while he may have been cold, domineering and opinionated, he'd done his best for his children in the only way he knew how. Just as she had for Danny. Perhaps, in his way, he had loved her, Emily and Jesse.

Honey sat back in the rocker. As it always did, when she allowed thoughts of her father to penetrate the wall she had erected to keep him out, the odor of cigarette smoke drifted to her. This time, however, it did not alarm her. This time, she understood.

In her mind, she stood outside the living room in

her old home, looking in at a man sitting in the dark, a man whose pain was so acute that even he couldn't identify it. A man who kept his emotions buried so deep he couldn't pull them out to share them with those around him.

In this most important way, she would not become her father. She loved Matt, but if she kept that love buried inside her, someday it would be too deep even for her to find. She couldn't and wouldn't take that chance.

For the first time in years, Honey felt a peace come over her that seeped down to her soul. She closed her eyes and let the silence of the night envelop her.

MATT FOUND HONEY SITTING on the porch, her feet curled beneath her, her head lolling back, her eyes closed. Her blond hair picked up the stray beams of light from the lamp inside the window. How many times had Matt envisioned her like this, as if waiting for him to kiss her? Too many to count.

Impulsively, he leaned forward and laid his mouth lightly against hers. She moaned. Quickly, he retreated before she awoke. Her eyes fluttered open. She smiled up at him.

"Hi."

"You probably would sleep better in a bed," he commented, slipping into the other rocker, then propping his feet up on the railing and bracing both hands behind his head for a pillow.

She yawned and stretched her arms above her head. Her breasts pressed against the fabric of her blouse. "I hadn't planned on camping out on the porch. It just kind of happened."

He turned away before his imagination began

working against him. "It's the excitement. The same thing used to happen to me after a rodeo. It's like someone pulled the rug out from under you or siphoned off your energy supply."

She turned to him. "Were you good at it? Riding horses in the rodeo?"

He glanced at her before answering. Genuine interest shone in her eyes.

"I guess I was. I got a few trophies," he answered.

"Where are they?"

"I pawned them." He grinned at her. "You see, there were times, mainly in the beginning, when I wasn't so good, and I got hungry."

Moving his gaze to the outline of purple mountains framing the night sky, he realized that this was the first time they had ever talked about his time away from her. He liked sharing it with someone.

"And later?"

"Later I got better and the money got pretty steady."

"And those trophies? The ones that you didn't have to pawn for food money. What happened to them?"

He shrugged. "I gave them away." He could still see the smiles on the faces of the kids in the hospitals he'd visited, as they showed their parents the shiny trophies topped with cowboys and horses.

"Then you didn't do it for the trophies and the fame."

He shook his head.

"What did you do it for?"

Matt had never had to think about that before, or maybe he'd never wanted to think about it. "I guess to prove something."

She had swung around in the chair, all her concentration on him. "To whom?"

"To myself, I guess."

"And did you?"

He stood, suddenly uncomfortable with the conversation. "I proved I'm stupid enough not to get out of the way of a damned angry bull." He rubbed at the faint throb in his leg. He couldn't talk to her about any of this yet. He wanted to, but he needed to sort through it in his own mind first. "I'm going to bed, and I suggest you do the same. If I know your sister, Danny will be here bright and early."

Honey watched him go through the door, but she didn't make a move to get up and follow. It appeared she wasn't the only one in this family who needed to do some soul-searching. Matt hadn't said he wasn't leaving, and that made her heart ache. But whether he stayed or not, until he started facing who he was, he wouldn't be any happier a thousand miles away than he was right here in Bristol.

She recalled something Amanda had said a long time ago in explanation of Stan's need to be constantly on the go. *People can keep moving for any number of reasons, but there's one thing they can't escape. They have to take themselves with them, and that's usually the very person they're running from the hardest.*

Chapter Sixteen

Eager to see Danny, Honey came downstairs early the next morning. As she stepped off the bottom stair, her gaze came to rest on something next to the door that made her falter. Tucked into the corner and nearly out of sight, but still visible, was Matt's suitcase. If she'd needed proof of his leaving, she now had it.

Disappointment flooded through her. A chilling pain crept around her heart. Until that very moment, she hadn't realized she'd been harboring a hope that last night and Danny's disappearance would have changed Matt's mind. Nor had she realized just how strong that hope had been.

Blinking repeatedly, she fought valiantly to hold back the threatening tears. Would she ever get used to saying goodbye to the one man who held her heart? She didn't think so, and if the agony sweeping over her was anything to go by, this time would be worse than the last.

Swallowing hard, she entered the dining room. Matt sat bent over a cup of steaming coffee. He didn't acknowledge her presence. She said nothing, but went to the sideboard and poured coffee into a china cup. It was if they both knew that speaking would cause more hurt, more anguish. Anyhow by now they had said all there was to say.

Except I love you, a little voice taunted from the back of her mind. *Tell him. Don't let him walk away without knowing.*

But she ignored it. What good would it do? Would he stay?

You won't know unless you try, the voice encouraged.

Still she ignored it. Just wanting something with every breath in you wouldn't make it so.

"Emily called a few minutes ago. She said she'd be bringing Danny by soon." Matt didn't look at her.

"Will you be here?" She couldn't hold the words back.

"I won't be leaving until after he comes home." He finally glanced up at her, and she noted the dark circles rimming his eyes. "I told you I wouldn't go without saying goodbye to both of you."

Evidently she wasn't the only one who'd found sleep elusive last night. The thought lightened her spirit just a bit. If he didn't care, he wouldn't have worried. As far as his promise to say goodbye, well, she'd heard him, but she hadn't believed him.

They sipped their coffee in silence.

Honey stared at the dark liquid, musing about what her world would be like once Matt was gone again. Oh, she'd live. She knew from experience that she could do it. But when would the color come back into her world? When would she be able to hear Matt's name and not feel like an arrow had pierced her heart?

Matt played with the jelly knife, then smeared a dollop of purple jam on his cold toast. He laid the knife and the plate aside. He had no appetite.

During the endless hours of the previous night, he had lain awake wondering why his answer to everything was to run. He'd spent his life doing it in one way or another, and he was tired. He wanted roots, a home, a life that didn't come out of a suitcase. The problem was, he couldn't have it in this house and he couldn't have it with this woman.

If he had learned nothing else from last night and Danny's disappearance, he'd learned that staying here was only making things worse for both the boy and Honey. His house was done and it was time he moved into it. The ghosts were gone, and he no longer had an excuse not to.

He'd gotten up in the middle of the night and finished the packing he'd started before Honey came in to ask him to have a talk with Danny. Matt wasn't sure this would classify as running away, as he wasn't leaving town—but it sure felt like it. As long as he stayed in Amanda's house, however, Danny would believe there was a chance that they could become a real family. Matt knew that had about the same likelihood of happening as a snowball's survival in hell. The longer he stayed here, the harder it would be on Danny when he left—and on him.

The sound of a puppy barking excitedly and a car motor alerted them to Emily's arrival. They rose simultaneously and headed for the front door.

As Emily drove up, Honey and Matt waited in silence on the porch. He felt her hand slip into his. He looked down at their clasped hands, then into her eyes. Her need for him to share his strength was clear in those blue depths. Gently, he squeezed her fingers, trying to convey that he needed her strength, as well.

"It'll be all right." He smiled to reinforce his words.

Seeming to absorb courage from his words, she returned the smile with a tentative one of her own, then turned toward the driveway and the parked car.

The door opened and Buddy shot out. His stubby puppy legs carried him across the lawn at breakneck speed. He stopped short, skidding in the dew-wet grass, then crouched down, as if preparing to pounce. He looked at Honey and Matt and barked, his tail wagging fiercely, as if he was the advance guard heralding the arrival of his best friend and master.

Slowly, Danny emerged from the passenger seat. Over his shoulder hung a superhero knapsack. He held his Yankee baseball jacket in one hand and carried his lunch box in the other. He kept his eyes downcast and walked toward the porch.

"Hi, sweetheart," Honey said, holding her arms out to him.

He sidestepped her and climbed the stairs without saying a word, Buddy romping along at his heels, oblivious to the tension between the adults and his friend. Opening the screen door, Danny glanced down at Matt's suitcase just inside. Turning back to Matt, he glared.

"W-w-why d-d-don't y-y-you j-j-just l-l-leave?" He slammed the door behind him and Buddy.

Matt stared blindly at the closed door, feeling decidedly like the worst kind of monster on earth. The disappointment and anger mirrored in his son's eyes had the same effect of a knife buried in his chest, sending pain to all parts of his body.

"He's not happy that I brought him back," Emily said, coming to stand at the foot of the stairs. "He wanted me to take him to the bus station in Albany.'' She grinned. "He said he had five dollars, and he was going to California.''

Honey stepped off the stairs, then wrapped her arms around her sister. "Thanks so much for bringing him home.''

Matt joined them and delivered his own hug. "Ditto,'' he said, his voice betraying the emotion produced by his son telling him to leave, and the obvious return of his stutter.

At that moment, Matt made a decision that hurt one hundred times more than the bull goring a hole in his thigh. It hurt more than any wound he'd ever had inflicted on him. This, no matter how necessary, was a wound that would probably never heal.

"Hey, one day one of my kids may decide to take off.'' Emily's voice interrupted his thoughts. "I just hope they have the good sense to come to you.'' She smiled, then sobered. "If I can do anything else, just holler. Okay?''

"I think we can take it from here,'' Matt said. Emily nodded, then headed toward her car.

"You want to come in for coffee?'' Honey called, obviously trying to put off the time they would have to go in and talk to Danny.

"Thanks,'' Emily called back. "I have a hot date for breakfast at The Diner with a handsome vet I know.''

Honey waved her sister off, then turned to Matt. "Well, I guess we'd better—''

"Honey, before we go in to speak to Danny, I want to say something, and it might be better said out here where he can't overhear it.''

"Yes?''

He swallowed hard, then summoned the words. "Maybe we shouldn't tell him who I am."

Honey couldn't believe her ears. For weeks, ever since he'd found out about Danny, Matt had wanted one thing, worked toward one thing—telling Danny he was his father. Now he had suddenly changed his mind.

"Why?" She searched his face for his reasoning.

"I've done enough damage. Telling him is only going to confuse him more. He'd be better off just thinking of me as Uncle Matt, the crazy guy who couldn't stay in one place long enough to get the soles of his feet warm. Let him continue to remember Stan the way he does, as his dad.

"You and Danny need a hero and I'm just not hero material. I could never measure up to your expectations or his. I'd disappoint you in one way or another. I couldn't live with that."

For a long time, Honey could say nothing. Then she forced a question through her numb lips. "Who are you trying to measure up to?" She didn't wait for an answer. She wasn't sure he had one. Turning away, she went into the house and up the stairs to their son's room, scarcely noticing that Matt followed.

She knocked gently on the closed door. "Danny?"

She was met with silence.

"Danny?" Matt called. "Your mom and I want to talk to you. We're not mad at you."

Again there was silence.

A soft whine drew Honey's attention. Buddy lay at her feet. Danny had shut them all out, even his very best friend.

"Danny, please, sweetie, let us talk to you," she called, then waited. When there was no answer, she added, "Don't you want to talk to us?" She tried the knob. The door was locked from the inside. She glanced helplessly at Matt.

"Young man," he called, his voice having lost its pleading quality. "You open this door now!"

"Y-y-you're n-n-not m-m-my d-d-dad. You c-c-can't order m-m-me." Danny's voice came to them, muffled and choked with tears.

Matt digested his son's words, feeling as if an arrow had pierced his chest. He never glanced at Honey, just turned and walked away. The only thing worse than the pain of his son's rejection would be seeing the accusation in her eyes.

A DAY LATER, after he and Honey had tried unsuccessfully to speak with Danny, Matt sat in his father's bedroom gathering the strewn newspaper clippings and placing them back in the box. He recalled Honey's question.

Who are you trying to measure up to?

Before he could answer that, he had to find out who he was. But after searching through his mind, he found it easier to ascertain who he wasn't.

He wasn't a father or a husband. He wasn't his dead brother, Jamie.

But while he wasn't many things and might be lacking in many areas, neither was he a bad person. Through his rodeo appearances, many charities had benefited, and he'd been able to help others. He'd been instrumental in helping Danny nearly overcome his stutter. Matt had every reason to be proud of the life he'd led.

He glanced down at his father's clippings. It would appear that he wasn't the only person who'd been proud of who he was and what he'd done. If only he'd known! If only, just once, his father had said how proud he was of him and not led him to believe he'd been in competition with his brother.

But had he? Or had Matt only assumed that, too?

He searched his memory for the exact time he'd heard his father say "Why can't you be more like Jamie?" Not one instance came to mind. He'd said things like "Remember how Jamie caught the ball?" Or "Remember what Jamie taught you to do." But never had he actually compared them.

The only comparison had been in Matt's mind. And when he hadn't lived up to what he saw as his father's expectations, he'd seen himself as a failure and unlovable. A disappointment.

He picked up the lid to the box and noticed a photo stuck against the cardboard, facedown. Carefully, he peeled it off and turned it over. His breath caught and memories came rushing back to him.

It had been his sixth birthday and he'd entered a rose he'd nurtured and babied in the competition at the Bristol County Fair. He'd won first prize and been presented with a blue ribbon. The picture had been taken shortly after the awards ceremony, just outside the main tent. It was of him and his father. His father's arm was slung around Matt's small shoulders and the grin on the older man's face conveyed to the camera the overwhelming pride he felt in the little boy tucked against his side.

Going back to that day, Matt tried to recall if he had asked his father if he was proud of him or if his father had offered the words, but he found no trace of either.

Silence had torn their lives apart. Because neither

of them had offered the words that would heal the other's heart, each had lived believing the other didn't care.

Matt's thoughts veered to Danny. Was that how he wanted Danny to grow up? Believing his father didn't care enough about him to claim him as his son? Was Matt making the same mistake his own dad had made? The same mistake he seemed doomed to repeat?

Years of living with the idea that love was beyond his reach and that he was destined only to hurt those he loved were hard to shed, and he couldn't do it here, surrounded by reminders of his and his father's mistakes.

Matt put the box aside, then walked from the room, down the stairs and out of the house. Needing space to think, he climbed into his truck and backed out of the driveway. He drove aimlessly for a while over roads he'd ridden as a kid on his bike, past his old school and the athletic field where Jamie had been a star.

The truck seemed to steer itself to the roadside near the athletic field. He put it in park, not bothering to shut off the motor. For a long time he stared at the empty field, hearing the cheers that rang out for his brother echoing in his mind. Jamie had been a good boy, a fine athlete, but he, too, had made his mistakes. The worst of them being sneaking the plane out before he was ready to solo. When Jamie died, Matt had felt as if part of him had died as well.

Now, he could see that, after Jamie's death, he had unconsciously decided to try to make up for the loss by being everything that Jamie had been. It hadn't been their father, it had been Matt who made the decision that changed his life.

He put the car in drive and steered toward The Diner, hoping that some familiar faces would draw him from this introspection. But when he arrived there and found it closed, he knew it was the hand of fate telling him he had to make some changes, and it better be soon, before he lost everything he loved.

As he turned back toward his truck, a bright yellow sign, written in what looked like a child's scrawl, caught his eye. It was an advertisement for Danny's school play. Matt had forgotten all about it.

Would Danny still want him there or would it be too late to regain his son's love?

HONEY SAT IN THE LAST ROW of straight-backed, wooden folding chairs assembled in the elementary school auditorium for the big show. Beside her, in the side aisle where it wouldn't get in the way, they'd tucked Amanda's wheelchair. When she and Amanda had arrived, later than Honey had wanted to, she had found most of the auditorium filled with parents and relatives eager to see the performance.

She laid her purse on her lap, crossed her legs and waited for the show to begin.

"When does Danny come on?" Amanda whispered.

"At the beginning of the second act. About ten minutes into the play. Right after the farmer chases the rabbit out of the garden."

"Was he nervous?"

Honey shook her head. "He still wasn't talking to me, but he didn't seem nervous."

For that matter, he hadn't said much all day yesterday or today, but when she'd gone over his one and only line with him, the stutter seemed to be as pronounced as when Matt had first arrived at Amanda's. Silently, Honey prayed he'd do well. She shuddered to think how he would feel if anyone laughed at him.

The lights dimmed and the noisy chatter died down slowly until silence reigned over the big room. The stage lights came up and the curtain slowly opened to reveal a small girl in a white rabbit suit, kneeling in the center of a hand-painted backdrop of an over-size garden, munching a make-believe carrot.

She spoke her lines, but Honey didn't hear them. All her thoughts were on the little boy who would make his public debut on stage as a tomato, and on the man she'd loved and lost again.

Where was Matt? Miles from here, no doubt, on his way back to the life of riding dangerous horses and bulls. Strangely, while the idea of Matt risking his life on a daily basis still scared her, she felt a deep-down confidence that he would not take the unnecessary chances that Stan had. Matt had a good head on his shoulders. He'd proven it over and over to her, with Danny and his concern for him, with her and since he'd been back the way he'd always been there when she needed him.

If only he'd been able to stay and face his doubts about himself. If only he'd given her the chance to help him. If only...

Applause filled the auditorium and dragged Honey from her thoughts. She joined in, having no idea what had just taken place on stage. The curtain closed slowly and the farmer and several barnyard animals bowed and smiled. Moments later, the farmer came on the stage holding a sign that said The Vegetables Come Alive, then exited stage left.

"Danny's about to come on," Amanda whispered, pride filling her voice.

Again the curtain slid open. The stage was empty. A large red tomato entered from the back and came to center stage. The stuffing inside Danny's costume had shifted to one side and he gathered it up in his hands and tried to reposition it. The audience giggled. He looked out beyond the footlights. His attention seemed centered in the front row. Even stretching, Honey couldn't see who or what he was looking at.

He frowned. For a moment, Honey wondered if he'd forgotten his line, then his face took on that expression that she knew meant *I'll show you.*

Confused, she sat back, held her breath and waited.

"Tomatoes are good for you, especially in scapetti sauce." Danny's words rang out loud and clear, without a single stutter.

Honey exhaled the breath she'd been holding.

She felt the warmth of Amanda's hand squeezing her arm. "He did it."

"Yes," she said, grinning until it felt as if her face would crack, "he did it."

The rest of the play went by quickly. Parents applauded their young prodigies and rushed forward to collect them as they exited from between the curtains. Honey held back, waiting for the crowd to thin, but keeping her eyes on the curtain for Danny's appearance.

"I'll wait here," Amanda told her. "You go up there so he doesn't think we left without him."

Honey handed Amanda her purse and pushed through the crowd of parents and kids heading toward the door. She'd almost made it to the stage when Danny stepped out, dragging his tomato costume behind him. He didn't look for her, but peered toward where he'd been gazing just before he spoke his lines. Now that she was standing and nearly to the front, she could see who he was looking at.

Matt!

She blinked to make sure her eyes weren't playing tricks on her. Standing at the edge of the stage with his arms out to help Danny down was Matt Logan. She drank in the sight of his dark hair, one wave dropping over his forehead, and his broad shoulders straining at the seams of a turquoise shirt. She couldn't see below his waist, but knew he wore jeans, the kind that molded his hips and backside just right to tempt a woman beyond endurance.

Danny walked to the edge of the stage, then balked for a moment before allowing Matt to lift him to the floor.

"You were good, sport," Matt exclaimed.

Danny looked up at him, a small smile curving his lips. "You think?"

Matt nodded, then ruffled Danny's dark hair. "Better than Mel Gibson, I'd say."

Danny pulled back, out of reach of Matt's hand. Honey saw the pain shoot across Matt's features. Enough was enough! She knew what had to be done.

She stepped into their line of vision. "Well, now that you've made your stunning stage debut, how about if we celebrate with some ice cream cones at the Twist 'N' Freeze?"

Matt looked at her with pain-filled eyes. This time it was her turn to comfort and assure him. "It'll be all right," she said softly. "Trust me."

He continued to stare at her, then nodded. ''I do.''

Honey took Danny's hand and Matt took the costume. They met Amanda at the back of the auditorium and made their way through the crowd to the parking lot. Matt left his truck and climbed into the passenger seat of Honey's car. She smiled at him, then started the vehicle. She was doing the driving tonight, in more ways than one. And if that meant she was taking control, then Matt Logan and his son would have to live with it.

Chapter Seventeen

Amanda, tired from the long evening, opted out of the ice cream celebration. By the time they dropped her off at home, then returned to the ice cream stand, the crowd of proud parents and would-be Broadway stars had thinned to almost nothing. Danny ordered his favorite, a cone of vanilla-chocolate twist with rainbow sprinkles. When Honey ordered a banana split with two spoons, Matt eyed her warily.

"You never used to object to sharing one of these obscenely fattening things with me," she said.

He grinned. "I still don't." Then his eyes grew warm. "I guess I was surprised that you remembered."

The way his voice softened on the last words sent a pleasant chill up Honey's spine. Was there a chance for them? Well, she'd soon have an answer to that question. Honey had made up her mind in the auditorium, when she had seen Danny flinch from Matt's touch and the pain reflected in Matt's expression, that tonight they would settle everything, once and for all. If he wanted to accuse her of taking control again, then so be it.

Matt got the ice cream orders and returned to the

car. As soon as he was inside with the door closed, Honey put the car in gear and steered out of the lot. The car tipped with the quick movement, and Matt juggled the ice cream for a moment. He passed Danny's cone and some napkins back to him, then shot an inquiring glance at Honey.

"Were you Stan's second on the race track?"

She ignored his sarcasm.

"Where we going, Mom?"

She ignored her son's question.

"I guess she's not talking to us, Danny."

"I guess."

Honey glanced in the rearview mirror to make sure Danny had secured his seat belt and saw a half grin surface on her son's lips. The first in days. The knot that had formed in the pit of her stomach loosened a fraction.

"I'm talking, just not answering questions." She sent a sidelong look at Matt.

What was she up to? Matt continued to divide his attention between her and the rapid progress of the car. He'd never seen Honey drive like this before. Speed had never been something she particularly liked, even before she'd met Stan. A car with Honey at the wheel, careening around corners on a dark road, made him more than nervous. He held on to the melting banana split with one hand and the door handle with the other.

"I think she's kidnapping us, Danny." He hoped his amusing comment might ease any discomfort Danny was having at his mother's driving.

Danny leaned forward as far as his seat belt would allow and stuck his head between the bucket seats. He had a smear of vanilla ice cream on his cheek, a few sprinkles stuck to his lips. He swiped them off with his tongue. "Are you kidnapping us, Mom?"

"Yup."

"Why?"

"Because this little group has a way of dodging issues that need to be talked about and until we talk about them, neither of you is escaping my clutches." She added an evil laugh that made Danny giggle.

Matt didn't find this amusing. In fact, a distinct feeling of unease that had nothing to do with her driving began to creep over him. As she veered to the side to avoid a rather large pothole, he swallowed hard. What in hell did she have up her sleeve?

"Honey—"

"Not now, Matt. I'm trying to drive."

"*Trying* being the operative word here." The car careened to a stop. Several yards beyond them, he could see Lover's Leap. "Nice landing."

She glared at him. "I got us here, didn't I?"

"Only because this car has a good center of gravity." Matt handed her a spoon. "Now that you have us out here in the middle of nowhere, what is it exactly you want us to do? Besides eat, that is."

He held out the banana split, and she scooped eagerly into the strawberry topping. He knew she would. Most women loved chocolate, but Honey would kill for strawberry anything.

She removed the plastic dish from his hand and scooped out more of the ice cream. "I'm going to enjoy this ice cream. You two are going to talk."

That wary feeling invaded his body again. "About anything in particular?"

She lowered the spoon from her mouth and looked him directly in the eye. Light from the full moon cast the planes of his face into deep shadows, making it impossible to read his expression. "Yes. You're going to tell Danny who you are."

"Aw, Mom, I know who he is. He's Uncle Matt. Right?" Danny unhooked his seat belt and leaned forward again. "Tell her, Uncle Matt."

Honey continued to stare at him. "He deserves to know the truth, Matt. And you need to tell him."

The dashboard lights illuminated her expression. This was not a joke. She wanted Matt to tell Danny he was his father. Of all the things he'd expected, this had definitely not been high on the list of possibilities.

"The truth?" Danny's voice sounded as if he'd picked up some of Matt's wariness.

"He's not ready, Honey."

She shook her head. "He's been ready since the day he was born." For the first time, she truly believed that.

Danny sat back, as if distancing himself from the conversation in the front seat. Alarmed, Matt turned to assess Danny's reaction and saw a glob of vanilla ice cream drip from the cone onto his new school pants. Danny ignored it and stared out the window into the darkness. In his gut, Matt knew the boy had picked up on the tension.

For once, Honey didn't reprimand Danny and shove a napkin into his hand. Instead, she took another spoonful of vanilla ice cream and strawberry topping and then raised an eyebrow at Matt. "Well?"

For a moment, he was distracted by her pink tongue licking a drop of strawberry syrup from her spoon. His gut tightened.

Like a butterfly emerging from its chrysalis before his eyes, she'd changed. No longer did she seem unsure of herself or defensive. This was the Honey he'd always loved and admired, the one who saw a problem and stepped in to solve it, come hell or high water. The Honey who knew what she wanted and wasn't afraid to go after it. The Honey who had fought for her own survival, and that of those she loved.

She set the half-eaten ice cream aside. "Are you going to let this moment escape? Are you going to miss this chance to start a new relationship with your son?" Her words were said very low and very quietly, but there was an edge of challenge in her voice.

Matt glanced at Danny to see if he'd heard her. Preoccupied with wiping up the ice cream dripping all over his hand, the boy seemed oblivious of the adults' conversation. But Matt knew better. The tactic rang with familiarity. He'd used it many times as a kid when his parents argued about him, and he was using it now, ironically, to avoid what he wanted to do more than anything—claim his son. Just as he and his father had done for all those wasted years.

Honey was right. The time was now. Otherwise, like him and his father, they would find a wall separating them that was too high to scale.

He set his unused spoon on the dashboard, then nodded at Honey. She smiled encouragingly. Half turning in his seat, he glanced at Danny, then took a deep breath.

Honey put a hand on his sleeve. "Let's get out."

Matt nodded, then opened his door. He stepped onto the uneven ground. A twig snapped beneath his foot and he was reminded of the fragility of this situation and how easily he could blow the whole thing with one wrong word.

Honey rounded the car, opened the trunk and drew out a plaid blanket. She snapped the trunk closed, then spread the blanket on the ground beside a big rock.

Danny emerged last. He looked from one of the adults to the other, then wandered over to sit on the rock. Shoving the last of his cone in his mouth, he chewed, and waited for Honey and Matt to join him.

Matt sat at his feet. Honey dropped to the grass next to Matt, then slipped her hand into his. The warmth of her grasp gave him the strength he needed to start talking.

Matt reached for Danny's hand. He pulled it away. This wasn't going to be easy. "Danny, you know what love is, right?"

Danny nodded, but kept his eyes downcast.

"Well, sometimes, love makes you do funny things."

Danny finally looked at him. "What funny things?"

"Oh, like hurt the people you love most."

Danny frowned.

"Okay, let me start again. Awhile back, I met this girl and fell in love with her. She was the most beautiful thing I'd ever seen." Honey's fingers tightened around his.

The frown on Danny's face turned to a wrinkled nose, as if he'd just gotten a whiff of something very offensive. "Girls aren't pretty. They're dumb."

Matt laughed. "Not all girls. Not this one. Not your mom."

"My mom?" Danny's gaze shifted from Matt to Honey. She smiled and nodded.

"Yes, your mom. She was the girl I fell in love

with, but being in love with her scared me so much, I ran away.''

The frown returned and deepened. ''Why?''

''Because I thought I'd disappoint her, and I couldn't stand the thought of doing that. But running away hurt her a lot, and I hadn't thought of that.''

''Like me running away the other night?''

''Exactly. I'm sure you didn't mean to hurt your mom or me or your grandmother, but you did.'' Matt touched his small hand tentatively, trying to reassure him that he'd been forgiven. This time, Danny allowed the familiarity without recoiling. ''I didn't mean to hurt anyone, either,'' Matt continued. ''But I did. I had to learn that running away doesn't make the problem go away, does it?''

''Uh-uh.''

''Well, I hurt your mom so much that she married somebody else.''

''My dad?''

Matt nodded, but didn't comment further. It hurt too much. ''What I didn't know when I left was that your mom was going to have you.'' He waited for his son to digest his words. ''If I had known, I would never have gone. I would have stayed and married her so we could have had our baby together. I would have loved him and been here to watch him grow into a young man—one who makes me very proud.''

Silence descended on the threesome.

''But mom only has one kid.'' Danny searched their faces. ''Right, Mom?''

Honey nodded, but remained silent to allow Danny to work through what Matt had just told him. As she watched the changing expressions pass over her son's face, she held her breath.

Please help him to understand, she prayed, even though she knew Danny was a bright, sensitive kid and could figure this all out, given time.

"No one should be afraid to love, Danny," Matt added, his voice taking on a note of desperation. "And no one should be afraid to be loved."

Honey's heart sang at his admission. Hearing him say that ranked right up there with hearing her son say her name without stuttering.

Suddenly, Danny stood up, comprehension written on his youthful face, and stared down at them. "Am I your kid? Are you my dad?"

Matt nodded. "Yes, I am."

The knot of tension that coiled deep inside Honey loosened and vanished. It was out. Now all they had to do was wait for Danny's reaction. When it came, it shocked both of them.

"I wanna go home now." Silently, he walked to the car, opened the back door, then climbed in.

Honey had expected anything but this. She started to follow. Matt stopped her with his hand to her arm.

"Let him go. He needs time to think. This is a hell of a blow to him." He released her arm, then dragged his hand through his hair and looked at the star-studded sky. "I should feel better, now that it's out in the open, but my insides feel like they've just gone through a blender."

"It's been quite a night," she said, noticing for the first time the smell of wild roses drifting on the night air and the hypnotic rhythm of the chirping crickets. "I think we should all sleep on it."

Smiling down at her, Matt bent and kissed her gently on the lips. "Thank you for giving me my son back."

"He was always yours, Matt, you just had to claim him." She only wished that this circle of love included her. "I hope you'll stick around and be there for him, now." She started to walk away, but he held her arm.

"For what it's worth, I didn't leave town. I just moved into my house."

Honey's heart stopped, then started up in double-time. She grinned.

"Let's take our son home."

Matt dropped his arm around her shoulders. "Let's do that."

AMANDA HEARD the threesome come in. "Hello, you night owls."

They came to the door and she felt like a hundred pounds had been lifted from her tired bones. Matt had his arm around Honey, and she appeared more radiant than she ever had before. Then Amanda looked at Danny.

"Why don't the two of you go check on Matt's house to make sure he locked it when he left?" she suggested.

At first they looked at her as if she'd lost every scrap of sanity she possessed. Then realization dawned on Matt's face. "You know, come to think of it, I'm not at all sure I did lock it."

"But—" Honey looked from one to the other. After a moment, she, too, understood. "Oh, right. Sure."

Shaking his head, Matt led her out the door.

"Danny?"

Timidly, he peered at Amanda around the door casing.

"Come in here and talk with me," she said.

He walked into the room and sat in the big chair opposite her. The evidence of his ice cream celebration showed on his pants and shirt. But the evidence of something else was reflected in his face and posture. He looked so small and lost in that huge chair. As if the problems of the world rested on his slim shoulders.

"Want to talk about it?" she asked gently.

He shook his head. Then he stared at her. "Gram, did you know Uncle Matt is my dad?"

Amanda nodded. "Yes, I knew."

"How come you didn't tell me?" Tears welled in his blue eyes. His expression clearly disclosed that he felt betrayed by yet another one of the people he'd trusted.

"It wasn't my place to tell you. Only Matt could do that."

"He shoulda told me," Danny shouted. "He shoulda."

"Maybe he didn't because he had good reasons not to." Amanda straightened the afghan throw on her lap. "Come here."

Danny rose and moved to stand beside her knees. She grabbed him under the arms and guided him onto her lap. Most of the time he protested such a gesture, by saying he was "too old for that mushy stuff," but tonight, her grandmother's intuition told her that a little cuddling was in order. When he snuggled against her chest, she knew her instincts had not failed her.

Wrapping her arms around him, she kissed the top of his head. His silky fine hair tickled her lips. She inhaled the scent of fresh air that still clung to him.

"When your dad first came home, he couldn't tell you because he was afraid that it would make your stutter worse." Danny tried to raise his head, but she held it against her with the palm of her hand. "Let me finish. The doctor told your mom that any shock wouldn't be good for you. So he didn't say anything."

"Why didn't he tell me after I quit stuttering?" His voice was muffled against her dress.

"Because he loves you so much, he was afraid he'd hurt you if he told you. Especially if he and your mom couldn't make a family for you and he had to leave again." This was mostly guesswork on Amanda's part, but she knew her nephew well enough to assume her guess was fairly close to the mark.

"But he did leave again." This time Danny sat up and looked straight at her,

"Did he? Or did he just move into his own house?"

Danny eyes brightened. "You mean he's not gonna go away again?"

So that's what had been troubling him. He was afraid to accept Matt because he was afraid he'd leave again. Amanda shook her head. "Your dad is not going anywhere." She chucked Danny under the chin. "Now, climb down off my lap. You're too old for this mushy stuff."

Giggling, Danny slid to the floor. "Aw, Gramma, you can do that mushy stuff with me anytime you want." He stopped laughing and stared at her with an intensity that shocked her. "Are you still gonna be my gramma?"

She took his cheeks between her palms, kissed each in turn, then his forehead. "I will *always* be your gramma. For as long as you want me.'' She released him and quickly turned away to hide the tears in her eyes. ''Now, I'm going to bed. You've tuckered me right out.'' She wheeled the chair toward the door, then paused. ''In case you feel the need to make a phone call, the number is on the pad beside the phone.''

Turning, she rolled the chair over the threshold. As she steered it toward the stairs, she heard Danny call to her. ''I love you, Gram.''

''I love you, Grandson,'' she called back, then smiled when she heard the sound of the phone being dialed.

As MATT STEPPED OVER the threshold of his front hall, he could hear the phone in the kitchen ringing. ''I wonder who that can be,'' he commented, striding toward the phone. Honey followed. As he lifted the receiver from the wall cradle, he slipped an arm around her and pulled her close to his side. ''Hello?''

A silence greeted him from the other end, and he was about to hang up when a small voice said, ''Dad?''

Matt swallowed hard, then tried to speak, but it came out a whisper. ''Yes, Danny?''

''I called to say good-night.''

''Good night…Son.'' The word tasted like ambrosia on his tongue.

A long pause followed. ''And, Dad?''

''Yes?''

''I love you.''

Matt's throat closed. He had to force the words from his lips. ''I love you, too.'' When he hung up the phone and turned to Honey, it was to find her with tears running freely down her cheeks. "You heard?" She nodded, then wiped the moisture from his face. He hadn't even known he was crying.

With a whoop of delight, he snatched her up and twirled her around the kitchen. She threw her head back and laughed out loud. Matt couldn't recall the last time his world had seemed so perfect, if it ever had. He had his son's love. He'd heard him call him "Dad" and he had the woman he loved more than life in his arms. What more could he want?

Then Honey showed him.

She placed her palms on either side of his face. He stopped moving and let her slide down his front, enjoying the feeling of her body so close to his.

"I love you, Matt Logan, and nothing, nothing you could ever do will change that." She kissed him hard and long.

Contentment. Peace of mind. Tranquility. Happiness. Fulfillment. Whatever word he wanted to call it by, the feeling raced through him, warming all the corners of his soul that had been cold for so long. To think that his fear and his silence had nearly robbed him of this made him blurt out the feelings hidden deep inside him. Feelings he hadn't dared admit even to himself for a long time.

"I love you, too, Honey Logan."

"Then make an honest woman of me."

Her grin showed him the pure happiness coursing through her, as well. But old fears didn't die that easily. Could he do it? Could he be the kind of father and husband he wanted to be?

As if reading his mind, she kissed him again. "We can do it, if we do it together, with love and honesty and as a family."

The doubts vanished. He knew that with Honey at his side, he could do anything. "I accept your proposal," he said with a grin.

"Then let's seal it to make it official."

"Want to measure those curtains?"

She giggled, then pulled back. "I have a better idea. Don't move."

He watched as she raced upstairs, then reemerged moments later, towing the quilt off his bed behind her. She held it out to him. "By the way, you don't have any doubts about disappointing me, do you?"

His laughter filled the kitchen. "If your reaction in the past is anything to go by, disappointing you at this particular responsibility is the least of my worries." Scooping her up in his arms, he started down the hall toward the stairs.

"No. Outside, where the pool used to be."

Grinning down at her, he pressed a quick kiss to her lips, then turned and headed toward the back door.

THAT NIGHT, they did make love where it had all started. The preliminaries of slowly undressing each other were dispensed with, as they tore off their clothes, eager to feel flesh against flesh.

When Matt's body touched hers as she lay on the quilt, his warmth contrasted sharply with the cool air around them, lending the night a hint of eroticism. Everything seemed magnified to her: the sound of the wind through the trees, the song of the night creatures, the twinkle of each star, the perfume of blooming plants. It was as if the universe was putting on a special show for lovers.

Then Matt began to skim his hands over her and everything else faded. She could only hear the beat of her heart in her ears, feel the hard planes of Matt's body fitting snugly against the gentle curves of hers, his heated breath fanning her kiss-dampened skin.

How had she survived without him? As if to assure herself this wasn't some wonderful dream that she would awaken from, she learned his body all over again. She ran her hands over the bunching muscles in his shoulders and back. Then she tasted his skin, the salty flavor reminding her of other nights, long ago, when she hadn't been able to get enough of the man she loved.

Then he was in her and the world spun away, lost in a cloud of thick sensuality that promised other nights in his arms.

For the first time he could remember since he'd left Honey, Matt felt whole again. Her body welcomed him with the same undeniable love that her heart held for him. How had he ever thought he could live his life without this, without Honey to lose himself in?

The years seemed to fade away, bringing back to him the joy of the first time he'd ever made love to Honey. Once more he stroked her skin and aroused her to the pitch of passion. She was his and his world had righted itself forever.

When it peaked and the stars came down to bless their joining, he told her he loved her and would love her forever. She tightened her grip on him, wrapped her legs around him and arched her body against his.

"No matter where you go or what you do, I will always be a part of your soul," she whispered.

Afterward, they lay in each other's arms for a long time, just savoring the peace and love they'd found again and had come so close to losing. They had each been trying so hard to be someone else that they'd almost lost one another.

As he held her and stroked her moonlight-bathed body, Matt knew in his heart that he'd found the happiness he'd searched for everywhere but in his own backyard. The ghosts of his old home were indeed gone forever, chased out by the enduring and unconstrained love of the woman in his arms.

Honey had finally found her hero, not one but two. A man who loved her enough to take a chance on their love and make a life with her, and a little boy who loved them both enough to forgive their mistakes and help them start over as a family.

Coming in April 2002
from

HARLEQUIN®

AMERICAN *Romance*®

and

Judy Christenberry

RANDALL RICHES
(HAR #918)

Desperate to return to his Wyoming ranch, champion bull
rider Rich Randall had no choice but to accept sassy
Samantha Jeffer's helping hand—with a strict
"no hanky-panky" warning. But on the long road home
something changed and Rich was suddenly thinking of
turning in his infamous playboy status
for a little band of gold.

Don't miss this heartwarming addition to the series,

Brides
for Brothers

Available wherever Harlequin books are sold.

HARLEQUIN®
Makes any time special ®

Visit us at www.eHarlequin.com

HARRR

Meet the Randall brothers...four sexy bachelor brothers who are about to find four beautiful brides!

WYOMING WINTER

by bestselling author
Judy Christenberry

In preparation for the long, cold Wyoming winter, the eldest Randall brother seeks to find wives for his four single rancher brothers...and the resulting matchmaking is full of surprises! Containing the first two full-length novels in Judy's famous *4 Brides for 4 Brothers* miniseries, this collection will bring you into the lives, and loves, of the delightfully engaging Randall family.

Look for WYOMING WINTER in March 2002.

And in May 2002 look for SUMMER SKIES, containing the last two Randall stories.

HARLEQUIN®
Makes any time special ®

Visit us at www.eHarlequin.com

PHWW

This Mother's Day Give Your Mom A Royal Treat

Win a fabulous one-week vacation in Puerto Rico for you and your mother at the luxurious Inter-Continental San Juan Resort & Casino. The prize includes round trip airfare for two, breakfast daily and a mother and daughter day of beauty at the beachfront hotel's spa.

INTER·CONTINENTAL
San Juan
RESORT & CASINO

Here's all you have to do:

Tell us in 100 words or less how your mother helped with the romance in your life. It may be a story about your engagement, wedding or those boyfriends when you were a teenager or any other romantic advice from your mother. The entry will be judged based on its originality, emotionally compelling nature and sincerity. See official rules on following page.

Send your entry to:

Mother's Day Contest

In Canada
P.O. Box 637
Fort Erie, Ontario
L2A 5X3

In U.S.A.
P.O. Box 9076
3010 Walden Ave.
Buffalo, NY
14269-9076

Or enter online at www.eHarlequin.com

All entries must be postmarked by April 1, 2002.
Winner will be announced May 1, 2002. Contest open to Canadian and U.S. residents who are 18 years of age and older. No purchase necessary to enter. Void where prohibited.

PRROY

Two ways to enter:

• **Via The Internet:** Log on to the Harlequin romance website (www.eHarlequin.com) anytime beginning 12:01 a.m. E.S.T., January 1, 2002 through 11:59 p.m. E.S.T., April 1, 2002 and follow the directions displayed on-line to enter your name, address (including zip code), e-mail address and in 100 words or fewer, describe how your mother helped with the romance in your life.

• **Via Mail:** Handprint (or type) on an 8 1/2" x 11" plain piece of paper, your name, address (including zip code) and e-mail address (if you have one), and in 100 words or fewer, describe how your mother helped with the romance in your life. Mail your entry via first-class mail to: Harlequin Mother's Day Contest 2216, (in the U.S.) P.O. Box 9076, Buffalo, NY 14269-9076; (in Canada) P.O. Box 637, Fort Erie, Ontario, Canada L2A 5X

For eligibility, entries must be submitted either through a completed Internet transmission or postmarked no later than 11:59 p.m. E.S.T., April 1, 200 (mail-in entries must be received by April 9, 2002). Limit one entry per person, household address and e-mail address. On-line and/or mailed entries received from persons residing in geographic areas in which entry is not permissible will be disqualified.

Entries will be judged by a panel of judges, consisting of members of the Harlequin editorial, marketing and public relations staff using the following criteria
• Originality - 50%
• Emotional Appeal - 25%
• Sincerity - 25%

In the event of a tie, duplicate prizes will be awarded. Decisions of the judges are final.

Prize: A 6-night/7-day stay for two at the Inter-Continental San Juan Resort & Casino, including round-trip coach air transportation from gateway airport nearest winner's home (approximate retail value: $4,000). Prize includes breakfast daily and a mother and daughter day of beauty at the beachfront hotel's spa. Prize consists of only those items listed as part of the prize. Prize is valued in U.S. currency.

All entries become the property of Torstar Corp. and will not be returned. No responsibility is assumed for lost, late, illegible, incomplete, inaccurate non-delivered or misdirected mail or misdirected e-mail, for technical, hardware or software failures of any kind, lost or unavailable network connections, or failed, incomplete, garbled or delayed computer transmission or any human error which may occur in the receipt or processing of entries in this Contest.

Contest open only to residents of the U.S. (except Colorado) and Canada, who are 18 years of age or older and is void wherever prohibited by law all applicable laws and regulations apply. Any litigation within the Province of Quebec respecting the conduct or organization of a publicity contest may be submitted to the Régie des alcools, des courses et des jeux for a ruling. Any litigation respecting the awarding of a prize may be submitted to the Régie des alcools, des courses et des jeux only for the purpose of helping the parties reach a settlement. Employees and immediate family members of Torstar Corp. and D.L. Blair, Inc., their affiliates, subsidiaries and all other agencies, entities and persons connected with the use, marketing or conduct of this Contest are not eligible to enter. Taxes on prize are the sole responsibility of winner. Acceptance of any prize offered constitutes permission to use winner's name, photograph or other likeness for the purposes of advertising, trade and promotion on behalf of Torstar Corp., its affiliates and subsidiaries without further compensation to the winner, unless prohibited by law.

Winner will be determined no later than April 15, 2002 and be notified by mail. Winner will be required to sign and return an Affidavit of Eligibili form within 15 days after winner notification. Non-compliance within that time period may result in disqualification and an alternate winner selected. Winner of trip must execute a Release of Liability prior to ticketing and must possess required travel documents (e.g. Passport, photo ID where applicable. Travel must be completed within 12 months of selection and is subject to traveling companion completing and returning a Relea of Liability prior to travel; and hotel and flight accommodations availability. Certain restrictions and blackout dates may apply. No substitution of p permitted by winner. Torstar Corp. and D.L. Blair, Inc., their parents, affiliates, and subsidiaries are not responsible for errors in printing or electron presentation of Contest, or entries. In the event of printing or other errors which may result in unintended prize values or duplication of prizes, all affected entries shall be null and void. If for any reason the Internet portion of the Contest is not capable of running as planned, including infection by computer virus, bugs, tampering, unauthorized intervention, fraud, technical failures, or any other causes beyond the control of Torstar Corp. which corrupt or affect the administration, secrecy, fairness, integrity or proper conduct of the Contest, Torstar Corp. reserves the right, at its sole discretion, to disqualify any individual who tampers with the entry process and to cancel, terminate, modify or suspend the Contest or the Interne portion thereof. In the event the Internet portion must be terminated a notice will be posted on the website and all entries received prior to termination will be judged in accordance with these rules. In the event of a dispute regarding an on-line entry, the entry will be deemed submitte by the authorized holder of the e-mail account submitted at the time of entry. Authorized account holder is defined as the natural person who is assigned to an e-mail address by an Internet access provider, on-line service provider or other organization that is responsible for arranging e-mail address for the domain associated with the submitted e-mail address. Torstar Corp. and/or D.L. Blair Inc. assumes no responsibility for any compu injury or damage related to or resulting from accessing and/or downloading any sweepstakes material. Rules are subject to any requirements/ limitations imposed by the FCC. **Purchase or acceptance of a product offer does not improve your chances of winning.**

For winner's name (available after May 1, 2002), send a self-addressed, stamped envelope to: Harlequin Mother's Day Contest Winners 2216, P.O. Box 4200 Blair, NE 68009-4200 or you may access the www.eHarlequin.com Web site through June 3, 2002.

Contest sponsored by Torstar Corp., P.O. Box 9042, Buffalo, NY 14269-9042.

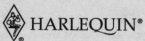 **HARLEQUIN®**

makes any time special—online...

eHARLEQUIN.com

your romantic life

——Romance 101——
♥ Guides to romance, dating and flirting.

——Dr. Romance——
♥ Get romance advice and tips from
our expert, Dr. Romance.

——Recipes for Romance——
♥ How to plan romantic meals for you
and your sweetie.

——Daily Love Dose——
♥ Tips on how to keep the romance
alive every day.

——Tales from the Heart——
♥ Discuss romantic dilemmas with other
members in our Tales from the Heart
message board.

All this and more available at
www.eHarlequin.com
on Women.com Networks

HINTL1R

A royal monarch's search for an heir leads
him to three American princesses in

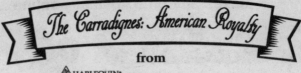

The Carradignes: American Royalty

from

HARLEQUIN®

AMERICAN *Romance*®

King Easton's second choice for the crown is
Princess Amelia Carradigne, the peacekeeper of
the family. But Amelia has a little secret of her own…her
clandestine marriage to a mercenary—
under an assumed name. Now news of her unlawful union
has been leaked to the press and her
"husband" has returned for some answers!

Don't miss:
THE UNLAWFULLY WEDDED PRINCESS
by Kara Lennox   April 2002

And check out these other titles in the series:
THE IMPROPERLY PREGNANT PRINCESS
by Jacqueline Diamond   March 2002

THE SIMPLY SCANDALOUS PRINCESS
by Michele Dunaway   May 2002

And a tie-in title from
HARLEQUIN®
INTRIGUE®

THE DUKE'S COVERT MISSION
by Julie Miller   June 2002

Available at your favorite retail outlet.

HARLEQUIN®
Makes any time special ®

Visit us at www.eHarlequin.com

HARAR2